D0189849

THE CHALLENGE

Geoffrey pondered the voice he had heard and wondered if he was perhaps a little mad.

Still, he had to admit the voice had never led him astray. He had stopped at its command on the road and seen half a hillside tumble onto the track where he would have stood if he had gone on. He remembered now how he shook all over and sweated and knew himself for a coward as the dust rose from the cascading earth. No wonder his father could hardly bear the sight of him.

Geoffrey discovered his hands were clenched into fists. He wished he were strong and brave and able, and that his father cared for him even if he was not. If only he could prove himself . . . if only . . .

Avon Books by
Adrienne Martine-Barnes

THE FIRE SWORD
THE CRYSTAL SWORD
THE RAINBOW SWORD

Coming Soon

THE SEA SWORD

Avon Books are available at special quantity discounts for bulk purchases for sales promotions, premiums, fund raising or educational use. Special books, or book excerpts, can also be created to fit specific needs.

For details write or telephone the office of the Director of Special Markets, Avon Books, Dept. FP, 105 Madison Avenue, New York, New York 10016, 212-481-5653.

THE
RAINBOW
SWORD

ADRIENNE MARTINE-BARNES

AVON BOOKS ◆ NEW YORK

THE RAINBOW SWORD is an original publication of Avon Books. This work has never before appeared in book form. This work is a novel. Any similarity to actual persons or events is purely coincidental.

AVON BOOKS
A division of
The Hearst Corporation
105 Madison Avenue
New York, New York 10016

Copyright © 1988 by Adrienne Martine-Barnes
Front cover illustration by Romas
Published by arrangement with the author
Library of Congress Catalog Card Number: 88-91526
ISBN: 0-380-75455-X

All rights reserved, which includes the right to reproduce this book or portions thereof in any form whatsoever except as provided by the U.S. Copyright Law. For information address Harold Matson Company, Inc., 276 Fifth Avenue, New York, New York 10001.

First Avon Books Printing: September 1988

AVON TRADEMARK REG. U.S. PAT. OFF. AND IN OTHER COUNTRIES, MARCA REGISTRADA, HECHO EN U.S.A.

Printed in the U.S.A.

K–R 10 9 8 7 6 5 4 3 2 1

For my sons, Simon, Geoffrey, and Steven,

and for Jeffrey D. Yablonsky

and Robert Hugh Fagin Forgue,

who were real heroes

A NOTE TO THE READER

This work is an historical fantasy set in an alternate earth. Lest certain confusions arise due to the absence of some events that figure largely in our own record, let me state at the outset that this is a world in which Mohammed was of no particular note and in which Islam does not exist. This is a world without any Crusades and the vast economic and intellectual impact that followed them, and also a world without a Greek Orthodox Church. The Roman Church is, here, much less dynamic and authoritarian, less inclined to heresy hunting and other excesses. It is, in short, a world less war-wracked than our own.

"And after Dylan d'Avebury had given the Crystal Sword to King Louis of Franconia, he wished only for peace. But rest was not yet his, for Louis, ever righteous in his service to the Savior, demanded that Dylan keep his vow to help drive the Darkness out of all Franconia. For two years he labored in this task, with his lady Alianora beside him, for he could never bear to have her from his sight, until Franconia, and much of Italia as well, was cleansed of all Darkness except that which lives in men's hearts, and he was weary and ill of killing.

Then he laid down his sword, and took the three mares and the stallion he had won from the last remnant of the White Folk, and his lady wife; and found a haven outside Brescia, not far from the shores of the Lago de Garda, and settled down to the making of children and the rearing of foals. Never did he speak of his exploits to his three daughters and his son, and if he communed with his beloved Lady of the Birches, he told no one. For twenty years he dwelt in silence, living simply and growing wealthy from the sale of the almost magical steeds he bred, for his work for King Louis was a wound which never healed.

And his spouse called herself Aenor, wishing to forget that once she had been a prize for kings and counts to bicker over, and made a great garden for him, and hoped that his service—and that of his mother before him—was sufficient, and that her offspring would be spared the attentions of the goddess in her many guises, for her long captivity and her labors beside her husband had injured her great heart.''

Excerpt from the *Chronicle d'Avebury,*
by Rowena d'Avebury

I

Geoffrey d'Avebury crossed the large, sunlit courtyard of his family's holding outside Brescia and barely noticed the fat pigeons waddling over the cobblestones, or the ache of his thighs from a lengthy and unaccustomed ride on horseback. A dream had sent him scrambling from his bedclothes in Milan three days before—pulling the first tunic that came to hand over his linen shirt, and saddling his horse amidst the protests of startled grooms—and brought him back to the well-remembered home of his childhood. Now he felt a bit foolish. What would his father say?

He paused in mid-stride to consider this question yet again, and decided that Dylan would probably say nothing, just look at him as if he'd lost his wits, the way he often had when Geoffrey was a boy and wished to know what made the sun shine or the sky blue. They had never gotten along well, and it was with relief on both sides that he had gone off to Milan to study the answers to such questions and the many others that occurred almost daily to his curious mind.

A quiet, sober man, devoted to raising the unique and beautiful horses which had made the family wealthy, and given to terrible nightmares and strange, black moods was Dylan d'Avebury, a man who ate no flesh and turned his eyes from the hearth as if he saw something terrible in the flickering flames. Sometimes Geoffrey had wondered what had happened to make his father so sad, but he was not as much interested in people as in ideas, and Dylan did not welcome inquiries.

A woman, a stranger, appeared in a doorway, dark-haired as his father or his youngest sister Orphiana, slender

1

as a willow wand and very tall. Geoffrey, his eyes a bit dazzled from the sunlight and exhausted from his ride, wondered for a moment if she were real, for her body seemed to shimmer with more light than was common. Then she smiled and seemed quite human. He had not broken his fast since the night before last, when the bread and cheese he had brought with him was finished, and he found he was a trifle dizzy.

She came forward, her hands extended. "You must be Geoffrey. We were about to send for you. But I see there is no need. Your eyes tell me you already know. I am your aunt, Rowena, and I have only just arrived myself." The woman caught his still ink-stained fingers in a cool grasp, as if the sun had no power to warm her, and drew him towards the house.

"I had a dream," he admitted, barely aware he spoke, "though I am too old to be frightened of such things."

"Shh! No one is ever too old to be frightened of dreams. Your mother is very ill. Time has caught up with her, as it must with us all, and my brother . . ."

"What? He isn't sick too, is he?"

"Only in his heart. He loves Aenor very much, too much perhaps. Sometimes it is better to love lightly."

Geoffrey looked at her and felt a hundred questions rise in his mind. He asked the simplest one. "What is mother ill with?"

"Time, only time." The words were a whisper above the cooing of the pigeons as she led him out of the light and into the relative dimness of the central hall.

"That is not a sickness. And Mother is not very old. What do you mean? I am too tired for philosophical riddles." He felt angry and confused and hungry, though the latter shamed him deeply. How could he be thinking about his stomach when his mother was sick, and perhaps his father as well? He gave a little sigh. Geoffrey had discovered years before that his body had no finer feelings, that it demanded food and rest and warmth no matter what the circumstances, and he could not comprehend the ecstasies the monks obtained by constant fasting and praying a great deal. Prayer, in his opinion, was an occupation best suited to dull, believing minds. Besides, he had never felt the slightest need to pester God with petitions for the salvation of his soul or anything else.

Rowena looked at him, her height but a handspan less than his own, so she did not crane her slender neck back the way most people did, a grey-eyed gaze that seemed to pierce his skin and search his most secret self. Geoffrey wanted to draw away from her gaze, and found he could not. Her eyes held him frozen for what seemed an eternity, as if he was falling into pools of still water, deep endless pools that drew him down into fathomless depths of stillness.

Finally, she released him, and said, "First, you will eat and get a clean tunic. Aenor sleeps at present, though she will be glad to see you when she awakens."

He felt very young and small somehow, and safe in his aunt's grasp. Geoffrey discovered he did not want to turn loose of her hand, which made his fair skin redden with embarrassment. He was no child, to be clinging to a woman's apron strings. "Will she? She has never been so before." The words, however true, sounded pettish and ugly, and he wished he could reclaim them.

Rowena sighed and walked him towards the table. A servant, old Giuliano, appeared, grinned toothlessly at Geoffrey, and vanished towards the kitchens. He returned with a steaming stew of chicken and quinces, fresh bread and sweet cheese, and muttered a greeting. Geoffrey grunted a reply as he scooped an almost too hot mouthful into his lips. Giuliano brought wine and cups, and Rowena poured. When his hunger was a little sated, Geoffrey noticed how delicious the food was compared to the endless bowls of boiled millet he dined on in Milan. The widow he rented a room from was a fine woman, but an uninspired cook.

He paused and drank a little wine, a flinty white which was almost sour after the sweetness of the stew, and tried to order his thoughts. His mind, well disciplined in logic and rhetoric, refused to obey, and he was left with a hopeless muddle of questions and emotions. He examined these, and discovered he was frightened. Horses had died, and servants, and one student at the university, but his parents were supposed to be immune to mere mortality. It shocked him a little to realize that he thought this, for it was not at all logical and he took a great pride in the clarity of his mind. Geoffrey drained his cup, refilled it and took some bread. He found he was almost afraid to break the comfortable silence that had grown between them.

"What do you know of your parents?" Rowena asked quietly.

Geoffrey wondered at this, but shrugged and answered, "My father raises the best horses in the world and my mother . . . brightens it with her song. Neither of them is native to Brescia, for she came from Franconia, and he from Albion, but that was before I was born. They have never said why they settled here, except it is good horse country." He turned his cup around restlessly. "I have no gift for horses or swords or such, which is a great disappointment to my father. My sister Beth is a better son than I."

Rowena gave a little nod. "Some of us are scholars, but not my brother, and he has never valued learning overmuch. But has he never spoken of how he rescued your mother from the White Folk, and claimed the Sword of Earth, and helped to drive the Darkness out of Franconia, or how our mother bestowed the Sword of Fire upon the house of Albion, or that it is the task of our family to do such deeds?"

"No. Perhaps he thinks me unsuited to such things. He jokes sometimes that his grandmother is a snake, and says he named my sister after her because she was such a wriggly babe, but only in his cups, so I always thought it was the wine speaking. Of your mother he has only said that she is a great lady in Albion, and that she kept him close by until he fled her reach, and that he would never do that to his own children."

Rowena clucked her tongue and shook her head. "Dylan never did have a dram of sense about people. My mother could hardly bear to have him from her sight, so he must needs attempt to ignore you as much as can be. And you, no doubt, feel unwelcome and unwanted."

"I feel like an ass in a herd of horses, yes. Do you

mean he was a great hero? Is that why he screams in his sleep and goes off to the mountains for weeks at a time?"

"Some wounds never heal, nephew."

"Then I am glad that Beth is the man in the family, for I think I have no talent for daring deeds, or for anything but seeking knowledge. But what of my mother? How does time afflict her?"

"Were you not destined for other things, I would take you back to Albion and Oxford with me. Your mother is old, Geoffrey, for the White Folk kept her captive for forty years, and although her body did not age, her time still passed."

Geoffrey wondered if his aunt were not just a little mad, for she spoke like some ancient sibyl. Surely she must be mistaken, for it was not possible that his mother was closer to eighty than to forty. He tried to think of a polite way to express these doubts, but she spoke.

"Come. Your mother awakes. Tonight you may read the chronicle I have written of my parents and yours, and learn what my foolish brother has denied you of your birthright, and, goddess willing, I shall someday add your own story to the tale."

Geoffrey froze in mid-motion and stared at her. Mad and a believer in the old gods, and, worse, the ancient goddesses. Then Margaret, his middle sister, came in, pale and strained, her exquisite goldenness faded with anxiety, her blue eyes red with crying, and said, "She's awake now. Oh, Geoffrey, I am so glad you have come."

Margaret, always his favorite, leaned against his shoulder, and he felt her tremble as he tried to puzzle out how his Aunt Rowena had known his mother was awake. Geoffrey felt as if the world he had known all the twenty years of his life had somehow tilted, shifted, and expanded, and he found he did not care for the sensation at all. He comforted his sister as best he could and tried to ignore the thoughts which swirled in his mind like a nest of wasps, stinging him.

Geoffrey followed his aunt up the narrow stairs off the two-story great hall to the bedrooms. His parents' room was at the south end of the house, overlooking the loggia and the gardens, away from the racket and the smell of the stables. The sun pierced the long windows and made splashes of gold on the floor.

The high bed into which he had often crawled as a boy—when summer lightning rent the night sky and sent him scurrying from his small cot in the adjoining chamber, terrified of the noise and the brilliance—was still hung with long blue linen curtains, pocked with white stars, a little worn and shabby, but reassuring. The room smelled of flowers, roses now. In other seasons it was scented with marigold, and in winter by bowls of dried petals, so any thought of his mother made him think of flowers and stars. But now it had a sickroom smell beneath the roses, the odor of sour herbs.

Aenor lay under the covers, and he was shocked. All the vitality seemed drained out of her body. Her thick, golden hair was like dried straw, and her skin was sere and colorless. Only her eyes seemed to have any spark of life. They raked him up and down, and her pale lips curved into a ghost of a smile. *She is like a poppet*, he thought, *like one of my sisters' dolls*.

Geoffrey sat on the edge of the bed and took his mother's hand very gently in his own. The skin felt dry and brittle under his fingers, and he could see a network of tiny lines around her eyes. It was as if she was growing old while he watched.

"You should be in the gardens, Mother," he said gently. "The roses will not know what to do without your command." He bent forward and kissed her brow awkwardly.

"Do you think I make the flowers grow, my son?" It was a reedy murmur quite unlike the strong, sweet voice he had expected, and he felt his chest tighten at the sound. "Margaret will have to do it now."

As a small boy, still in leading strings, he had toddled beside her on short, plump legs as Aenor tended her plants. He remembered how she often kissed the dirt, and turned her face up towards the golden sun and just laughed, and how the blossoms seemed to turn to follow her progress. No garden ever was as verdant as his mother's, no orchard so fruitful year after year, no fields so rich. It was as if the earth rejoiced to bear her tread.

"No one can fill your shoes, Mother."

"How are your studies?"

Geoffrey stared at her a little stupidly for a moment, because Milan and the university seemed a distant dream. "Each day I learn a little more and realize how much there is left."

"I am sorry to drag you away from them."

"It matters not at all." He was acutely uncomfortable that his mother could ever imagine he would think his studies more important than her health. As always, he felt shut out somehow, excluded from her love and laughter, a barely tolerated intruder.

Dylan d'Avebury turned from where he had been standing by the long windows and came towards the bed. "Don't tire your mother, Geoffrey."

Geoffrey was too stunned by his father's appearance to respond for a second. It wasn't the faint silvering in the lustrous curling black hair, but the dark circles beneath the blue eyes, the loss of weight and the sag of massive shoulders that spoke of the cost of Aenor's illness. The pang of sorrow was followed by a stab of old anger at being driven away, but he banished it as he did many feelings. His mother was dying, and it was killing his father as surely as some slow poison, and all he wanted to do was prevent both events. He felt helpless, the way he always had before his father's enormous strength, and knew himself as weak and useless, except for nosing through old books.

"Wait!" Aenor's voice was a weary whisper. "I want Geoffrey to play for me." She sounded like a child then, a sick, complaining child. She clutched at his hand. Dylan glared at him, and Geoffrey flinched as he always did beneath his father's gaze. He always felt so useless and unworthy when his father looked at him.

Music had always been a bond between Geoffrey and his mother, and he had tried to fit his piping toddler's voice to her splendid garden song, and, when that would not serve, had taught himself the flute as soon as his pudgy fingers could reach the holes. Now his hands were long and slender, like the rest of him, all leg like a young colt, and his flute was never far from his person. He pulled it from a sheath in his belt—where it lay beside a short sword he barely knew how to manage despite hours of sweaty, clumsy training with his father and Angelo, the arms master—and blew a single clear note.

Geoffrey never knew where the music came from, for while he knew by ear the many tunes that the peasants sang and danced to, he rarely played them unless asked. It always seemed in any given moment that a particular melody rested on his breath, awaiting release. He thought of roses, and, strangely, of poppies now, and the song rose from his heart, passed along his lungs, and left his lips and fingers like a breeze. The melody unwound into the still air of the sickroom, and after a time Aenor drifted back into slumber, a hint of a smile gracing her features.

Go to Byzantium. The words rang like crystals in his mind, spoken in a woman's voice, a voice he barely believed in, but which he knew had saved his life at least once. It was, he realized, that voice in his dream which had brought him rushing home. He liked to regard himself as a logical man, a scholar and a rationalist, and succeeded except when the voice intruded. It was an undeniable command, so urgent and so strong he nearly stood up from the bed and walked directly to the stables.

"That's enough, Geoffrey." Dylan's voice interrupted his melody harshly.

He felt a sharp, irrational flare of anger, unfamiliar now because he had not suffered it in over a year, and he wished he had the strength to knock his father down. He quashed the feeling as he had since he was small, lowered the flute, and said, "Yes, sire." The coldness lay between them like fresh snow.

Geoffrey kissed his mother again, and withdrew from the chamber into the small bedroom which had been his since childhood. To his surprise, his face was wet with tears. He brushed them away on his sleeve, curled his nose at the rank smell of his body, and yanked open a chest which stood against the wall. His tunics lay neatly folded, each with a bundle of lavender upon the breast, and he crushed this evidence of his mother's affection between his fingers, and wept until soundless sobs shook his entire body.

Geoffrey forced himself to breathe slowly and led his mind away from his sense of sorrow and pain. Byzantium. He concentrated on remembering everything he could about the place as he snuffled his nose clear and chose fresh clothing. He walked downstairs, through the great hall and the kitchen, and into the bath house, which was unique as far as he knew. The public baths in Milan were never so splendid, and he had never seen another in a residence. Dylan, in a rare moment of garrulousness, had confessed it was something he had copied from his mother's house in Albion, but Geoffrey knew no more about it except that it was the greatest blessing on earth after a long day in the fields or on horseback.

He scrubbed himself pink, poured several buckets of water over himself to wash away the harsh soap, then settled into the huge wooden vat full of steaming water to soak and think. It was one of the few things he missed at the university.

What did he know of Byzantium? He let his scholarly mind roam across tale, rumor and historical fact. It was the city of Julian the Mage, known as the Apostate in monkish records, who had been Emperor hundreds of years before, and had rejected the teachings of the Savior in favor of those of the antique deities of old Greece. He was said to be yet alive, by spells and strange magics, teaching a council of other mages. The city itself was purported to have streets of gold, with towers carved of jewels, but these fancies he dismissed. Still, the mages had reputations as excellent physicians, makers of elixirs which prolonged life and youth. He was not certain he believed in such things, for surely if they existed at all, some would have reached Milan or Rome. Surely if the elixir of life was real, the Pope would get some.

Geoffrey chuckled despite himself. Milan had been awash in rumors of yet another scandal in Rome, where the College of Cardinals was divided into two rival camps, each electing a pope. Three of the last four holders of the office had been assassinated, and the remaining one was almost a prisoner in his residence. There was even a wild tale that Louis, King of Franconia, was planning an invasion in order to set *his* candidate upon the Papal Throne. Two years before, when he had been eighteen and had just moved to Milan, there had been open revolt, and the monks had taken to the streets in warfare until the Duke of Milan had put a stop to it. Nothing was permitted to halt the trade which filled his coffers.

Stewing pleasantly in the heat of the tub, his travel weariness leeched away, Geoffrey pondered the voice he had heard and wondered if he was perhaps a little mad. His priestly instructors assured him angels spoke to men, but this had always struck him as wishful thinking, not unlike fantastic elixirs from Byzantium. The Cosmos must be an orderly place. Anything else was unthinkable.

Still, that voice had never led him astray. He had stopped upon its command on the road and seen half a hillside tumble onto the track where he would have stood if he had gone on. He remembered how he shook all over and sweated and knew himself for a coward as the dust rose from the cascading earth. No wonder his father could hardly bear the sight of him. Dylan was afraid of nothing in the world—except losing his beloved wife.

Geoffrey discovered his hands were clenched into fists beneath the water. He wished he were strong and brave and able, and that his father cared for him even if he was not. If only he could prove himself.

Go to Byzantium, echoed the voice.

II

Geoffrey lifted his eyes from the pages of his Aunt Rowena's *Chronicle d'Avebury* as the candles guttered and the hearth smoldered redly. He rubbed the ache between his blue eyes and flexed his shoulders, then regarded the object on the table before him as if it might become a venomous serpent at any moment and strike him dead. She had, he noted relentlessly, a fine chancery hand, and if her style was not formally correct, it certainly held his attention. In fact, it was all he could do to resist the urge to plunge back into the remarkable adventures of his grandmother and his father. Still, he needed time to digest what he had read, as his stomach required time to digest the excellent supper the family had shared a few hours before. Except for his mother's absence, it had been as pleasant a meal as he could recall in a long time.

Rowena had a wonderful influence on her brother, teasing him gently under the astonished gazes of her nephew and nieces, reminding him of childhood foolishnesses and mischief. Dylan countered with stories of his own, until the hall rang with laughter. Geoffrey had never seen his father so relaxed and almost cheerful.

He looked back at the book which Rowena had given him after dinner and wondered how much of it was true. It was more fantastical than Homer or Virgil, and he tried to maintain a healthy skepticism. It was not easy, for it seemed very real, as if Rowena had been there herself, which was impossible. Wasn't it? More impossible than a great-grandmother who was some sort of great serpent, a grandmother who sent fire from her hands, and a father who had the power to become a beast, who was a Lord of

Beasts. It explained the way the horses, even the stallions, bent their heads as Dylan passed along the stable or walked through the pasture, and it also offered a reason for his father's absences in the mountains.

It was the presence of the goddesses in the tale which disturbed him. Bridget, at least, was a saint—though not a very proper one—but Saille and Beth, the Lady of the Willows and the Lady of the Birches, were neither proper nor saintly. He scratched his unshaven chin thoughtfully. Only simple country folk still believed in such spirits, burning their bonfires at midsummer or harvest time, and his aunt was anything but simple. She was, in fact, the best educated woman he had ever met, displaying a knowledge of Greek and Latin and a clear familiarity with classical literature. He ran square fingers through his curly brown hair and poured himself a glass of wine.

The book, at least, explained his father's frequent nightmares and his distaste for meat. As Geoffrey had read the tale of the cleansing of Paris, he could almost smell the choking odor of funeral pyres and hear the sound of slaughter. There was a vividness in Rowena's words that was almost magical. But Geoffrey d'Avebury did not believe in miracles or magic or anything he could not see or smell or taste. The Masses he attended daily in Milan held no power for him, and he had never experienced any sense of the transubstantiation of bread and wine into the flesh and blood of the Savior. He went because he enjoyed the music, and because people would have noticed if he had not. Had his mother really learned her song from a magical race, and had his father actually slain an entire people who lived beneath the earth? It seemed possible, for Aenor's song was unlike any other in the world, and his father's remoteness was less puzzling in light of the tale.

Geoffrey rose and put another small log on the fire, and got a fresh candle from the chest which stood on the table. When he turned to set it in a candelabra, Dylan was standing, staring at him. The younger man started and hot wax spilled on his knuckles. He stifled a gasp of pain and completed his task with trembling hands.

Dylan d'Avebury watched in silence, then folded his

long inches into the high-backed chair at the center of the board and poured himself a glass of wine. Geoffrey took his seat across from his father and felt acutely uncomfortable, as if he had been caught doing something wicked.

"Do you plan to sit here studying all the while your mother dies?" Dylan's voice was harsh as the rooks which gathered on the rooftops.

"I am reading Aunt Rowena's book."

To his surprise, Dylan smiled. "Clever, isn't it? I cannot see how she did it, for it is almost as if she was there. As if she rode on my shoulder and felt my heart. I have no gift for words, except plain ones. Your way with them, even when you were small, always made me feel like a bumpkin. I used to listen to you singing in the garden with your mother and want to throttle you for doing what I could not." He knitted his work-roughened hands together around the stem of his goblet and hunched his shoulders. "The words and the music leapt over me and came to you. Sometimes the gods are less than fair."

"I regret I have been so bad a son, sire."

"Bad? Whatever gave you that notion? No, just unlike me. I do not understand you. I never did, even when you crawled around the flagstones at my feet. The first time you looked at me, still wet from your mother's womb, I could hardly believe we were connected. I used to hate to see your head upon her breast where only mine had lain. Jealousy is a terrible thing, Geoffrey. Rowena says it is because you were born at Midsummer and I at the depth of winter, and we are rivals and opposites. I wanted to love you and I could not."

"Rivals? What nonsense. One must be equal for rivalry, and I have never measured up to you, nor do I hope to. Beth should have been your son. Did you name her after . . . after this Lady of the Birches?"

"Yes, I did. Your mother's only rival, my sweet Beth."

Geoffrey was not sure if his father spoke of the tree goddess or his sister. "Why have you never told me of these events?"

"I had no wish to remember them. After I claimed Aenor, I wanted nothing but quiet, to raise horses and children. But I had given Louis my word to help drive the Shadow out of Franconia, and it was two long, endless years of killing and burning before we came here. Take my advice and be careful how you make your promises, son. I was almost glad you showed no talent for the sword—well, a small talent, then—and no burning desire to be a knight. I grew up listening to tales of my parents' heroism and bravery, and yearning to do some deed to win renown. I got my wish, but it was a bitter gift, in the end. I killed a whole people to rescue your mother, a whole nation older than man, and it weighs upon my heart still. I learned too late that all, even the worst, deserve life. Your father is a bit of a fool, Geoffrey. I denied you your history because I cannot bear my own.''

Geoffrey had the oddest feeling, that he had crossed some invisible barrier in that moment, that he was less a boy and more a man than ever before, and it made his eyes prickle. It was the longest conversation he could remember with his father since the night before he journeyed to Milan, when Dylan had felt moved to warn him to avoid a certain sort of woman who took money for favors. Solemn at the time, it was hilarious in retrospect, for he had never had the least inclination to patronize the painted women who strolled the littered streets of the city, although a number of his fellow students seemed to enjoy their company. At the time he had wondered how his father knew about such females, but he now realized that being raised at the court of the King of Albion had given him a very cosmopolitan upbringing.

Geoffrey studied his father in the flickering light, noticing the loss of weight and the dark circles around the vivid blue eyes. He could not bear to lose the man he felt he had just found, and he knew in his bones that Dylan would follow Aenor into the grave as surely as winter followed summer. How could he save them? Three words whispered in his mind.

He reached across the board and grasped Dylan's large, roughened hand. His father squeezed back, but it was a half-hearted response, as if all the enormous strength had drained out of him, and Geoffrey could almost sense the presence of the Angel of Death nearby. He felt a senseless, peculiar desire to seize the phantasm by the throat and throttle it.

Rowena appeared from the shadows, her long dark hair unbound and her thin linen shift barely concealing the slender body beneath it, and touched Dylan's broad shoulder with a pale hand. "Aenor is calling for you."

Dylan stumbled to his feet, scraping his chair across the stone floor, his face dazed, and was halfway to the staircase when he turned back and looked at Geoffrey. "I love you very much, son," he said, then vanished into the shadows.

For a moment the younger man felt quite convinced that so trusty and sturdy an organ as his heart might indeed break into a thousand pieces like a fractured crystal. Rowena took Dylan's abandoned chair and commanded his attention, and the feeling passed under her steely gaze.

"Well?" she said. She refilled her brother's cup and took a sip.

"What? Oh, yes, your book. A remarkable document." Geoffrey shifted his gaze to the carved decorations on the chair, because the rosy glow of his aunt's breasts above the table made it difficult to remember they were close kindred. He was shocked at the carnal course his thoughts seemed quite eager to take, as if she was not a woman old enough to be his mother, but some Milanese lightskirt to be had for a few coins.

"Pray, do not play the scholarly fool with me, dear nephew. I would prefer not to demonstrate what gifts I received from my parents, but I will do so if you continue your rationalist posturings." Her face seemed to shift a little as she spoke, a trick of the unsteady light no doubt, until she seemed less a woman and more some sharp-toothed woodland creature, a fox or ferret.

The hair on the back of his neck bristled and the chamber seemed very cold suddenly. That accounted for the gooseflesh crawling up his arms. But his throat was parched and his tongue felt thick and lifeless. Geoffrey reached a shaky hand out for his wine cup and decided he never wanted to see his aunt angry. Did fire leap from her fingers as it was purported to do from his grandmother's? The tidy, orderly cosmos he believed existed around him seemed disordered by her gaze.

Geoffrey drank some wine and glanced down at the open page of the book. His eye followed the words for a moment, for he had never been able to resist the lure of the written language, and he almost saw his father in the maw of a great, eyeless worm. Then he drew his gaze away, looking at his own slim, smooth hands where they curled around the wine cup. "Forgive my skepticism. I trust not in visions and miracles, but only in what is real." He heard faint laughter, and glanced up. Rowena's face was solemn, and he realized the sound he heard was only in his mind.

Geoffrey clenched one fist and tightened his jaw, remembering the times as a child when he had seen a strange lady in the garden, a dark-haired woman who vanished when he reached for her with small dirty hands. In spring she stood amongst the irises, and in summer favored the poppy bed, and she shimmered. A fear had chilled him then, as it did now, recalling it, that some strangeness lurked within him. He had fled the garden and the presence, and ignored the voice he sometimes heard until he learned to pretend the words came from some friendly angel. Milan had destroyed any belief in angels, friendly or otherwise, for the corruption of the clergy disgusted him. The fear of madness faded a little beneath the effort of his studies, and he had come to believe the lady in the garden was simply the result of too much imagination. He had never spoken of her to anyone, not even his confessor, but he was sure it was she who laughed at him.

"If you do not invite the Lady in by the door, she will come in by the window, and if you bar the window, she will fly down the chimney. She will not be denied, Geoffrey."

Rowena spoke quietly, and in a voice he recognized as one of sincere belief. He looked up, examined the coruscating aura which surrounded his aunt, and wished he had stayed in Milan, dreams or not. Geoffrey felt he was being dragged off the long, narrow path of scholarship he had devised to keep himself sane, onto some perilous track suited only to heroes. He knew he was inadequate for anything but the patient sorting of information. Go to Byzantium, indeed. That was madness. He wanted no manifestations of the divine in his life, not suffering Jesus nor the alchemical Mercurius who ruled the hour of his birthing, and certainly not those capricious ancient jades, lewd Venus or solemn Minerva.

"What do you want of me!" He spoke loudly enough to waken a faint echo in the great hall

"*I* do not want anything, Geoffrey."

"Leave me be, curse you." He pushed back from the table, trembling, stumbled away into the entry hall and through the door into the night. The gardens were limned with moonlight, and he almost flinched as that maker of madness enveloped him. Geoffrey paused on the path, his head throbbing with wine, and lifted a fist towards the lunar orb. Then he remembered he did not believe in such things, lowered his arm, hunched his shoulders, and strode defiantly towards a nearby bench, determined to resist superstition and overcome a lifelong fear of the moon.

He glared at it for a long time, and it shone serenely back, as if to show it was not troubled by the fearsome scowl of one young mortal. The smell of night curled around him, the sickly sweet scent of belladonna, the rich odor of damp earth, and the lingering fragrance of his mother's roses. An owl hooted softly nearby, and several crickets began a concert. Geoffrey almost forgot the moon as he listened. It was a soothing music, and he wished for his flute, to accompany it. The air seemed almost alive around him, and the wine he had drunk seemed to clear from his head.

A woman walked towards him from the lower gardens, and for a moment Geoffrey thought that his Aunt Rowena had somehow slipped past him and was returning, for her hair seemed part of the night. Her face was shadowed, and after a moment he realized she was dressed in a draped gown like one of the old statues the Duke of Milan collected so avidly. An armful of poppies the color of blood lay across her breast.

Geoffrey felt his breath cease and his stomach knot. He wanted to rise and bow, but he knew his long legs were trembling too much to support him. She lifted her face from the poppies and he knew her for the phantasm of his childhood, her expression so infinitely sad he could hardly bear it. Torn between a desire to run and hide and another to comfort her in some fashion, he did nothing but gape at her, wordless and breathless, until his aching lungs expelled what they held. A sound like a mouse squeaking escaped his throat.

She took another step forward, and Geoffrey drew back, over-balanced, and fell into a flower bed, banging his head smartly on a stone. A number of new constellations swam in the sky for several seconds, and then her face and shoulders blotted out the moon as she bent over him.

"Am I so hideous you must go to earth like a badger, young Geoffrey?"

This expression of vanity lessened his terror, but not his tongue, so he just shook his head violently and sat up on one elbow. She reached a long white hand towards him and he shrank back. His heart pounded and the blood thundered in his ears. She gave a sigh and sat down on the empty bench, laid her poppies to one side, and folded her hands in her lap patiently.

"Most men are honored by my presence," she began musingly, "or were. The world has perhaps changed too much. We change not at all, or so slowly it is imperceptible, while you mortals alter almost with each breath you draw. At first it was amusing to watch your hustle and bustle, and then alarming, as we were neglected and then finally denied for newer and more terrible avatars. You cannot quite forget us, as much as you might wish to, but we can only reach you in sleep, in dreams ignored under the sun's golden light. And you, my young friend, are very stubborn. I have been trying to speak to you these twenty years, but your ears and mind were shut and locked. Why is that? I merely wished to be your friend."

Despite what he had read in Rowena's book about his father's and his grandmother's friendships with their goddesses, Geoffrey did not quite believe her. Some deep instinct told him that friendship was the smallest part of what she wished, that beyond it was homage and some sacrifice that he could hardly conceive. At the same time he found himself quite intrigued by the problem of the interaction of man and god and curious about time and immortals. He would, he realized, have chatted with the Devil himself to learn new things. Which was, of course, how Satan lured men from the paths of righteousness. Knowledge was good, but also perilous.

"Why me?" he blurted. "I'm no hero, and I never will be. My sister Beth is better suited to great deeds."

"I spoke of no deeds, only companionship."

"Forgive me if I believe you not, *ma donna*, for when immortals meddle in the affairs of men, it is *always* about deeds. Take Beth and leave me to my books."

"That hoyden." The woman chuckled. "No, she belongs to wild Artemis. I need a thoughtful man, and I chose you."

Geoffrey sat upright and folded his knees into his clasped arms. "I am a coward." He forced the words out from behind clenched teeth.

"I know. Most good men are."

Geoffrey found his eyes brimming with tears at this calm acceptance of his greatest failing, as if some heavy burden had been lifted from his slender shoulders. He blinked rapidly, but they slid down his cheeks anyhow. He rubbed his face against the cloth of his sleeve and choked back sobs that pressed against his throat like wild animals. After a long silence, he looked up, half expecting her to have vanished as she had done when he was a child. She remained, serene as stone, the moon a halo behind her head.

"That mortals can bear such heart-hurts and still live has always been a wonder to me. Such passion. It is almost terrifying. If you could have your heart's desire, my Geoffrey, what boom would you ask?"

"That my mother would not die," he replied.

"Not to be brave as a lion?"

He shook his head. "I can live with being a coward, but

I cannot bear to lose her, and more, it is destroying my father. And this is only a game between us, is it not?"

"A game? Perhaps. I cannot prevent your mother's passing, but you might. But you must hasten."

"There are no magical elixirs in Byzantium, or anywhere else."

"Are you certain?"

Geoffrey felt a half smile cross his lips. *"Ma donna,* I am no longer certain the sun will rise in the east. I have learned tonight such wonders as I thought only happened in old tales, and I barely believe them. I almost expect to awaken in my bed in Milan, to the sound of matins, at any moment."

"Yes, I know. I never approved of the ignorance in which your parents kept you. But you were chosen for the task before you, and therefore you must do it."

He laughed bitterly. "The gods must be fools, *ma donna,* to pick such a poor fellow as myself except to fetch and carry. Well, then, that is what I will do, fetch a potion and carry it back. I suppose I cannot do that too badly."

"You will accomplish more than you think."

"This is madness. I do not even know your name."

"Three times you have called me 'Lady,' and for the present that will suffice. Go, quickly." She seemed to expand into the moon, to grow transparent, and then she faded into the night. But the poppies remained on the bench to mark her manifestation, and Geoffrey grasped the prickly stems until they broke and sticky fluid crept onto his fingers. It had not been a dream, but it still seemed some moon madness. He rose, brushed the leaves and dirt off his backside, and picked up the flowers before he returned to the now sleeping house.

III

Geoffrey paused in the empty great hall and realized how tired he was. His eyes felt filled with grit, and the muscle aches from his long ride had returned with renewed fervor. He longed for nothing but his bed. Except for the poppies he still clutched, he could have dismissed his encounter in the garden and his foolish decision as too much wine and moon. Already he found himself doubting the incident. A good night's sleep would mend his mind, and in the clear light of morning the trip to Byzantium would seem quite foolhardy, a boy's silly dream.

He climbed the stairs as quietly as possible, and slipped through the door to his parents' room with no more than a minor creak of hinges. Moonlight poured through the high windows, silvering the floor stones and casting huge shadows. The fire had almost died, and he looked towards the great bed. Aenor lay pale and still, and only the faint movement of her breast assured him she breathed yet. Her beautiful hands rested on the counterpane, and he remembered the many times they had brushed his thick hair off his brow, soothed scuffed knees and scraped elbows, and gathered armfuls of fragrant roses. Geoffrey turned his gaze away from her image and saw his father, sleeping upright in a chair near the embered hearth, his fearsome eyes hidden beneath black-lashed lids. He seemed a statue, the effigy of some ancient monarch. He was so old.

Almost breathless, he slipped into his small, familiar chamber and did not see his aunt emerge, ghostlike, from the shadows beside the long, high windows. Rowena looked after him, and shook her head sadly. Then Aenor stirred, fretful as a child, thirsty and complaining, and she hurried to the bedside.

For a moment Aenor looked at her without recognition. Then she drank the cool barley water Rowena offered her, and permitted her pillows to be smoothed and turned. A little refreshed by the draught, she clung to Rowena's hand and looked at the moon.

"I never thought I would be such a long time at this business of dying, sister. I can see the gates, you know, but I cannot pass them. But I always imagined I would simply fall asleep one night and waken in another place— not this endless waiting between the worlds." She made a feeble ghost of a smile. "I have spent so much time between worlds. Once—no, many times—I longed for death, when I was a prisoner, and then I saw so much of it I believed I would never wish for it again. But I do, dearest Rowena, even though I can hardly bear to leave my beloved. You will take care of Dylan for me, won't you?"

Rowena bit her lip to stifle a cry of anguish which would have roused her serpentine grandmother, the earth snake Orphiana. She thought she had resigned herself to her fate, to being a spinster, an aunt to her nieces and nephews, a chronicler of great deeds. Now it seemed a vast emptiness, like the barrenness of her womb, that she would know no touch except the occasional rough kiss of her grizzled father or her brother. She envied Aenor her doubtless sweaty couplings, her odd brood of children, her quiet domesticity. It was a bitter draught, that the interfering goddesses had planned great destinies for her brother and her nephew and given her nothing but the chance to serve without question. She would have raged against it—she had often done so when she was younger—but now she just swallowed the anger and the grief.

"I will take care of Dylan as long as he needs me," she promised.

"I wish I could have made him happy," Aenor whispered.

"You did, goose. As happy as anyone can make a son of my father. I think they have very little talent for it." But Aenor had slipped back into sleep, and Rowena was

left to her futile musings in solitude. After a time she left
Aenor's bedside and returned to stand in the shadows she
felt she had always lived in. She looked out at the garden
and recalled something her mother had once said. *There's
nothing like having a good melancholy to make an Irishman
feel right with the world.* Rowena smiled in spite of herself, and found that silent tears had been dripping down
her cheeks unnoticed for some time. It is not fair, she
thought.

No, it isn't, came the unmistakable tart voice of Sallie,
the Lady of the Willows, in her mind. *It is life, that is all.*

Geoffrey stretched out on his narrow bed and waited for
blessed sleep to overtake him. His eyes felt like coals in
his head, and his mouth was sour with wine. The blood
throbbed in his skull, and after a short while he sat up and
swung his feet to the floor. He rested his elbows on his
knees and held his pounding head between shaking, sweaty
hands. He was filled with a strange urgency, like the
desire for a woman, and he knew that if he waited for
morning he would never leave. Already his logic and his
cowardice conspired to dissuade him from even trying.

Clenching his teeth, Geoffrey stood up and opened his
clothes chest. He pulled out his oldest, roughest garments,
still smelling faintly of the horses he had broken wearing
them, hose and boots, a serviceable cloak, and a battered
wide-brimmed leather hat, and stuffed them into a bag.
The pounding in his head subsided. He took his sword,
then counted out his small store of money. It was not
enough, not nearly, but he knew where his father kept the
family coffer. It struck him, for a moment, that he was
acting like a thief in the night, but he shrugged the thought
aside. He added his wooden flute to the bag, reached for
one of his precious books and rejected it. Finally he folded
his blanket into the bag, and cautiously opened his door.

Dylan snored lightly in his chair, but the room was
silent otherwise. Geoffrey tiptoed to the bed and lightly
kissed his mother's brow. "Please, stay 'til I return," he
whispered. Aenor stirred a little in her sleep and seemed to
smile. He half crossed the room, then came back and

brushed Dylan's cheek with another kiss. The salty taste of tears stung his lips, but his own eyes were dry. What dreadful dreams Dylan must have, to cry in his sleep. Geoffrey's resolve almost melted, but he started to leave again.

He stopped, halted by some invisible force. Puzzled, he turned his head from side to side. He felt he had forgotten something important. The poppies! Geoffrey pondered the madness of dragging flowers along on his adventure, then decided it made as much sense as creeping off in the middle of the night. He retrieved the flowers and left the room without another look at either of his parents, sure that if he looked over his shoulder at them he would turn to salt or be forever lost like Euridice. And I am certainly no Orpheus, he thought bitterly as he climbed down the stairs.

Geoffrey stood for a second, looking at the familiar room, at the long table where they dined, at the glossy tiles where dogs and his younger sisters had frolicked, and felt a pang of loss. His eye fell upon his aunt's volume, still open on the table. He had not finished reading his father's tale. On impulse, he closed it and thrust it into his tunic, knowing it for an act of thievery—and a foolish one at that—but unable to resist. Perhaps it will give me courage, he thought, and I will bring it back. Then he took food from the kitchen and silver from the coffer, and headed for the stables.

Rowena watched her nephew stride purposefully down the path, and felt a pang of envy. She gazed up at the moon accusingly for a moment. *Why could I have no great adventures? Or even a child? Good fortune, nephew. I barely had time to know him. Oh, goddess, why, if you love me, is my fate so cruel?*

There was no answer. Dylan snorted and woke up. "What? What is it? Is Aenor all right?"

Rowena turned from the window and gave a little shrug. "Everything is as it should be, I think, brother."

"Umm. Well, you always were the knowing one, weren't you?"

"Perhaps." She came towards him and put her arms across his shoulders, seeking a little warmth, and after a look of surprise, Dylan put an arm around her waist, and gave her an affectionate pat on the bottom.

"You are a handsome woman, 'Wena—enough to make me wish you weren't my sister a few times. I cannot understand why half the chivalry of Albion hasn't been sniffing around you all these years."

Rowena was quietly pleased at his crude suggestion, not for herself, but because it was the first glimmer of her vigorous, healthy Dylan, the energetic boy she had adored as a child. A speck of hope filled her heart. Perhaps he would survive. Perhaps fate would be kind for a change. Tomorrow she would tell him that Geoffrey was gone, and bear the rage she knew would follow. For now, she wished only to comfort herself against him, as she had so often when their parents shook the rafters of Avebury Hall with their stormy arguments. What disagreements had Dylan and Aenor had, she wondered. Explosive, she imagined, for she could not believe a man of her father's line and a woman from the fractious Plantagenet one could dwell in perfect serenity. And young Geoffrey, named for the Prince of Albion and also for the Count of Anjou, was startlingly like Arthur, King of Albion, in his look and lineaments. Too much jaw and too much nose for a young man, especially one so frightened of himself. She could have slapped Dylan and Aenor silly for keeping the boy in ignorance. When a god or goddess put their finger upon one, they would have their way, no matter how long it took. They were so patient. Rowena envied them that.

Geoffrey entered the stable and several horses thrust their heads out of stalls and knickered soft, equine greetings. He breathed the warm smell, comfortable and familiar, and stroked a soft muzzle here and there, wondering which horse to take. Not the lazy slug he had ridden from Milan, an ill-tempered steed he had borrowed from a sleep-muzzied groom. It was so dull and stupid he could hardly believe it was of the same race as the animals who watched him curiously from their stalls. And if he believed his aunt's chronicle, they were not quite, but an almost unnatural breed with qualities that were a little magical.

His father had crossed them with the best horseflesh he could get, dainty mares from Egypt and fiercer ones from Iberia. Most were grey, a few black, and rarely one as white as the snows of winter.

Geoffrey ignored the old stud, Vengeance, now a little grey around the muzzle but still a masterful stallion, and those mares he could see were in foal. He knew most of the stock, even after a two-year absence, as well as he knew the various monks who instructed him, though a few were new to him. He moved quietly down the central aisle, pondering a choice.

A moon-white muzzle poked across a stall door, and grey ears flickered attentively. Odd eyes, as blue as his own, regarded him intently, and Geoffrey looked up at the carved plaque that hung over the stall. *Marina,* it said.

"I knew you when you were still wet from your mother's belly," he told her. "You have grown up very pretty for such an unlikely foal." He extended his hand and she lipped the palm, hoping for some sugar, while he remembered her birth a few nights before he left for Milan. It was difficult to believe that this handsome mare was the same wobbly and undersized foal he had helped deliver. Her body was grey, with a white mane, tail, and showy feathers above the dainty hooves. She was a good fourteen hands high and more, leggy and elegant, but a little young to be bred yet. He was torn between his father's displeasure at the loss of a mare and the fact that his heart warmed to her as it rarely had to any steed. He had grown up with horses, bred them and birthed them, curried them and mucked out their stalls, broken them to saddle, but in his heart he was still a little frightened of them. He ran a hand along the long, sleek neck and was lost. Marina nosed his shoulder and blew a warm, damp breath into his ear.

Geoffrey walked down to the tack room, got his old saddle—still clean and polished—bit and bridle, blanket and feed bag, then led Marina out of her stall. She stood patiently while he saddled her, stamping a hoof occasionally as if eager to be underway. He arranged his belongings, got a bag of grain from the storeroom, and led her out to the yard. The clop of her hooves against the cobbles seemed loud enough to rouse the dead, but neither the grooms who slept above the stables nor the inhabitants of the house appeared to hear anything. For a moment he wondered why a robber could not make away with his father's precious stock, then realized that a stranger would have been greeted with a challenge from Vengeance. It was vaguely comforting that he was not a stranger.

He hesitated, wondering what he might have forgotten. Then he picked up the poppies from the mounting block where he had laid them, wound their prickly stems into a rough garland, and thrust it around the crown of his leather hat. He clapped the hat on his brow, felt foolish, and swung up into the saddle. Marina almost danced beneath him as he urged her across the moon-dappled cobbles and onto the path to the road. Once, he looked back over his shoulder. He could see the long windows of his parents' room high in the house, and the shadows of a woman enveloped by a shining aura. A fair, pale hand seemed to wave farewell, but it might have been the moonlight. Geoffrey turned Marina east, towards the sea and far Byzantium, and gave her sides a light touch.

IV

"Damn you, ill-favored wretch, why were you not the boy child I strove so mightily for?"

Helene, sitting with one leg curled under her tight bottom, stirred a goblet of wine with a languid finger and gazed dispassionately at her father with cool green eyes, pretending to a calmness she was far from feeling. She was being aggravating and she knew it, knew it as well as she knew "ill-favored" meant ugly and that her being female was a source of rage to Hiram, and had been since the moment of her birth.

Of her mother she knew nothing, neither name nor race, for she had died as Helene had gasped her first breath, and she had been raised by indifferent servants. Hiram rarely emerged from his sanctum, and then only to rain displeasure upon her head. It was difficult to imagine him striving mightily on the couch of Ishtar—or any other of the lusty deities whose names were forbidden in Byzantium. Great Julian had banished them all long ago. But Helene had tried many times to picture her father coupling, or indeed, without his reeking, symbol-adorned robes, without success. She coiled a small finger into her wildly curling, cinnamon-hued hair, and pouted her lower lip out to show her complete indifference to his abusive tongue.

Before she had fully understood just how worthless a girl child was to a mage of Byzantium she had learned all the skills of a male—to ride, use arrows, a sword and shield, to read in half a dozen scripts, though she was no scholar, and much else. It had availed her nothing, and she had learned to keep her feelings under an iron discipline.

It was cold, despite the arrival of summer some weeks

before, and the city was like a tomb. The stillness was pleasant, for there had been riots in the streets and arcades below since the sickness had begun and the ships had ceased to come. Worse, the fields refused to sprout, and all around the city the earth lay barren. Helene could see a thin column of smoke rising between two wizard towers and knew it came from another pyre. A flash from a narrow window told her some mage was making another attempt to remedy the situation. The wind carried the scent of burning and a faint clamor of voices.

There was an enormous cracking sound followed by a boom, and they both rushed to a window, standing closer together than was their custom. The round dome of the tower of Demetrius was shattered and the masonry crashed down into the street below. Some red substance spilled out of the ruined tower and ran down the sides, then burst into flames.

Helene shivered. "What do you think has happened?"

"His elemental must have gotten free. The wards are becoming weaker and weaker." Hiram frowned. "I do not understand. Those spells have stood a thousand years, from father to son passed down, and suddenly they are snapping like dry kindling."

Helene ran small fingers through her short-cut hair. That anything should elude her father's understanding he took as a personal affront, and she ached to be able to assist him. But women had no powers over the elements except the power of fertility, and then only when the mages commanded it.

"Perhaps they are worn out, like old boots. Can you not make fresh wards?"

Hiram glanced down at her. He was a very tall man, thin as a reed, and pale as a winding sheet, for he rarely saw the sun. Helene barely came to his chest, for she was tiny, small-boned and spare, her breasts almost invisible under the soft silk of her quilted tunic. She passed for a boy of twelve, though her sixteenth birthday was but a week away.

"Old boots, indeed! Your metaphor is most inept."

"Not as inept as spells that are falling to bits in front of our eyes. You and your fellow wizards seem quite help-less. The sickness is everywhere, the fields lie fallow, and what have you accomplished? I ask you a logical question and you criticize my metaphor! Is this the sort of intellec-tual behavior of your rivals? I am not surprised the city is dying.''

''Logical question! You do not know the meaning of the concept. Women do not think—let alone think logically.''

Helene felt her skull would burst with rage, and she grasped the goblet in her left hand tightly. There was a faint sound and the bowl shattered under her fingers, the glass cutting the flesh. The wine, however, did not splatter onto the floor, but coiled like an amber serpent, spread flaming wings, and flew straight at Hiram's astonished eyes. The thing fastened itself to his face as Helene watched, horrified. Hiram gestured, and the serpent turned back to wine, running down the front of his garments.

Thin scratches marred his cheeks, and blood welled in them. Helene reached out to dab them, then snatched her hand back. She had never touched her father's person—nor he hers, for a mage must remain inviolate—and this did not seem a good time to begin doing so.

The hand she extended was cut a little, but blue fire danced along the flesh, and the cuts closed and vanished as she watched. Helene turned her hand back and forth as the fire faded, curious and bemused. When she looked at Hiram again he was regarding her with greater interest than she had ever seen him evidence before, an avid, hungry look she did not find reassuring.

''How did you do *that?*'' His long fingers ran across the broad collar of his robe, touching the symbols worked there with a lover's caress.

Helene shrugged. She was too surprised by the manifes-tation to offer any explanation. ''I don't know.''

''Who has been teaching you? Who is the renegade?''

She laughed. The thought of any of the solemn, dour wizards of the city instructing her in their secrets was perfectly ridiculous.

''Father, I am *only* a woman. A worthless, useless female. Remember?''

Hiram looked at her for a moment. "You may be more valuable than I thought." His brows drew together, making a deep furrow between them, and blood rilled down his pale cheeks unnoticed. "Perhaps the spells can be renewed."

Helene stared at him. "I have read every work in your library—not with complete understanding, but enough to grasp the drift of your thoughts—and I will not be your blood sacrifice."

"You will do as you are told. You will be useful! Finally. And then perhaps I can get the son I so greatly desire. Yes, yes. It was meant. It is part of the great plan. I see it now. How could I have been so blind? I must inform the Council immediately." He turned and strode out of the room, leaving Helene as if certain of her obedience.

For several minutes she stood motionless at the window, looking at the shattered tower beyond without seeing it. The street below was an inferno which she barely noticed. Slowly her stunned mind recovered and gave way to near panic. He would slit her throat without hesitation! She wanted to run, but where or how eluded her.

V

"I wish to buy passage to Byzantium."

The clerk looked at Geoffrey insolently, and he realized he should have found the public baths and shaved the beginnings of a beard off his square chin before approaching the shipping offices. Then the clerk smiled, and Geoffrey realized he was still wearing his battered old hat with the red poppies wound around it, and must look quite moonstruck. The poppies were as fresh as they had been three days before, the delicate petals unblemished. He glared at the clerk to hide his embarrassment, and the insolent grin faded into sullenness.

The man hunched his shoulders and bent his head over his tallies. "That is not possible."

"Why?" Geoffrey demanded.

"Plague." He paused and looked up a little nervously. "The whole city is closed and we are turning back any ships that have sailed from there. Byzantium is dying. It could be dead by now, for all I know."

Geoffrey was tired, dirty, and hungry. He had ridden the leagues from his home to Venice with the best speed Marina could provide, three days and most of the nights. He felt a sort of fury rising in his chest, a sense of frustration and urgency, as if he had been offered a gift only to have it snatched away when he reached for it.

He gazed out towards the wide harbor and realized there was very little activity for one of the greatest ports of the world. The smell of the sea was overlaid with the scent of pilings and tar—and, he realized, rot. Men loafed around long wharfs, and stacks of goods sat in sad piles, going nowhere. If Byzantium died, Venice would perish as well, for it was the clearinghouse for most trade with that distant city. He remembered the chronicle he had read of his grandmother's and his father's exploits and wished he had their curious ability to transform into some creature which could swim, though the foul waters of the harbor were not tempting.

"Athens, then, or Tripoli."

The clerk looked almost ill, and shook his head. "Nothing has moved here for most of a month—and by the Doge's order, nothing will. Now, be off. It is worth my job if I am caught gossiping about it."

The fellow was frightened, which puzzled Geoffrey. "Can you tell me a decent inn, then?"

The clerk almost beamed with relief. "Now, that I can. Cross the second bridge," he said, pointing over Geoffrey's shoulder, "and go on until you see the sign of the rose. It is clean and they won't cheat you—well, not much. There is a stable too." Geoffrey handed him a small Milanese coin out of his pouch and turned to go. "Thank you, sir, thank you. If anything changes, I will send word to you."

"Good. Good day to you, then, and thanks."

Geoffrey found the inn with little difficulty, then got Marina stabled. He inspected the stalls and gave the grooms a good looking over before he surrendered her, though his thighs ached and his belly growled. After three days and nights she was as much family to him as one of his sisters, and he rightly put her comforts before his own. Exhausted and depressed, he wondered if he should retreat from this fool's journey and go home. *Go to Byzantium,* the voice inside him insisted.

How? Swim?

Silence answered him.

He put his things in a small chamber, and went down to the general room on the ground floor to get something to eat. A plate of rice covered with an overly sweet mixture of vegetables and fowl was half consumed before he noticed the flavors. Geoffrey slowed his eating and began to pay attention to the conversations around him.

Two merchants—Franconians by their accents—hunched together conspiratorily at the table to his right, and a man and a veiled woman sat on the left. Their clothing was strange, elaborate pleatings and patterned fabric making a gaudy display in the dim light of the inn. This, plus the woman's veil, proclaimed them to be from the east.

"I want more wine, Antonio." The woman spoke in Greek, a different Greek than his monkish instructors, but recognizable.

"You have had enough already."

"Get me more," she whined. "How long are we going to sit here? I want to go home. I hate this city." She went on with a stream of complaints about the food, the bedding, the weather, and the folly of her companion in a querulous tone.

Geoffrey turned his attention to the other table. "We cannot sit here forever while the Doge hides under his covers. If we do not get that wool shipped, we are ruined, Martin."

"Then we are ruined, for the fat old fool will not budge. Between the war and the plague he is immobile."

War? Geoffrey pricked his ears at the words, for he had heard no rumor, unless they meant the continuing conflict between the two factions in Rome. That hardly seemed a reason to halt shipping from Venice. There were so many things he did not know, he realized, and the world was such a large, complex place. It had never seemed that way before, until he had read his aunt's chronicle and discovered that his parents and grandparents had consorted with kings and performed great deeds. I am just a dull scholar, he thought wearily. No fire leaps from my fingers and I cannot transform into a beast. I cannot even buy passage on a ship. He thought about the long overland trek north and east that would bring him to Byzantium's gates in half a year, if he was not killed by bandits or did not break his neck in a mountain pass, and was halfway to hopelessness when he heard the words "smuggler" and "revolt."

It took him a moment to realize that the merchants had used the first, and the Greek-speaking man the second. He lifted his wine glass and listened intently.

"It is like chasing a ghost, Martin. One man tells me to speak to another, and he to a third, and always the ship has just gone or something. The Venetians are robbing us blind on our hopes."

"Keep your voice down, Anna. The Doge has spies everywhere. If he gets even a hint of trouble from our people, it is the dungeon or the ax for all of us. Also, I do not believe there is anyone in the enclave with the heart for such a venture. We *buy* swords, not use them."

"And look what it has gotten," she shrilled "Dirty desert men swarming up from Araby to the very walls of Damascus. My poor babies may be dead already."

"Tarsus is a long way from Damascus."

"Men are such fools," she answered bitterly. "I wish you had never convinced me to come with you."

"As I recall, you insisted, sister."

"Even if we get to a smuggler, how can we get our goods out of the warehouse without arousing suspicion?" the merchant called Martin hissed.

Geoffrey scratched his beard thoughtfully. South, along the coast and out of Venice's influence, there were probably dozens of small ships eager to make a profit from the embargo. He was unencumbered by goods. Except Marina. Still, a man and a horse ought to be able to find some means to cross the sea, if only as far as Greece. The sour wine had made him light-headed and sleepy, so he left the tap room for a lumpy mattress that felt like paradise, content that he would find a way, somehow, and save his sweet mother.

The following morning dawned with the loud sound of voices. Geoffrey sat up, knuckled his eyes, and wondered where he was. After a moment it came back to him, and he swung his lanky legs out of the narrow bed and stood up. Shouts echoed up the stairwell—angry, outraged shouts—and Geoffrey wondered what was going on. He pulled on a tunic and his boots and went below.

The landlord was bellowing like a stuck boar and gesturing widely to a yellow and maroon clad soldier who listened impassively. When the innkeeper began to slow down, the guardsman said, "No one is to leave the inn except by permission of the Doge. If any do, you will be executed along with them. Do you understand?"

"I understand. *Dolce Maria,* I understand. I understand that this will ruin me. What will my guests think? You do not care. All the Doge thinks of is his own precious skin. What good will it do him if Venice dies?"

"Silence!" The guard spoke sharply, but he was not very much older than Geoffrey and it sounded rather forced. "Do not speak treason."

"Treason. I will give you treason, you silly pup. I knew you when you were peeing in your swaddling bands and squalling. The only real treason is to cut off the blood of this city—which is trade! If there is no trade, how will the Doge pay you to save his cowardly flesh?"

"Please, Uncle Marco—"

"No Uncle Marco, Romeo. You cannot come into my inn and tell me I must lock my guests in their rooms because his Eminence has eaten too many beans and has a flux and still be my nephew. If you have any sense, you will leave the Doge's service before you get hurt."

"What do you mean?"

"I mean, Romeo, that a few more weeks of this silliness, this closing of the harbor, and there will be trouble. Bad trouble. Do you understand?"

"If you know of any plots or schemes to disrupt the peace of the state, it is your duty to inform me."

"Plots? Schemes? I am only an old man with an inn that is to be a prison for my guests. What do I know of discontent? I am not some young hothead. But, Romeo, you be careful, because the people will not be patient forever."

Geoffrey listened to this conversation with a sinking heart. Now what would he do?

The door of the inn opened and a slender man entered. He wore a flat-brimmed hat and a brief cloak of bright green over yellow tunic and breeks, and was altogether a curious figure for so early in the day. He glanced about avidly, eyes darting everywhere, and when his eyes met Geoffrey's they widened and smiled, just for a moment, in

the most conspiratorial fashion. "Do you have a room?"
the stranger asked languidly, flipping the cloth of his short
cloak back in a graceful gesture.

Both the landlord and the soldier looked at the new-
comer a little suspiciously, but Marco could not resist the
opportunity to earn a little money, so he bowed slightly
and said that he had; quoting a price that was somewhat
more than he had asked of Geoffrey the day before. The
stranger seemed to find this acceptable, and the young
soldier used the ensuing negotiations to slip away quietly.
Geoffrey took a seat in the taproom and commanded a
breakfast of bread, cheese, and watery beer.

"May I join you?"

His mouth full of mildly dry bread, Geoffrey could only
nod at the stranger. He had removed the flat-brimmed hat,
and without it his face was almost too pretty for a man. He
had the appearance of a youth, and his chin seemed never
to have known the razor's kiss, but his eyes were at
variance with this. They were old eyes, somehow, wise
and perhaps even cynical, and no color Geoffrey had ever
seen before, a grey that was almost amethyst.

The stranger seemed unaware of any scrutiny on Geoffrey's part and gazed around serenely at the beams in the
ceiling, the stones in the hearth, and the other appoint-
ments of the room. "Not what I would have chosen, nor
what I am used to, but it will have to do. I am Mercutio di
Maya."

Geoffrey swallowed his mouthful and washed the crumbs
down with a little beer. "I am Geoffrey d'Avebury. What
are you accustomed to, pray?"

"Nothing quite so . . . Spartan as this, I assure you."
At this he chuckled, as if some private jest amused him.
"And you?"

"I find nothing to complain of, except I cannot get out
of Venice. I have been at my studies in Milan for the last
two years, rooming with a widow woman of uncertain
temper who burned the porridge if she did not serve it
uncooked, so I am quite content."

"Still, you wish to depart upon your business."

Geoffrey did not remember mentioning any business,

but he nodded anyhow. "Yes, but it seems that I cannot. The Doge has stopped all shipping, and just before you arrived, that young soldier came to inform our host that no one would be allowed to leave the inn. I do not know if he meant we must stay inside or just continue to reside here, but I am sure the news will be unwelcome to the other occupants." He ceased his chatter for a moment, surprised at himself. There was something so charming about Mercutio, seductive almost. Startled by his chain of thought, Geoffrey munched another dry mouthful. Books and music pleased him more than people, except that he found watching people quite interesting.

"Oh? And why is that?"

For a moment Geoffrey was confused, lost in his ruminations. "Oh. The other people. There is a merchant who wishes to ship his wool—a Franconian, I think—and a man and a woman who wish to go to Tarsus in Antioch. Greeks."

"And you?"

"Me?" Geoffrey felt a flush of dismay, and then disgust at his plan to journey to Byzantium in search of a cure for his mother. "I am just a fool—or perhaps a madman."

Mercutio smiled, and his grey-violet eyes danced with mischief. Geoffrey was certain he had never seen anyone so charming. "All mortals are foolish betimes. As for madness, who can say? To desire something greatly is a sort of madness, but a fine madness. Every man should follow his heart."

Geoffrey shook his head. "I am not impulsive—or I never was before—and now I have made a muddle of everything and cannot think what to do. Short of sprouting wings and flying away or swimming across the sea like a fish, I cannot see any way to go on, and I cannot even return home."

"Change is always possible. If you desire it enough."

Geoffrey felt there was some special significance to this statement, if he could only discover it. He felt bewitched by his companion's eyes, by the youthful smile that curved across his lips.

"Change?"

"I am only a messenger."

VI

Helene left the chamber and walked down several sets of stairs, leaving the working and living areas of the tower behind her. She passed through the storerooms and stables without a glance and went below, to the abandoned and crumbling arcades, and even lower, into the brine-scented conduits that carried refuse to the sea.

There was a moderate walkway beside the rushing waters, and the sounds and smells of the city were drowned in its gurgle. The tide was coming in. Helene had discovered this place as a child, hiding from the rod of her caretakers. It had been a long time since she had come there, and she had almost forgotten how peaceful it was. The clean salt air from the sea swept away the stench of burning that covered the city, and the reek of her father's robes as well.

She turned into a side passage and found dust lay thickly upon the worn stones. A little ways beyond was a small room where she had often spent long afternoons, though it had no comforts to recommend it but some stone benches and a niche in the wall with a small figure of a woman in it. The face was sweet and serene, and sometimes she had pretended it was her unknown mother.

It was still there, with the withered remains of a few flowers she had placed there years before. Helene blew the dust away and coughed as it caught in her throat. The eyes seemed to rebuke her for her neglect. She brushed the curling tresses with a finger, and traced the smooth flow of a shoulder down one slender arm to a hand which had once held a graceful bow. The drapery of the gown fell from the opposite shoulder, leaving one small breast revealed. Sandalshod feet and long, strong legs stood under the folds of a brief skirt, and the head of a hare crouched between them. A wolf stood pressed against the leg, the other hand resting on its mane.

Helene had never wondered who the woman was, or why her statue should be hidden away here. She ran dusty fingers through her curling hair and left streaks of dust along her brow. Then she sat on a bench and rested her back against the wall. Tears welled up and slid down her cheeks. Sobs rose out of her throat despite her efforts to suppress them, and she covered her tanned cheeks with her hands. Finally the crying stopped, leaving her exhausted, and she curled up on the bench, pillowed her head on one arm, and slipped into an uneasy slumber.

Helene woke, startled, then disoriented. She was stiff from sleeping on the cold stone, but her skin was sheened with sweat, as if she had been practicing with the sword. The small, dusty chamber confused her for a moment, and then memory returned. With it came the realization that during her sleep she had dreamt. A sense of complete astonishment very nearly overcame her. Then her stomach rumbled, and she laughed at herself. She surely had *not* dreamed. No one dreamt in Byzantium, not even the mages. She only knew of such things from prowling about in her father's library.

Then what, she wondered, *what* were those peculiar flashes of memory which had begun to trouble her a few months before? She drew her brows together, concentrating on recalling when each strange memory had occurred, and finding that they always followed sleep. With a gasp, she realized that the dreams had begun just before the sickness came to the city.

It was her fault. Helene suddenly *knew* that something she had done had brought the sickness to Byzantium. Hiram was absolutely right to feel he should sacrifice her. She wondered if it would hurt a great deal, and tried to feel happy that finally she would be able to do something which would please her father. Much to her surprise, Helene discovered she did not wish to die, not for her father, and certainly not for a chilly city full of mages. She tried to think of the poor innocents who were perishing in the streets and arcades, the merchants and craftsmen, not to mention their wives and children, and found only that she had an even greater reluctance to die for strangers than for people she knew. This final proof of her unnaturalness left her feeling oddly exhilarated instead of properly sorrowful, and she felt no desire to rush back into the tower and beg her father to dispatch her as soon as possible.

You are, without question, the most exasperating child, but at least you have a little sense left in that head of yours. I did not bring you into this world to perish on some stinking altar presided over by doddering old eunuchs who have gotten quite above themselves. Self-sacrifice never answers, as I know from bitter experience. Nine days and nights I held my mother while she labored to bring forth my beloved brother, wiping the sweat from her high brow, and hearing the screams of her torture, and she was not in the least grateful. A sound like a sniff of displeasure punctuated this remarkable recital as Helene looked around the small chamber for the source of the voice. The room was empty of all but herself and the little statue. *She adored him—well, everyone did, except poor Daphne and a few others who found his amorous attentions distasteful—and gave to me such scraps of affection as were left over.*

Helene realized that the voice was entirely within her, and also that it was a voice she knew from sleep. A demon? There was a largish volume filled with those in her father's library, all male as far as she could remember. A ghost? That seemed more likely, although they were supposedly excluded from the city. Still, if the warding spells were in disarray, who knew what might have gotten in.

I am not a ghost—though with as little attention as I've gotten over the last several hundred years I might have easily dwindled into one, had I been of lesser resolution. I never should have revealed myself to that boy Julian. He was so charming—just like my brother. You are fortunate that the men in your life are not charming.

Helene could not recall ever being exposed to any male who could be termed charming, or even pleasant, nor any woman either. The servants were subservient because it was their job to be, the mages arrogant as suited their calling, and her instructors were simply stern taskmasters. She had never felt more than abstract affection for anything or anyone except her father and her horse. She looked at the little statue in the niche and enlarged her list to include it. In her reverie she almost forgot the voice in her head.

Oh, do stop chasing butterflies in your head and pay me your entire attention, you vexatious child.

Helene recognized that tone of voice, even if it only existed in her mind, as one of unmistakable authority, and she made a mental bow in acknowledgment.

That is better. You certainly have neglected me these past few years.

"I am sorry," Helene said to the empty air. "I did not intend to."

No, you did not. You really do not remember how we used to talk when you were younger. It is all right. Everyone neglects me until they want something—and you, at least, came seeking comfort, not a favor. But it is a long time since you brought me this withered posy, and I have missed you. I could not reach you in the realm above, for my brother rules there, and in his blinding light no other illumination is possible. When the moon rises in the day, she is but a pale ghost of herself. And I have been buried here, trapped within these walls for so long, so long.

The plaintive tone of this last statement made Helene almost squirm with discomfort. She had the wretched sensation that somehow it was her fault, and that she had the power to have changed matters, if only she had known how. It was a familiar feeling, one that had driven her to explore the contents of her father's library even though she had no interest in demons or spells or the myriad other matters which filled the parchment pages of those volumes. She liked horses better than people and riding better than reading, but she had been driven by the conviction that somewhere there must be an answer to the question that she could only dimly frame in her mind, an answer she would recognize when she found it. Surely there must be some reason she existed, and within her must be some clue to the woman who had birthed her and died.

She was my last servant. My only companion, until you found your way here. We are alike, you and I, abandoned in the moment of our beginnings.

"Who was she? What was she like? And why did she die?"

The dusty chamber was very still for a long moment. *We killed her, you and I and Hiram. I because I could not succor her as I did my mother in her travail, you because you were such a fierce, strong babe.*

"And my father?"

His is perhaps the greatest fault, for he used her to his own ends without thought, seeking only a mage son, looking for power and taking any he found without consideration. He filled himself with his need and his pride, took her unwilling at the moment of your conception, and locked her up afterwards. She perished of loneliness, I think, and I would have followed her had I possessed the capacity to cease. But while we can dwindle until we are no more noticeable than the murmur of bees among the wild thyme, we never end entirely. It is one of the cruelties of fate, that we can be alone, can suffer the endless torment of solitude, and yet never escape it. We come to love our brief-lived companions, our priests and priestesses, our servants and worshippers, and their deaths betray us afresh. And while in death you come to us, finally and utterly, still it is your lives that are our joy and wonder.

Helene found this was rather too complicated and mysterious for her mind to grapple with. "What was her name?"

Phyllis. She was small and fair. You have her hair and eyes—and the same square, stubborn jaw. I would that you had known her, but you are so alike that you would have disagreed on many matters.

Helene thought about that for a second and decided the being who spoke in her mind must be mistaken. "Who *are* you?'' She paused a moment. ''And what do you want from me?''

Your mother was not nearly so sharp-witted as you are. I wish to be taken out of this . . . this tomb. I need to be in the forests once again. The voice seemed a little desperate.

''But, who are you?''

I cannot tell you! Do you not think I would have revealed myself to you long ago, had I been able? You must discover me for yourself. All men must. There was a sort of sigh. *That is the nature of the war between men and women, the war of which this dreadful, dying city above us is a sorrowful example. My brother made here a revelation, and the first mages took it for the only truth—which, indeed, is what he hoped for. But revelation is continuous, not stagnant. It changes with the season, the very moment, and with each individual. Each of my worshippers finds me by his own way—as you did. And I am always the same and never alike.*

''Well, you certainly are confusing,'' Helene replied impatiently. ''You sound an awful lot like the arguments in some of my father's books, full of promise but never really explaining anything.'' Her stomach growled.

Language is a great barrier to communication.

Helene suppressed a desire to laugh at this peculiar idea, and realized that she had to come up with some sort of plan, and quickly too. Her father would come looking for her soon, a knife in his hand and murder in his heart, and she had to decide what to do. Should she trust the voice within her?

''If Hiram sacrifices me, will the sickness leave the city?''

No. It will not save a single life, and it will only deprive me of your fellowship.

Helene heard the anguish within the calm words, and felt her heart swell with the pain of her own loneliness. ''Whoever you are, I won't leave you alone. I do not know why. But I know what it is to be lonely.'' A sense of warmth suffused her, as if she was being hugged. A vague sparkle thickened the air within the niche for a second, then vanished. The little figure seemed almost alive. She picked it up, stroked the smooth cheek of the face with a grimy finger, then tucked the statue into her tunic. It made an awkward lump as she turned back into the sewers, but she barely noticed, so busy was she trying to plan an escape.

VII

Geoffrey d'Avebury leaned his head back against the stuccoed wall of his chamber and rubbed the bridge of his nose to ease the ache of his eyes. Then he rubbed the back of his neck and twisted his head from side to side. The light was fading at the end of another long, hot, and frustrating day. The guests, the Franconian merchants and the Greek brother and sister, had greeted the announcement of their house arrest in different ways the previous day. The Greek woman had fainted dead away and the merchant called Martin had favored the landlord with an exhibition of profanity that Geoffrey had thought perfectly remarkable. He himself had paced, played dice, eaten, and slept until he was thoroughly bored, then pulled out the book he had taken from his Aunt Rowena and started to read it over again. He got an occasional glimpse of the man Mercutio during meals, but had no further congress with him after their peculiar conversation.

It came back to him now, that conversation. Change is always possible, he had said. Geoffrey looked down at the pages of the book on his knees, at the fine chancery hand of his Aunt Rowena and the exquisite illumination done by his Aunt Beatrice. It showed a man recognizably his father in the process of turning from a man into a huge wolf, and it was a masterful piece of work. Around him capered a pack of red-eared white hounds, their tongues lolling out. He wondered how Dylan had managed the trick. How disappointed it must be to have such a dreary, inept son. He couldn't even manage to get out of Venice!

Something very like anger pulsed along his veins. Geoffrey was not given to bouts of rage, unlike his father, or even the milder tempests his mother and sisters were occasionally inclined to. He had trained himself to think calmly and behave logically years before he ever left for Milan to pursue his studies. He could barely remember why—an argument with the son of one of the stable hands when he was perhaps seven. Something had happened during the clumsy swinging of fists which had terrified him. The other boy was larger and stronger, and they had grappled and rolled in the sweet-scented hay of a clean stall, Geoffrey getting much the worst of it, until he had fastened his teeth along the bare neck of his opponent and felt his whole mouth lengthen and enlarge. It had lasted only a few seconds, just long enough to bite a chunk out of the boy's flesh and taste the warm, strange flavor of the blood. Franco had screamed, Geoffrey had released his grip and felt his face return to its ordinary proportions, and both of them had been terrified.

Now he felt as if all the times he had been angry since that day—the occasions when his father ignored him or his mother seemed preoccupied, when he had fallen off his horse or tripped over his own clumsy feet, when his sisters or his fellow students had teased him—had gathered into a huge knot under his chest bone. Geoffrey could barely breathe. The sense of his own madness which had plagued him since childhood seemed about to choke him.

There was a firm knock on the door, and Geoffrey carefully set down the open book and stood up. He opened the door and found the enigmatic grey eyes of Mercutio di Maya examining him. They appeared to dance with merriment at some unspoken jest, and he was struck again by the seductiveness of the stranger.

"May I come in?"

Geoffrey stood silently for a long moment, wondering if Mercutio were one of those odd fellows who cared for men instead of women, and if perhaps he was that sort himself. There had been a few among the students in Milan, and he had found them as puzzling as the students who paid gold for women along the Strada Magdalena. But, indeed, the whole matter of love seemed a rather peculiar thing to him, and as for wedding and bedding, he had never felt the least desire. His mother he regarded as the most beautiful woman in the world (though he mentally conceded that the Poppy Lady met by moonlight might rival her—and heard, he thought, the faintest echo of laughter), and his sisters fair enough in their different styles. The whole matter was quite illogical, and Geoffrey was profoundly suspicious of anything which did not submit to the strictures of rationality. Such as dashing off to Byzantium to get some elixir. Arguing with himself was very unsatisfactory—and Mercutio still stood in the corridor, impatiently whirling a small baton that hung from his belt.

"Uh, come in."

Mercutio glanced around the little chamber, his eyes darting here and there. He seemed to pause over the wide-brimmed hat with the poppies still fresh around the crown, and over the opened book which Geoffrey had set down on the corner of the table. The rest of his meager belongings, his spare tunic and hose, his flute and cloak, were folded neatly in a pile on the sill of the single, tiny window. The other man gave a nod.

"You tarry. Why?"

Geoffrey had a sudden sense that he was being pushed, herded, or somehow forced into a path not of his own choosing. His square jaw clamped at the thought, and he glared at the other man. Mercutio did not seem at all discomforted by his look. In fact, he smiled and nodded.

"You are quite correct, of course, young Geoffrey. When the fates play the tune, we all must dance to it. No, you do not like it. No man enjoys being told to do this or that, and ask not the reason. I, myself, have chafed at being an eternal errand boy, and at being so slight beside my grander brothers. It hardly seems fair, does it?"

"I do not know what you are talking about."

"Do you not? Have you sat over your purloined volume with no understanding then? This surprises me, for I had the impression you were mentally quick. Still, you stole the book, and that is a good sign. It shows . . . initiative." He smiled sweetly.

"I did not steal it," Geoffrey began, feeling wretchedly

guilty. "I merely borrowed it—and how did you know? Who *are* you?"

"Borrowing is stealing for a little while, is it not? But all borrowings and stealings are mine. Though I died not on the cross with the sweet Savior, yet I am the good thief." His eyes fairly danced. "They say I invented lies and thieving on the very day of my birth, and that is true. I did. It was great fun. You don't know much about fun, do you?"

Geoffrey was still puzzling over the matter of borrowing being a form of thievery, and the question caught him off guard. "I have never had much time for foolishness," he replied carefully.

"I know. You are a very serious fellow. And yet, you stole the book and summoned me, and not my stuffy brother. *All* my brothers are terribly stuffy—not a shred of humor in the lot. It makes life very dreary." Mercutio folded his knees under him and sat tailor-fashion on the end of Geoffrey's narrow bed. "I cannot conceive where I got it—not from my father, to be sure. A boring fellow. Here, sit. I promise I will not bite you." He smiled and Geoffrey once more felt the sense of seduction and enchantment about his curious guest. He sat, leaving a distance between them, comfortable and uncomfortable at the same time.

"What do you want from me?" Geoffrey asked, after a silence had filled the space between them for what seemed like an eternity.

"Me? I do not want anything. I am not that sort of fellow, always demanding sacrifices and prayers and other claptrap. It's not me. It's *her*."

"Who?"

Mercutio looked over at the blood-red poppies, and pointed with his baton. "You know perfectly well who I mean, and you are being deliberately cloth-headed." He sounded sharp and impatient. Then an expression of surprise filtered over his youthful features. "No, you are not. You do not believe. How peculiar. That you should be the son and grandson of two of the most profound devotees of all recorded history, and yet you do not believe. And without belief, we are powerless. Not me, of course. People will always lie and steal and make me present in their lives. But you. You believe neither in God nor in gods.''

This was a fascinating intellectual argument, and Geoffrey examined it with his usual care. He decided it was correct after a minute, and nodded. ''I never thought belief was wise, because so much that people believe seems to me quite foolish. The priests believe that the Pope is God's bishop—and yet he is only a priest and a man, often a miserable man at that. How can one believe in a God who chooses such unworthy servants?''

''Poor Geoffrey. A cynic at only twenty. Look at those poppies. They are a manifestation of the divine, fresh after a week, and yet they are but flowers to your eye. You do not believe in yourself at all.''

''I believe in my mind. Until now, that has been sufficient. I never wanted more.'' As soon as the words were out of his mouth, Geoffrey knew they were a lie. He wanted more, much more, and could not recall a time when he had not yearned for something he could not put a clear name to. Courage, like his father, to be sure, and something of his mother's serene happiness in her flowers and her song, his sister Beth's skill with horses and the sword, or Margaret's cheerful disposition. He knew himself to be moody, cowardly, and physically awkward, fit only for a monkish life of study and thought. He had begun his journey, he realized, in the vague hope that he might become different—braver, surer. What folly. He was just a poor, foolish scholar, not a hero, not a savior. The poppies seemed to reproach him.

Mercutio watched him like a cat at a mousehole. ''Of course you wanted more. Everyone does.'' He chuckled. ''Even the gods want more.''

''What do you mean?''

''Aphrodite envies Athene her wisdom, and Hera envies Aphrodite's beauty. I would have the shining bow of Phoebus—not to mention his wide shoulders—if I could. No one is ever satisfied with what they have. It would be amusing if it were not so tragic.''

Geoffrey was about to dismiss the man as a charming

lunatic, but he kept looking at the poppies. They should have faded days before. He had brought them for no reason he could fathom, no logical reason. They defied all logic. He had managed to ignore that for several days. Something inside of him moved, as if his heart had staggered in its steady rhythm. For a moment he felt capable of saving his mother, of journeying across the world and returning with some potion to restore her to health, capable of anything. For an instant he believed in himself, and then came back to reality with a thump. He could not even manage to get out of Venice! He was a fool and a lunatic. And a thief. A hot tear rolled down his cheek. Geoffrey clenched his hands into great fists and glared at the poppies. This was no job for him.

"I did not ask her to choose me," he muttered sullenly.

"No, you didn't. But she loves you anyhow."

Geoffrey was quite certain his heart was going to crack in his chest, so great was the pain of Mercutio's words. He was not good enough to be loved by anyone, let alone the Lady of the Poppies. At the same time, he knew he was loved, and it was a sensation both joyous and painful. He did not even know her name. He couldn't imagine why she had picked him. His father had known Beth, the Lady of the Birches, and his grandmother her Willow Lady, with an immediate recognition, as if they had been expecting a divine manifestation. He had not wanted to know her. He was afraid of knowledge for the first time in his life. She had always been there, and he had always been afraid of her.

He closed his eyes, and her vision shimmered before him. She stood in a darkened place, a sliver of moonlight haloing her head. She smiled and held out a pale hand. *Let me help you,* she seemed to say.

"I do not know what to do," he whispered.

It struck him then that he had run away, like a thief in the night, from his mother's deathbed, that he had let the madness he had long hidden from everyone overmaster him and lead him into believing he could do something to save Aenor. The woman in the garden had been a dream, a delusion. He was, quite simply, mad.

The despair of that almost choked him. Then he opened his eyes and saw the poppies. Each fragile petal was fresh and glowing. The long, prickly stems which he had wound around the crown of his hat were not withered or dry. Madness could not account for that phenomenon. And if he was not mad, if the poppies were real, then the lady in the garden was real.

Geoffrey discovered that he liked this idea even less than the thought of his own madness. He had read the pages of his Aunt Rowena's book without belief, in the same manner he had read Robert de Boron's *Joseph d'Arimathie,* as a fable. If he accepted as actual all that he had previously attributed to his own concealed madness, then the world became a truly terrifying place where gods meddled in the affairs of humans as they had in the misty past. A goddess was interfering in his life, and he did not welcome it. He wanted her love, not her manipulations. Not even that. He just wanted to save his mother's life and escape back into the safe existence of a scholar.

He turned his gaze back upon Mercutio, and suddenly the bits and pieces fell into place. His mind seemed divided into parts, the one collating facts and arriving at conclusions, the others rejecting these conclusions for a variety of different reasons, not the least of which was that his companion might be the Devil himself. Geoffrey was almost startled to discover that while he nursed quite heretical doubts about the existence of God, he had none at all about His opposite. Why, I am as superstitious as a peasant, he thought. It annoyed him to discover he carried around that particular piece of impedimenta.

Mercutio laughed at him. It was, after the initial shock, a pleasant sound, a kindly noise. Geoffrey had almost no experience with the company of men other than his fellow students and his monkish teachers, and he had never given them cause to laugh either at him or with him. He felt somehow lighter, less solemn, and less bedevilled by his fears.

"You are such a serious fellow, young Geoffrey, that I cannot imagine how you have escaped the attentions of my

dull brother, who, for all his shining countenance, is as
stubbornly unhumorous as you."

"Yes, I suppose I am. You are . . ." He could not go
on for a moment. If he spoke the name, the word, he
would have to accept the truth that the old gods and
goddesses still walked the earth, and, more, that they were
interested in him, Geoffrey d'Avebury, scholar and madman. It was not a comfortable thought. He looked at the
book still open where he had left it. In his mind he named
the deities who lived in its pages, Bridget, Saille, and
Beth, and silently added one for his poppy-bearing patron-
ess. "Neither my grandmother nor my father ever encountered the god, only the goddess. Why are you here?"

"You flatter me. I am not *the* god."

"Aren't you, swift Hermes?" The name was out, said,
acknowledged. It was done. He felt almost brave for having overcome his doubts enough to speak his mind.

The beautiful mouth curved into a smile, and the eyes
gleamed. Hermes gave a little shrug. "Perhaps I am. I
have never thought about it. As to why I am here, I came
to speed you on your journey. I have not made a very good
job of it so far, but some journeys are slow to begin."

"Is that the only reason you are here?"

"No." He made a mocking face. "The ladies are not the
only ones who are susceptible to caring for the odd mortal,
now and again. You interested me. You made such lovely,
lonely melodies on your flute. They touched me."

Geoffrey was stunned. No one had ever praised his
music before except his mother. On the contrary, his
family called it depressing and unharmonious. How many
nights had he poured his pain and fear and loneliness down
the tube of his flute? "Thank you," he managed to say
from a strangled throat.

"No, I thank you. When I heard you play, I was less
alone."

"Alone?"

"Do you think Olympus was an affectionate home?"

"Well, no. What I have read makes it sound very
uncomfortable. Everyone always quarrelling. My mother
and my father never quarrel, though sometimes, when his

black moods come upon him, I wish they would. She can't die. I cannot let my mother die. Tell me what to do.''

"We were both alone in our homes. That was the first binding."

"No, the second. I was born in the sign of the Twins— which you rule.''

"I stand corrected, oh, scholarly younger brother.''

Geoffrey felt almost happy. He had always longed for a brother. He gave Hermes a shy smile, and clasped his hand for a second. Then he blushed furiously.

Hermes bent forward and put a light kiss on his cheek. "I may steal your heart from the Lady's toils yet. But first we must escape this benighted city and begin our journey. Will you have me for a companion on the road?''

Geoffrey considered that a long moment. His heart felt as if it was overflowing. Was this how his unknown grandmother had felt when she first encountered her Willow Woman? Complete safety and unbounded affection. He had never trusted anyone, not even his family, that greatly. And it was not logical that he should trust so utterly in the man beside him. He was the god of lies and thievery. For the second time in his life, Geoffrey rejected logic and followed his heart.

"I would follow you to Hell itself, I think.''

Hermes looked grave. "You may have to.''

VIII

Michael ben Avi turned away from the window and the panorama of Jerusalem beneath a leaden sky. Would the sun ever shine again? He glanced with disfavor on his wife, Rebecca, swollen with child, nagging and complaining, and tried to conjure up some feeling of affection for her. There was nothing, just vast weariness and the sour taste of expediency. He had married her for reasons that had nothing to do with the respect and care a man should bring to the wedding bed, but only because she was a Levite and could further his ambition.

He stroked his thick beard and made himself smile at her. "I must leave you now, dearest."

Rebecca looked at him, her moon-face bloated, her fingers bulging around her many rings. "Leave me. How can you leave when you are never here, never with me. All you think about is the city. Will you leave me when those—those creatures overrun the walls, break down the gates, smash through the doors, and flood into Jerusalem? You do not care what happens to me. All you care for is yourself."

"I care nothing for myself. I care only for God, and for the mission he has given me." Her accusation stung, for it was closer to the truth than he liked. He could persuade or charm anyone. Since his earliest childhood he had been able to bend everyone to his will, everyone except his stupid but cunning wife and his lunatic twin brother, Jacob. He had always known who he was, the Messiah, the Promised One, the Deliverer, and only these two refused to acknowledge it. Jacob, like his namesake, tried to usurp his role, and Rebecca tried to undermine it. A wife must support her husband in all things, must agree with him. Surely his mother, if she had lived, would have done so. Women had been created only to uphold men, not to think on their own, for they had not wit or wisdom.

"Rebecca, you are very foolish. Jerusalem will never fall. I will save the city."

"It took you long enough to answer. 'I will save the city,' " she mimicked, her lips twisted in distaste. "What a hypocrite you are. You believe yourself the Messiah. Pah! My only satisfaction will be in seeing you ground into the dust where you belong—and I shall probably be denied it. I will die in labor, or you will leave me to the Darkness when the city falls and pretend you had no other choice. I will almost welcome my own death to be rid of you and your ambitions."

"I am the Deliverer!"

"And I am the Virgin Mary," she replied. "There is no deliverer, you fool. You men make up tales of saviors and deliverers and angels! Camel droppings in the wind of your mouths. You will not save the city, and you will not save me. Leave me. You were never here to begin with."

Her words were whips across his mind, and he stormed out of the chamber in a black mood. Michael left his house and began to check the guard stations along the walls, although it was not his task. But the open adulation of the troops soothed his temper and calmed him. He looked out at the masses of foes gathered beyond the walls, and believed that he could stop them.

Michael was still troubled in his thoughts, because he had had a dream the night before that he could not interpret. Finally he walked to the restored Temple and made his ablutions before he entered. It was quiet within, and he bowed his head before the altar. He made a long silent prayer that sounded to his interior ear more like a demand than a petition, and he cursed Rebecca for making him doubt his purpose.

The dream came back to him. He saw a girl, a child almost, holding a great light in her hands. She stared at him adoringly, but when he reached for the light, she drew it back. He needed that light. It was his by right. No woman could withhold it from him. Certainly no little redheaded girl. He was humble before the Lord, but he bent his knee to no other power on earth.

When he emerged from the Temple he found his brother waiting outside. They glared at one another, exact replicas except that Jacob kept his beard trimmed shorter. They were both handsome, strong, hawk-faced men, men of great personal attractiveness, and they loathed each other. Michael was sure they had wrestled for supremacy within their mother's womb and so hastened her death, but that was Jacob's fault. If he could only have acknowledged Michael's authority, she would have lived.

"I thought I would find you here, begging for help. Have you ever noticed that your observances are quite infrequent unless you desire something?"

"I was asking for guidance as I always have," Michael answered with as much dignity as he could muster. Jacob always made him feel naked. His brother was mad, but only Michael seemed to realize it.

"Give me, give me, give me, I wager. I hope you were successful, for the assault has begun on the south wall."

Michael wanted to smash a fist into the mocking face as he had done so often as a child, but instead he turned and headed through the maze of streets, past houses, the small chapels and monasteries and pilgrim hostels whose taxes were so essential to Jerusalem's coffers, past workshops of coppersmiths and broiderers. The tumult became clearly audible as he neared the wall.

There was a rending sound and the gate shattered. A thing out of nightmare, a scaled beast which breathed frost, not fire, shoved its snout through, and a rain of arrows from above nearly caught him. For a moment, Michael was terrified. He stood frozen against a sheltering wall.

Then the divine fire which had first touched him on his sixth birthday coursed along his veins. He felt the archangel whose name he bore enter him, consume him, burn away the terrible fear, and fill him with hot certainty. He pulled his sword, barely aware that Jacob mirrored his gesture, and leapt forward to battle the monster.

Its cold touched him briefly, but his fire warmed him. Michael knew he blazed like the pillar of fire itself. He brought the sword down across a scaly limb. It barely cut the surface, and he sought some more vulnerable spot. At that moment, Jacob leapt forward and stabbed down into the dark eye of the beast as hundreds of gabbling nomads swarmed in behind it. The sword slid down into the great eye and the beast made a shriek. Michael had a moment to think, *Thief, always stealing my place* as Jacob killed the thing, and then he was too busy fighting the horrible creatures who had besieged the city for weeks to think of anything at all.

Afterwards Michael never had any clear remembrance of how long the battle lasted, nor when the tide turned against the defenders, when retreat became rout and the exhausted remnant of his forces got out of the city in any way they could. Jerusalem burned, brightening the night which was not so different from the day, as they re-grouped. He was almost too weary to stand.

A steady stream of refugees swelled the ranks of the fighters: women, children, and the old, plus horses, camels, asses, and snarling dogs. He croaked orders from a throat raw with shouting and smoke, and vaguely realized that Rebecca had been prophetic. He had not come for her. Michael had a moment's regret for the unborn child, hoped it had been a girl, and none at all for his wife. All his sorrow was for Jerusalem, *his* sacred city. He would return and drive out these Darklings. He would find that light, wrest it by force from the girl, and save his city. He was the Deliverer.

IX

Mercutio scratched his fair head in thought. "I may have to foment a revolution to get us out of Venice," he said quietly.

Geoffrey frowned and shook his head. "I hope not. People are bound to get hurt."

The young god smiled. "Is that important?"

"Certainly. You cannot just go around causing upheavals because it suits your purposes. Well, *you* can, I suppose, because you are a god. But it isn't right—interfering in lives. Don't you have any conscience?"

"None. I travel light—and that's a heavy bit of baggage."

Geoffrey was perturbed. "Do any gods?"

"No, I think not. We do what we can or what we must, and just suffer the consequences. It does not always come out as we wish—we are not that powerful. Even when we were at the height of our power, we could not always control what happened. Oh, there are most assuredly some gods who claim omnipotence—but they are bigger liars than I am. Vain boasters. A lie must always contain a bit of truth—and there's no truth in omnipotence."

"If you aren't all-powerful, and if you cannot make things come out the way you want, what good are you?" Geoffrey blushed furiously. "I mean, what is the purpose of being a god if you can't . . ."

"Provide miracles? Sweet Geoffrey, we gods are less than you think, and more than you can imagine. It is a mystery I myself do not comprehend." He looked as if he had considered the matter a great deal, and the resulting ruminations had not satisfied him. "Here I offer you a solution—a modest little revolution, which Venice sorely stands in need of, I assure you—and you prim your mouth like an old woman because it isn't a tidy solution. I should have expected it. Your whole family has an excess of conscience. I hoped you would be different. You made such an excellent beginning, stealing your Aunt Rowena's book and all.'' He made a comical face of disappointment.

"You are completely amoral,'' Geoffrey replied, in his most severe voice.

"Yes, I know. If you wanted . . . What's that?'' A distant murmur of voices came from somewhere outside. "Come on. Let's go look. People get up to a lot of mischief without my help, you know.''

They hurried down the narrow stairs to the public room. The shouts were clearer now. Cries to overthrow the Doge echoed up the canal. The sound of running feet pattered along the street. The landlord stood wringing his large hands in his apron, and the Greek brother and sister listened with the expressions of cream-fed cats.

"Oh, *signore*, it is terrible,'' began the landlord. "The sailors, they are revolting.''

"I have always found sailors revolting, myself,'' Mercutio muttered, *sotto voce*, and Geoffrey repressed a grin. His companion might be a liar and a thief, and quite amoral, but he was full of play, and Geoffrey was beginning to discover some of that quality in himself. He was not yet certain if he approved of it, but he did know he enjoyed the sensation. It was rather like being mildly drunk. "How foolish of them, to be sure, and inconsiderate as well,'' Mercutio added more audibly. "Why, we could have moldered here for years.''

The sarcasm was lost on Marco, the landlord, who continued his anxious plaint until the Greek man demanded some wine. Marco hurried away, and the four of them took seats around a common table. The two Greeks eyed Mercutio and Geoffrey suspiciously, and Mercutio gave them one of his heartwarming smiles. The racket in the street and along the canals increased as they sipped their wine in silence.

"I am sure the city guard will quell this disturbance quickly,'' said the man. His sister gave him a sharp glance.

"Not *too* quickly, let us hope," Mercutio purred. "I was getting rather bored."

A sharp-faced fellow in the garb of a servant dashed into the room and skidded to a halt. He made a nervous bow at the Greeks, and the man rose. They withdrew to one corner of the room and whispered together. Geoffrey caught bits and snatches—the words "horses" and "ships"—and gave Mercutio a glance. The young god had a beatific expression on his face. He was enjoying himself thoroughly.

Geoffrey. Mercutio's lips had not moved, but he "heard" the voice. *Go gather your things and take the back stairs out. Go to the stables. I will join you there.* He hesitated for a moment, then saw that the woman's attention was focussed entirely on her brother. He slid quietly out of his chair and made for the stairway.

He gave a quick glance back, and saw that he appeared to be still sitting at the table, listening to something Mercutio was saying. *Go!* The sharp voice in his mind was like a stab in the butt. Geoffrey scurried up the stairs, packed his things in a thrice, and crept down the rear stairs, through the empty kitchen, and out into the alley. His heart was pounding, and he could still hear the racket from the streets and canals. It seemed very misty, faraway and dreamlike.

The stable was warm and full of the homey smell of horses. He walked in as casually as possible, and passed a groom who did not appear to see him. Geoffrey was puzzled. Was he invisible?

He opened Marina's stall and she nickered a greeting, pressing her soft nose into his neck and lipping his shoulder. He stroked the smooth neck, glad of her comforting presence. Geoffrey set his pack down and pulled her tack off the wall. Marina jiggled happily as he saddled and bridled her. He was glad of something to do besides wonder who was sitting beside Mercutio in the inn, and why the groom had not acknowledged him. Too quickly it was done, and he hunkered down in the corner of the stall to wait and worry.

The day had advanced to evening before Mercutio made an appearance. Several times Geoffrey was tempted to simply get on Marina and try to ride across the long, narrow bridge that tied the city to the mainland. But it was a long way across Venice, and the noises of continued rioting dissuaded him from the attempt. He used the hours to ruminate, and was almost irritated when the young god interrupted him.

Mercutio's appearance was altered—he looked older and more serious—but the eyes were unmistakable. Geoffrey scrambled to his feet and brushed some hay off the back of his tunic. "I thought you might have left without me," Mercutio said quietly.

"I considered it, and thought it was a poor idea." Geoffrey felt mildly uneasy that he had even let such a notion enter his head. "But I wanted to ask you how I appeared to be sitting at the table when I was really climbing the stairs, so I stayed."

"That curiosity of yours will get you in a lot of trouble some day. The city is in quite an uproar—none of it my doing." He seemed somewhat put out. "Those Greeks . . . well, they have always been devious. They paid well to start a rebellion, and wasted their money because several groups of merchants had already done the same and various lots of sailors were organizing their own revolt—free of charge. Organizing is too nice a term for it. Come on. We are going to the arsenale."

"But won't there be lots of guards there?"

"Yes, but also confusion, and, at present, that is our best ally." Mercutio's eyes widened. "You were thinking of trying the Ponte della Laguna. Brave boy. You would never have gotten through."

"Why? I seem to be invisible. At least, the stable hand didn't see me."

"You are. Your lady friend here is another matter." He gave Marina a little pat on her neck.

"Should I leave her?" Geoffrey felt stricken. Marina seemed his last link to everything that mattered to him, his home and family.

"After going to all the trouble of stealing her? Certainly not." Mercutio grinned. "I must say, you made a very good beginning of it, taking the horse *and* the book."

"I took money too," Geoffrey said, eager to make a clean breast of the matter.

Mercutio shrugged. "Any lout can take money. It requires imagination to go beyond that, to see the value of other things. Come along. The streets are a tangle and it is getting dark."

The three of them went out to the narrow street and used back alleys as they worked their way down to the harbor. Each time they crossed one of the bridges they encountered bunches of people shouting and hitting each other with sticks or brandishing torches. The firelight cast strange shadows on infuriated faces, and blood ran down foreheads. Geoffrey remembered his father's work in the cleansing of Paris and felt slightly ill. Dylan had tried to protect him from the horror of this, or had tried to deny that it existed. He had a sense of both empathy and affection for his father.

Geoffrey watched as a city guard brought his halberd down across the skull of some unfortunate, and a moment later saw a long, wide-bladed knife enter the guard's kidneys. Blood spurted out as a work-roughened hand removed the knife, and his eyes met those of the murderer, an ordinary-looking man whose face was now twisted with something like lust. Then the look was gone, replaced by one of befuddlement. The man looked at his knife, at the guard dying at his feet, and turned away.

"I wish I had never come here," he told Mercutio when they found a quiet alley away from the clamor. "And I don't think much of your brother Ares' pastime," he added bitterly.

"No, I have never cared for it overmuch myself. Too noisy. And do not leave out my dear sister, Pallas Athene. She, too, looks upon war with favor."

"Why? I thought she was very wise."

"Oh, she is, but she has many aspects. We all do—even Ares. Still, I am glad you do not love him."

The harbor was almost day bright when they finally reached it. One great alder pile dock was ablaze, and the heat was enormous. Another was a glowing smolder, and the smoke was intense. Geoffrey coughed and pulled his cloak across his mouth to filter out some of the smoke. Groups of exhausted men battled the fire, pulling buckets from the sea, but it seemed to make no difference.

Mercutio led Geoffrey along the quay, where confusion reigned. Merchants argued with sailors while workers dumped bales of goods onto waiting ships. At one dock two groups of sailors were fighting over which of them would transport some goods, while a merchant wrung his smooth hands and the two captains screamed at one another. It was disgusting.

Mercutio watched him. "No, this is not how commerce should be conducted. But whenever trade is halted, war follows."

"How can people . . . be so hideous?"

"We all have many aspects," Mercutio replied sadly.

"I could never . . ." Geoffrey began hotly, and stopped. He no longer knew what he was capable of. A few days before he had never stolen anything. He had never had the courage. Why couldn't he have told his father about his meeting with the Lady of the Poppies and gotten his blessing instead of slipping away, a thief in the night, with a valuable mare, a book that did not belong to him, and money. He wished he could go back and begin again. Or, better, not begin at all. He wished he had never known his father's history.

Geoffrey followed Mercutio blindly through the confusion of the arsenale, loathing himself. He examined his motives with the same ruthless logic he applied to his studies, and concluded that he had done everything from an unspoken desire to rival Dylan's exploits and a stupid yen to have an adventure. Instead, he was having a well-deserved nightmare. He was not made of any heroic stuff. The sight of blood revolted him, and the destruction going on round him seemed somehow to be his fault.

"Stop," whispered Mercutio. "You torment yourself needlessly. Dylan would never have let you come."

"Yes. He knows how wretchedly useless I am."

"No. He does not understand you, but he thinks well of you. But he would wish to protect you from all this. When you are a father, you will have the same desire."

"Me? A father? What a joke! What woman would even look at me?" Even as he said the words he saw a long room, light playing along smooth stuccoed walls, and two small children rolling together on a mosaicked floor. They were the same age, and he could hear them squeal with delight, their dark hair tumbled across plump, rosy cheeks. They looked like him—or his father in the boy, and his sister Beth in the girl—and he loved them immediately. Were they ever to be, or were they just the products of too great an imagination? Geoffrey wanted them to be, as profoundly as he wished his mother to live forever. He wanted Aenor to see those frolicking toddlers, to hold them and cuddle them as he could not remember being snuggled. What sort of parent would he make, he wondered, and remembered how his sisters came to him with their small distresses. He remembered small, grubby hands entwined around his neck, and little tearstained faces pressed against his lean shoulder. He had loved that, and missed it sorely when they came to menarche and became somehow remote, withdrawn into the mystery of woman. Only Margaret had still sought his comfort and his counsel.

They came to the end of an almost deserted dock, to the gangplank of a very small boat that wallowed like a pig against its restraints. A sickly breeze blew smoke and ash around them. The oily waters of the arsenale reflected the still burning quay and the torches on others, the shapes of vessels large and small, and the blurry figures of men. The uproar had faded to a dull murmur.

A dark-haired, scoundrelly-looking fellow swaggered down the gangway, picking his rotting teeth with a blackened fingernail and tugging up a pair of tattered trousers tied around his sagging belly with a piece of rope. One eye had a cast in it, which increased the unwholesome appearance. Geoffrey found him perfectly terrifying.

"I was 'bout ready to shove off without you," the seaman grunted as he sucked his teeth. He blew his nose between his fingers and made a hacking cough. "You didn't say a horse. It will be more for the horse. Three more sequins."

"Three sequins," purred Mercutio. "What a droll jest.

One is more than sufficient.'' He balanced a bag in one slender hand and jingled it suggestively.

The seaman pulled up his rope belt again and wiped his hand on a pants leg. "Two. Rhodos is a long way off.''

Geoffrey bit back an angry reply. He had an instant dislike for the fellow, and he sensed Mercutio was engaged in some mischief. Two sequins was more money than he had with him, and most of his coinage was Milanese anyhow. And he did not want to go to Rhodos. He had said he would follow the young god into Hell, but he had never mentioned any actual places. He was quite mad, and no one seemed to notice. The thought struck him as funny, and he began to laugh uncontrollably.

The seaman took a step backward and stared at Geoffrey. Whatever he saw seemed to discomfort him a little. Then Mercutio suggestively jingled the bag again, and with a shrug they were waved aboard.

The sea foamed beneath the bow of the ship, and the slap of the water made its own gentle music. Geoffrey was sitting on the deck near Marina. Despite her name, she viewed the proceedings with disfavor and tended to become restive if he left her for any length of time. A brief stay in the foul-smelling hold that passed for a cabin below decks had given Geoffrey a great desire never to view it again, and he had spread his blanket beside the horse, glad of the companionship.

He had seen little of Mercutio since they got underway. The young god seemed to prefer the airless cabin to the breezy deck, and Geoffrey knew it was because something was wrong between them. He tried to think what he might have done to fall into disfavor—beyond being mad and a coward—and what he might do to mend matters, and found himself soothed and enchanted by the sea instead. It was a wonderful thing which he had never experienced before, and he re-read the various adventures his grandmother and father had had at sea. Strangely, none of the keen freshness of it, the pure exhilaration, came through in the pages of his aunt's volume. He looked hopefully for dolphins and was quietly disappointed when none appeared.

The sun was sinking behind them in the west on the third day out from Venice, and Geoffrey felt almost lulled by the rhythm of the waves and the sound the canvas made in the wind. A small melody rippled through his head. He pulled his flute out and began to play. The tune rolled on his breath, slipped down the tube of his instrument, and swirled into the freshening air.

It seemed to him it caught in the sails, swelled them, filled them, and glided too along the swollen timbers of the hull. The clumsy, wallowing ship seemed lighter, swifter. The *Swallow* lived up to her name and sped across the waters. He did not see the seamen crossing themselves anxiously, nor Mercutio emerging from below and leaning indolently against the gunwales. Geoffrey knew nothing but the music. It reminded him of Aenor's song and brought her somehow closer to him. As long as he played he felt he could preserve her. Then, as gracefully as it had come, the song departed, the wind shifted, and the sea took on a different rhythm. He lowered the flute to his lap and stared at the darkening sea.

Mercutio sat down beside him. "That was very beautiful, Geoffrey."

"Thank you." He felt his cheeks flush with pleasure at the praise and lowered his eyes to the worn deck. "I do not think I can take much credit for it. It was just there on the wind."

"Perhaps. But it takes a special ear to hear it." Mercutio paused. "I have come to crave your pardon."

"What?" Geoffrey was completely confused. "For what?" He felt an immense relief that he was not at fault, followed by a great sadness tht his friend felt guilty.

"For interfering, and then for doing nothing but demonstrate my own poor cleverness. I have taught you nothing but to await me in a stable like a servant. You don't need me, Geoffrey."

"But I do. I need you for my friend and to guide me."

"I have been a poor friend and a worse guide. I wanted you to love me." The quiet voice brimmed with bitterness.

"Well, I do, and I cannot see that you've done anything less than be a good friend."

"I delayed us in Venice."

Geoffrey went utterly still. He felt the mute volcano of his own rage rumble through his bones. He lifted his eyes from his lap and gazed at the young god coldly, holding in the anger, feeling it claw at his throat like a huge beast. He let the betrayal flower in his heart, analyzing it like a problem in logic. Time was a luxury he did not have.

"Is there an elixir in Byzantium which prolongs life?"

"Yes." Mercutio gazed out at the sea. "But it will not serve females."

Geoffrey looked at the book resting beside his knee, then at the poppies around the crown of his battered hat. His anger flowed away from Mercutio and focussed itself on the Lady. "So, there was never any chance for me to help my mother."

"No, not really, not directly." A single tear rolled down the beardless cheek of the young god.

Geoffrey reached out and touched a finger to the tear. It felt hot as molten lead against his skin. "Then it really does not matter how long we stayed in Venice, does it?"

"Do you forgive me?"

"There is nothing to forgive." Geoffrey felt his own withdrawal, his remoteness, cover him like a vast, heavy blanket. "If I cannot save Aenor, nothing else matters." He tucked flute and book into his bag, pulled his cloak about his shoulders, and stared sightlessly at the sea.

X

Hiram was waiting for Helene when she returned, filthy and ravenous, from her sojourn below Byzantium. "Where have you been?" he nearly screamed.

"Out," she answered as coldly as she could. Helene ran nervous fingers through her short hair and left a trail of smudges on her brow.

"Out? In the city? Are you mad? You might have been hurt."

"Your concern is touching, Father. No, I am not mad. I merely needed to think."

"Think! You never thought in your life, you stupid . . . I won't have you wandering the streets. You have to prepare for the . . . Go bathe. You are disgusting."

"Did you speak to the Council, then?" It was remarkable. She felt quite dispassionate, as if every human feeling had drained out of her body, leaving only an icy sense of calculation.

"Yes. They agreed." Hiram twitched his fingers along the embroidered symbols of his robe, uncomfortable.

"They agreed to murder me, at your suggestion."

"It is not . . . that. We all have to make sacrifices in this life. It is for the good of the city. You must understand that. It won't be painful. I promise that." His skin was a pasty grey and a light sweat beaded his brow.

"My death will not save the city." The little statue hidden in her garments felt warm against her belly.

"These matters are beyond your understanding, child. You must trust my judgment."

Helene gave a sharp, bitter bark of laughter. "Trust your judgment, you old fool? I will never trust a man again, I think. I find I am unwilling to make the sacrifice—for you, or the city, or any other reason you might offer." She waited to see his reaction, knowing quite well that an unwilling victim played adversely with the energies of magic. Helene wanted her father to acknowledge her rights in the matter, recognize her as a person, as a human being worthy of value and respect. No, she just wanted him to say he loved her. It seemed such a small thing to ask.

"Nonsense. You do not know what you are saying. Surely you are willing to do this for me." His face smoothed out, and he seemed kind and earnest and wonderful. Helene recognized a mild charm spell, an exercise of charismatic magic, felt it whisper across her mind and wrap little tendrils of power around her. She *was* willing to die for him. Of course. Then he would love her. It was so simple. Her head wanted to nod in agreement. Her lips wanted to say "Yes, I will die for you, Father."

For a long second she felt helpless, as if she was drowning in a fathomless sea of warmth, of affection she had never had and always longed for. She stepped forward and rested her body against Hiram's, head on his chest, her statue-heavy belly pressed against his hips. She felt him flinch.

Then he screamed, and the spell tore into rags of magic, little wisps of energy flickering between them like fireflies. Hiram wrenched himself away and slapped at his body as if he were ablaze. He hit his loins and howled and danced almost frantically. A bulge rose in his robes, and there was no doubt he was male.

"What are you?" he screamed. "Why are you doing this to me?"

Without the charm spell, hopping about like a puppet, he was revolting, a red-faced, wrinkled old man. His dark hair began to become white as she stared in astonishment. For the first time he looked every day of his seven hundred years. His skin began to droop, soft jowls falling from his chin, and wisps of hair cascaded from his skull. He clapped his claw-like hands to his face as a drop of drool slid out of the corner of his mouth. With a final cry, he dashed away towards his sanctum.

Helene stood stunned for a moment. What had she done now? Something had broken Hiram's unaging spell, the magic which kept him youthful. She bent and picked up a strand of white hair and stroked it between her fingers, bemused. Then, disgusted at the dust and grime on her body, she decided she was not going to escape without a hot bath. For some reason she laughed at that—a real chuckle—and felt almost lighthearted.

Her chambers faced east, and offered a view of the harbor. The thousand lamps of the House of Wisdom, Hagia Sophia, reflected through its marbled walls and reflected on the waters. So did the light of several fires, here and there along the shore. The air was heavy with the smell of ash and smoke. Byzantium was burning. She could hear the roar of the mob in the streets.

Helene stared out at the city for a minute, curling the strands of her father's hair between her nervous fingers. Then she turned away and walked to the enormous bathing pool. She walked in, clothes and all, and sank down into the warm waters up to her chin, then submerged her head entirely. When she came up for air, she pulled off her sopping tunic and held the little statue in one hand. She washed the tiny lady until the alabaster shone white. Then she set the statue on the step of the bath and removed her sandals and trousers.

Helene scrubbed herself vigorously, as if she was washing off more than just dirt. She hummed to herself. It was almost like a ritual, a cleansing of something more than her body. She felt wonderful. The noises of the dying city and the smell of burning had nothing to do with her. From time to time she paused and touched the statue and smiled at it. It stood half submerged and gazed back.

Finally, when her skin was beginning to wrinkle, Helene dashed through the cold end of the bath, and dragged herself out of the water. She drew a towel around her body and rubbed her flesh dry, enjoying the sensuous texture of the cloth across her skin. She noticed again how hungry she was, and reached for a withered apple which sat in a tray of miserable fruit as she rubbed her tumbled hair with a corner of the towel. The fine linen was damp beneath her fingers.

Hiram walked in as her hand closed around the apple. His hair was black again, his complexion unwrinkled. Helene was so busy noticing that he had renewed his rejuvenation spell that she barely observed the apple in her hand until she got it up to her mouth. The withered skin was gone, and the fruit had a golden glow and smelled as if it had just come from the tree. Indeed, the entire chamber fairly reeked of apple blossom, completely obliterating the smell of smoke from the city.

Hiram gaped at her, and Helene remembered she was naked. Oddly, she felt no embarrassment, as if her unclothed state was perfectly natural. This must be how Eve had felt in the Garden, Helene thought as she looked at the apple. *I wonder if it will bring me wisdom, and I wonder if I want it.*

"Cover yourself," her father croaked. His voice sounded old and tired. Helene looked at him and saw that the left eyelid drooped and the corner of his mouth was dragged down unnaturally. She felt oddly indifferent to his command, as if he were a distant figure, a phantasm from another life.

She put her teeth into the apple and took a bite. The taste filled her mouth and seemed to course into her blood. The smell rose in her nostrils, into her very brain, like the first wine of autumn. It was sweet, sweeter than anything she could recall, and bitter too, a faint tartness beneath the nearly overwhelming deliciousness. It almost choked her as she chewed, slowly, deliberately, as if it was the most important thing in the world. The taste filled her, and she felt she might never be hungry again.

Hiram was moving his hands in patterns, and Helene felt the luxuriant, pulsating richness within her begin to still. Her limbs seemed to be turning to lead, her heart to stone. She looked at him uncomprehendingly as her sense of her own power began to drain away. She felt hungry again—no, starved of something she could not put a name to. The apple smell curled into her nose, and slowly, painfully, she lifted the fruit to her mouth again.

Helene bit. It tasted horrible, like dung and blood and offal mixed together, nauseating and foul. She spit it out, and the morsel flew across the room and struck her father in the middle of his wide brow.

Hiram gave a soundless scream and clapped his hands to his forehead. A faint gurgle came from his throat, and he sagged to the floor. The gold embroidery of his robe tarnished and began to unravel as his flesh decayed across his bones. He struggled, waving his hands feebly, as his eyes rheumed, dimmed, and faded. In a few moments all that remained was a dried skeleton wrapped in a few moldy scraps of cloth.

She cried out and ran across the room. Helene knelt beside the bones and grasped a desiccated hand as tears splashed down her cheeks. The hand disintegrated in her grasp, and she stared down at the knucklebones. She flung them away.

"I did not mean to kill you! I only wanted you to love me. Why couldn't you have loved me?" She grabbed the eyeless skull and shook it, enraged and sorrowful at the same time. A tear splashed onto the white bone and trickled into a vacant orb like a drop of quicksilver. "I am sorry, Father," she whispered.

The jaw moved. "Accursed child," it hissed. "Murdering brat. You killed your mother, and you killed me. Why could you not have been the son I wanted?"

Helene lifted the skull and hurled it across the room. It smashed into pieces against the wall, and the whole tower seemed to groan. The stones gave an ominous rumble, and a large crack appeared in the ceiling. A large section of plaster crashed to the floor.

Helene froze for a second. She wanted to run, but she could not move. The skeletal remains of her father seemed to hold her enthralled. She could not take her eyes away from an object that hung around its neck. It appeared to be a cross with a large, glittering stone set in the top. Peculiar patterns curled across the crosspiece, dazzling, shimmering coruscations. Her hand reached down and tore the object away as a large stone shifted out of the wall.

Flee, child, flee. Run for your life.

She scrambled to her feet, snatched the small statue from the water, yanked a gossamer robe off the end of her bed, and dashed for the door. She tucked garment, statue, and cross into a clumsy bundle, and raced for the stairwell. Her bare feet slapped against the cold stone, stubbing and bruising her toes. The sound of falling masonry urged her on, and she could hear the shouts of servants here and there. The rumbling increased and the stairwell shook.

In a minute she ran the five levels of stairs, fleeing past startled servants, until she reached the kitchen level. Cook was transfixed by the crumbling hearth, and Helene slapped him on the shoulder.

"Get out, you fool!" she screamed as she scooped up a small loaf of bread and thrust it into her bundle. Then she darted past him and dashed for the stables. These were set apart from the tower proper, across a large courtyard which was littered with fallen stones. She cut a naked foot on a smashed tile and left bloody prints in the dust.

The grooms were peering out of the doorway of the stable. Their eyes nearly popped from their heads as they registered her nudity. One, Pedros, reached for her, and she aimed a kick at his manhood and felt the flesh connect with a satisfying crunch. "Saddle my horse—now!" she ordered his companion. "Hurry!"

Helene took a cloth bag off a hook and stuffed her belongings into it, then pulled on a quilted practice tunic and fighting trousers from the cabinet where she stored them. She tugged her boots on, shoved her hose into the sack, and pulled her well-worn sword and belt around her narrow hips. Helm and gloves she added to the sack, and with bow and quiver slung across her small breasts she turned to get her horse.

The groom was pulling the girth into place. She slipped the halter and bit into her steed's mouth, tied her sack behind the saddle with nerveless fingers, and mounted. Achilles lunged under her, reared once as the groom jumped away. Helene reached forward and put a reassuring hand on her horse's neck, then urged him towards the street. His shodden hooves clacked against the surface of the road.

An earsplitting crack made her look behind. Helene

could see the top of Hiram's tower above the surrounding buildings, where her father kept his library and workshop. It tore in twain as she watched, and books and stones cascaded into the smoky air. Then she rode like the wind.

XI

The wind faded and died, and the sails hung like empty bladders against the masts. Geoffrey roused from his vacant reverie as sailors scurried across the decks and peered anxiously over the sides. He heard their uneasy mutters and found them eyeing him. He turned to speak to Mercutio and found the place beside him vacant.

Geoffrey stared at the deck and wondered where his companion had gotten to. Perhaps he was down below decks. Then he knew with a kind of sick certainty that the young god had departed. He let the betrayal wash over him, through him, then let it go. He was not even angry, just a little sad that he had not said farewell. He was more immediately concerned that the sailors would believe he had dumped Mercutio overboard.

It was now very dark beneath the pale sliver of the moon, and the stars were almost dazzling. The little ship wallowed, and Geoffrey realized that there were large waves rolling across the sea. The waters made a strange moaning sound, and a big wave poured across the bow. The air was hushed and still, and the waves ran larger and faster. He could not imagine what would cause such contradictory phenomena, and the sailors seemed equally puzzled.

Then there was an enormous boom, like thunder but much more intense, and a light bloomed on the horizon. The stars went out like doused candles, and a burning smell swept across the deck, followed by a patter of rain. It was not until several small stones struck his forehead that Geoffrey realized that it was not rain but rock which fell, and ash.

The sea churned and rumbled, the waves increasing by the minute. The helmsman tried to alter the course, but the *Swallow* floundered as it took on more water. Geoffrey stood and put an arm under Marina's neck, feeling her trembling subside beneath his touch, and wondered what to do. Drowning held no appeal, he discovered. He just couldn't think of any immediate alternative.

Change is always possible.

For a moment it was as if the young god had returned, the memory of that first encounter like a brief caress. Then the bitterness returned. Change? To what? He could not imagine how his grandmother and father affected their transformations, no matter how often he read them in the book. Then, too, he could not bring himself to contemplate abandoning Marina. She snorted as if she understood his thought. Her eye was an orb of gold in the ruddy light which now colored the sea. Larger rocks crashed onto the deck.

Use the flute. Geoffrey could not tell if this idea came from his own mind or another's. He remembered the curious incident by his mother's bed, and the way his body had tingled as he played for her. It was if he had been given a part of Aenor's sweet song. He must have heard it from her very bones as he rested in her belly. It had always been a part of him, and he had never known it. What else had he denied himself knowledge of? He had a moment's brief insight of his connection to his father, the ways in which they were alike instead of all the ways they differed, and then a stone the size of a sheep's head smashed onto the deck and cracked into smaller pieces, smoking. He did not have time to stand around wondering. He had to do *something*.

Change is always possible. Use the flute. He ran the words through his mind as he pushed long fingers through his hair. Something prickly brushed his ear, and he looked around and saw his hat hanging from the pommel of Marina's saddle. The blood-red poppies seemed to glow and pulsate. He touched the delicate petal of one and "heard" a little trickle of melody. It was like one of Aenor's garden songs, but different.

Geoffrey pulled the flute out of his bag, took a hot, searing breath of smoky air, and set his lips to the instrument. He felt a little song swell in his chest and float down the column of the flute, and he barely heard the ominous crunch of wood on rock. The sea rushed over the bow of the *Swallow,* sweeping two crewmen overboard, and the deck split into three long sections. The center one began to sink almost immediately, leaving Geoffrey on the portside portion, and several hysterical sailors on the starboard.

He didn't know how he played, or even what, but the music poured out of him as he focussed on the flowers, barely aware of the mounting confusion around him. The poppies began to expand. Geoffrey pictured them in his mind as huge, enormous and strong. Then he noticed that his leather hat was keeping pace with the expansion of the blossoms, and appeared to be thickening. He paused for a second and put the hat on the quivering deck in front of Marina's hooves. A curl of foaming sea brushed the brim, and he fluted furiously.

The hat was as large as a shield when he set it down, and a moment later, the size of a table. A wave splashed over him, and the deck lurched under his boots. He almost panicked and lost the song. The smoky air burned in his lungs, and his eyes teared, but he grimly continued in a sort of stubborn desperation, until the hat was larger than a bed, a thick leather circle adorned with poppies as big as trenchers.

One of the sailors screamed, and a jagged rock thrust up through the waters. A wave caught the edge of the hat and lifted it above the sinking deck for a moment. With a sense of incredible serenity, Geoffrey grasped Marina's bridle and pulled her onto the curious craft. Her eyes showed white with fear, but she did his bidding and stood shivering, hock deep in flowers, her belly above the crown of the hat.

He took a hasty breath and stepped onto the hat beside her. The sea boiled up through the cracked hull of the *Swallow* around the rock, caught the hat, and swirled it over the sinking gunwales. Another wave smashed him against Marina's trembling side, and nearly tore the flute from his grasp. He clutched it close, pressed it to salty lips, and played on. It was not the flower song, but the wind tune he had made earlier. He felt some other element enter it, and caught the vagrant melody, interweaving it with the earlier one.

Geoffrey almost lost the song and the flute when he glanced back and saw the wreck of the *Swallow* and the bobbing heads of a couple of crewmen before the waves took them. They flailed about, unable to swim, and he wondered how any man could undertake the risky business of sailing without the knowledge of swimming. The song faltered as he contemplated this, and he realized they were drowning and that he could do nothing. A wave slapped him into the present and he returned to the task of his own survival, which quickly occupied his entire attention.

The hat was an ungainly craft, and the sea was in tumult as further convulsions erupted from the now visible volcano. Spindrift curled amongst the poppies and his boots were soaked. The air was hot and rank with the smell of sulfur. He felt in danger of capsizing, but he forced the fear back into a corner of his mind, like an unruly child, and ordered it to be still. It sulked and made hideous faces at him, until he began to find it almost humrous. A ghostly chuckle interrupted the melody for a second, and the vessel seemed to lighten. It started to spin across the waves in dizzying circles until he was nearly sick and closed his eyes.

Geoffrey concentrated on the song, only the song, and ignored the increasing ache in his lungs, the weariness of his arms, the trembling in his legs, and the constant battering of the waves. After a time he was too exhausted to continue standing and he lowered himself into a sitting position, resting his back against the sturdy crown of the hat. It felt wonderful, and he was struck by the utter ludicrousness of the situation. No one—not his Aunt Rowena, not the great, ancient Homer—could make a sober tale of so ridiculous an adventure.

He had a moment's thought of the two toddlers he had envisioned and wondered if he would live to tell them the story. Geoffrey decided that if these children ever came to be, he would indeed inform them how he had gone to sea in a hat, because they would never believe him. I am a fool, a clown, a buffoon, and there is not a heroic bone in my body, he thought, and felt oddly comforted.

He played on in a sort of waking dream until a whinny from Marina made him pry his eyes open.

The sea was calmer and the hat spun more slowly. He could see the rosy hand of Aurora brush the horizon, and realized he had not really expected to see another dawn. Of the volcano he could catch no glimpse, and the air smelled clean.

The dark bulk of an island loomed from the sea before him. The rising sun gilded the ridges of its mountains, and the hat spun over the waves until they entered a large bay. Geoffrey decided the rocky shore that spread out around him was the most beautiful sight he had ever seen, and played a happy tune to reflect his emotions. A final wave pushed vessel and passengers onto the streaming strand, and he staggered to his feet, pulled Marina onto the stony beach, and let the flute fall to his side. The hat shriveled back to its normal size, and the poppies rustled merrily in the morning breeze. He picked it up, hooked it on the pommel, and clambered up the beach to beyond the tideline.

Geoffrey wanted to sit down on a rock and never move again, but he was thirsty, and that drove him on until he found a tiny stream surrounded by a few bushes and a little grass. He removed Marina's halter, pulled off her saddle, and released her. Then he drank handfuls of water, thinking it sweeter than anything he had ever tasted. Finally, he pulled off his soaked, briny garments, washed them in the stream, and spread them to dry. Marina was munching a thorny bush, an expression of mild astonishment on her face that she should consume such fare. It is fit only for goats, she seemed to say, and Geoffrey found himself laughing. She gave him a hurt, haughty look and turned her flanks towards him and deposited a generous dropping on the ground, letting him know in no uncertain terms just how she felt. But this sent him off into fresh gales, and he was still chuckling as he stretched out naked on the ground and began to drift into sleep.

"Thank you," he murmured, as he fell into exhausted slumber, though he could not say to what powers he addressed his gratitude. He dreamed of children hanging around his neck, planting moist kisses on his cheek, and snuggling trustingly against his chest, and smiled as he slept.

XII

The ground rolled. For a moment Helene thought her eyes were playing games with her. Then she saw the dome of the House of Wisdom shiver, the lamps within it flicker, and she heard a deep rumbling sound. There was a terrible cracking noise behind her, and as Achilles reared and slewed, she saw the roadway behind her split into several sections. The arcade beneath it was falling to pieces.

She grasped the reins in both hands, leaned forward on the neck of her frightened animal, and spurred him hard once. Achilles leapt forward like an arrow and they galloped down the street. A large man in the livery of one of the mages jumped in front of her, shouting something she could not make out, and she smashed his jaw with the pommel of her sword. A column crashed into the road and her horse barely managed to leap across it. An enormous explosion boomed from somewhere within the mages' precinct, but she could not spare a glance to see what it was. Helene could barely hang on to her horse in the mounting chaos.

People ran screaming in every direction, women clutching children, old folks hobbling along as fast as they could, city guards weaponless and wide-eyed. Carts full of the bodies of the dead were abandoned here and there, making new fresh barricades beside the mounting rubble, and frightened Byzantines crawled over the decaying bodies, their fear of contagion forgotten in the face of the fresh calamity. Fires blazed and leapt from place to place as if alive.

Helen lost all sense of time as she strove to work her way across the huge city. The ground shook and shivered in agony. Dully she realized that the city wards must have collapsed completely, because no earthquake had disturbed its serenity for nearly a millenium. It felt as if every tremor that had been prevented for those centuries was happening all at once. She fought off several attempts to unhorse her by both men and women, laying about her with the sword without compunction. She barely noticed the blood on her blade, the wound she got on one thigh, or that she killed several people.

The night was broken by the sliver of an ancient moon and the glow of the spreading fire. Slowly she worked her way towards the outskirts of the city, towards the landwall with its many gates. The night had begun to fade before she reached it and joined a stream of exhausted survivors struggling to get through.

Remarkably, the wall still stood almost intact. The soldiers who patrolled and manned it were barring the way, shouting at people and prodding them none too tenderly with spearbutts. The frightened folk seemed to hesitate, to pause. Then a fresh tremor transformed them into a hysterical mob, and by sheer numbers they overran the soldiers.

Helene pulled back, and drew her horse off to the edge of the swarming road. She noticed the cut on her thigh for the first time and stared at the crusted blood. She was too weary to go on, and just sat, catching her breath as dawn began to gild the smoky horizon.

"Mistress Helene!" A grimy face appeared at her knee, a small, dark man with his helm askew. She recognized him. Jerome. The name came back to her. "Come this way." He reached for Achilles' bridle and nearly lost a finger as the horse nipped at him.

"I have to get out," she croaked. Her voice was rough, her throat raw, and she remembered that she had screamed at many people. The gate before her was full of frantic folk clawing and fighting their way out of the city.

"Not this way."

"Why?" She had worked out with him in the armory a few times and knew him for a sober, careful fellow. Helene turned Achilles' head and followed him away from the road. It was quieter, and she could feel her head pounding with pain. Her lungs ached, her whole body hurt, and she wanted to cry.

Jerome followed the line of the wall away from the gate and led her towards an almost deserted guardpost. A single horse stood in one of the dozen stalls. The thick walls shut out the sounds of the mob and the burning city almost completely, and the air smelled clean.

Helene dismounted and almost fell. Jerome steadied her for a second. Her legs trembled. She leaned against Achilles' shoulders and smelled his heavy sweat. She reached up and pulled his bridle off, patted his huge rump, and urged him into a stall. He sucked up some water sloppily, then poked his nose into the manger and came up comically munching wheatstraw. It was such a commonplace sight, so real and ordinary, she wanted to hug him.

"Come above," Jerome said. She followed him up the narrow stairs to the lookout. Hippolytus, arms-master and a captain in the guard, stood staring north across the enormous necropolis which abutted the wall. His grizzled hair was matted against his skull with sweat, and his mail was punctured in one place, though the quilted tunic beneath had prevented a wound. He turned and looked at her, and lifted his eyebrows. "Look who I found," Jerome offered.

"And what are you about, young woman?"

Helene shrugged, aware of a certain ambiguity in her position. She was the daughter of a mage in a city where females were inconsequential, a student of arms with the man before her as well as his social superior, all at the same moment. "I am not free to say," she temporized. She pulled off her helm and ran gritty fingers through her hair. It was damp and salty to the touch.

Hippolytus seemed satisfied with her reply, for he turned back to his lookout. "There," he said, pointing. "I warned them."

Helene peered out and saw hundreds of glowing fires on the plain beyond the burial grounds. "What is it?"

"That, child is an army. They've been gathering for days—a week almost. The commander has sent messages to the Council, but they have not seen fit to respond. I dare not hope you bring an answer."

"No, I do not." The rising sun illumined many small tents and the figures of men like insects gathering between them. "The Council has been occupied with other matters."

"The sickness continues?"

"Yes. And, as you have perhaps guessed, the wards are no longer . . . impenetrable."

Hippolytus gave a crack of laughter, like a tumble of small stones. "The wards. Ah, yes, the famous spells that made my vigilance unnecessary." The Mages' Council and the city governor had been at odds over the matter of the guards for as long as she could recall. "I knew they had failed when the first temblor came. If any of those old fools remains alive, they will be glad of my strong arm. But not grateful. Mages are never grateful."

"The city is badly damaged," she said. "That army may find little but a smoking rubble."

"I won't live to see it."

"You will fight, then?" She struggled to understand why, knowing he was outnumbered, he would choose to remain and fight. Males were such peculiar creatures.

"I have sworn to defend Byzantium, and I keep my oaths."

Oaths. Promises. Brave words. Honor. It made her sick to think that this man, whom she respected, would cheerfully die for a few meaningless noises. She looked out at the tents, at the insects forming into units around limp flags on poles, and realized that those too were men, and that they too would perish. A straggling group of Byzantines trudged through the cemetery, apparently unaware that they were proceeding headlong into fresh disaster.

Helene turned away. She was tired and filthy and almost overwhelmed with a terrible sadness. She wished only to retire to some quiet place where neither war nor magic existed. Perhaps she would become one of those peculiar Christians who shut themselves up in monasteries and spent their lives praying.

She sat down at the table with a thump, and reached for a hunk of bread and some cheese. Helene ate without tasting while Jerome conferred with the captain, washing the dry bread down with sour wine. A mild tremor shivered through the wall.

It was suddenly urgent that she leave. Her body seemed leaden and her muscles protested as she rose. Quietly, she slipped down the stairwell, rebridled Achillles, and lead him out of the stall. As she pulled herself into the saddle she heard Jerome shout something. Ignoring it, she turned Achilles south, along the wall, and headed for the sea.

This was a quarter of the city she had rarely entered, and she found it very quiet and relatively untouched by either earthquake or fire. Helene puzzled over that for a moment, then realized that it seemed almost deserted as well. The houses along the streets showed neither lamp nor torch in the screened windows, and no voices echoed from them. A lone dog trotted out of an alley, glanced at her curiously, and vanished into the shaodws. Her skin began to crawl, and she felt cold beneath her quilted tunic.

A rectangle of light like a plate of silver shimmered against the morning sky, and after a few seconds she could see the outline of a tower. It seemed to be made of mist. The whole district had a foggy, insubstantial look, and only the sound of Achilles' shoes striking the pavement assured her that the place was quite real. The silver rectangle seemed larger. Her scalp prickled under her helm and she strained both eyes and ears for some clue to her unease.

The rectangle moved. It appeared to slide across the face of the slender tower, vanishing on one side and reappearing on the other after a few moments. What mage dwelt there, outside the precinct? As far as she knew, every man of magic in Byzantium lived and worked in the same district, facing east beside the Horn of Gold. The Council of Twenty, their number reduced to eighteen by the deaths of her father and Demetrius, had always kept a firm hand on the establishment of towers as well as the number of mages in the city, lest any one of them should attempt to make himself supreme. They decreed that none might practice beyond the precinct.

There was no doubt in her mind as she watched the silver shape rotate around the outside of the almost invisible tower that some one of her father's peers had defied the Council's rule. He must be very strong to have eluded their notice, and she racked her weary brain for a likely candidate. The sun crawled above the horizon, and the tower vanished entirely, as if it had never been. Helene decided she did not like the neighborhood at all, and turned Achilles' head towards the landwall to the east.

Something huge squatted in the shadow of the buildings. Helene could make out a darker shape and she could hear a sound, a sort of rustling, that made the hair on her nape bristle. There was a little rattle, then a chittering clack, and an enormous spider rushed towards her. The great eyes sparkled, and the furred face seemed very human.

Helene wheeled Achilles around on a bezant, and felt his huge withers gather for a gallop as a great sticky strand of stuff looped around her body. She struggled to pull her arms up, but they were held fast to her sides. She was pulled out of the saddle, and she clutched at the bag tied behind it, pulling the cords loose with icy hands. Blindly she thrust her fingers in and curled them around the figured surface of the cross she had removed from her father's body. Then she slipped off her horse's rump and hit the paving stones with a bone-rattling thump. Stars of pain danced in her eyes.

Come, my bride. What lovely, strong mage sons you will give me. Your father was a fool to have thought to waste your blood on a sacrifice. Better to have coupled with you and gotten what he desired. But he was always so nice in his notions.

The voice hissed in her skull as she was dragged across the stones, revolted at the suggestion but more disgusted as she realized that the spider was a mage in beast form. A shape-shifter. No self-respecting mage would ever stoop to such a device.

What a foolish prejudice that is, child. You will see. You will learn to rejoice in this body, and in your own transformation into many forms. I will teach you how to wield your magnificent powers. You are such a delicious morsel.

Helene felt violated by the very words in her mind, sickened to near nausea. She gripped the curious artifact in sweating hands, her arms tied to her sides by coil after coil of sticky web, and tried desperately to drive the voice out of her. The coils rose, from waist to chest, as she was dragged across the paving stones, pulling and struggling. A strand slipped around her throat and she fell silent, only then realizing she had been screaming.

She clenched her teeth and pressed the flat jewel at the top of the cross against her groin and tried to concentrate on the object rather than the vile voice in her mind. A thrill of something played across her body, a sort of cold fire. She felt as if her bones were filled with light—blinding light.

What's this? The spider-mage's query sounded a little uneasy. Helene felt her body halt on the hard stones and opened her eyes. The cross in her hands was different. From the unjeweled end a long, slender stream of light issued. The colors in it shifted, dazzling her for a moment. Then it seemed to solidify into steel, but metal such as she had never seen, for the surface danced with red and blue and yellow. It was somehow both substantial and airy at the same moment. She did not pause to consider the metaphysics of it. It was a weapon, and Helene knew very well how to use those.

Dizzy and gasping for air, she touched the coruscating light to the disgusting strands around her body. As the strands parted Helene sucked in a breath and rolled to her feet with the ease of years of practice, although her head spun. A fetid smell filled her nostrils, and the spinners shot out a stickly strand that roped around her ankles as the great mandibles reached for her. She swayed and almost lost her precarious balance, then brought her strange sword across the web, slicing it, then up in a continuous arc against the closing jaw.

The sword sheared through the bony stuff. She kicked her feet free and hacked off the closest leg. The smell of blood joined the other odor as the spider-mage made a howling noise. The beast staggered for a second, and she plunged the scintillating blade into a great jewel-like eye. Light played across the huge, hairy body as it jerked.

Helene pulled the sword free and saw the fluid spurt

from the ruined eye. The spider-thing shimmered, then vanished, and she saw a bearded man naked on the stones. He seemed vaguely familiar, but she could not name him. A great weakness filled her, and she heard the thunder of hoofbeats and the sound of many voices as she sank to her knees and felt blackness engulf her.

XIII

The first rumble of the earthquake sent the ragged train of survivors from Jerusalem into near panic. Michael saw the ground rise and fall in front of him and assumed for a moment that it was sheer exhaustion, that his aching eyes were playing tricks on him. He had been up for three days and nights, organizing, bullying, comforting, and demanding. That his brother Jacob was doing these tasks as well was unimportant.

Ahorse, he did not feel the tremor, but behind him a wagon overturned, and a woman screamed. He turned his weary horse around and realized what was happening. He sat transfixed as the hard-won organization of the train shattered into chaos. If only the women would stop screaming. The sound cut into his mind. He wondered if Rebecca had screamed. Why had God given women such shrill voices? Or created them at all? Why had God listened to Adam when he said he was lonely? Surely loneliness was preferable to this unbearable shrieking.

Michael found tears swelling out of his aching eyes. He brushed them away and dismounted. The earth rolled beneath his feet and he nearly fell down. It faded away and he began shouting. Somehow he got them back together and underway again, but every fresh temblor set off new outbursts of hysteria. He was glad custom prevented him from touching any woman not related to him by blood or marriage, because he wanted to throttle the lot of them.

They camped uneasily at twilight, and soon dung-fed fires made a homey scene. Michael sat on a rock, too weary to move, and someone brought him food he ate without tasting. His eyes drooped, and his head fell onto his chest.

Rebecca screamed. A dozen black shapes hacked up her body, jumping up and down and laughing horribly. They cut the child from her belly, slapped it into life and tore it into pieces, gnawing on the warm flesh. A boy. It had been a son.

A woman stared up at him with great green eyes. Her hands held light, a sword of light, but when he reached for it, she drew away, and another woman, a stern, strong woman with one breast bare and a quiver of arrows over her shoulder, stepped in front of her. She seemed about to speak, but he shoved her aside and reached greedy hands for the green-eyed girl. He must possess that sword. It was his. He must have it to restore Jerusalem and drive away the Darkness.

Michael ben Avi jerked awake and felt enraged. He had had it in his grasp. Where was it? He looked at his empty hands, puzzled. He looked up and found Jacob standing nearby, watching him.

"You will never have it, you know," Jacob said. "I will not permit it."

"Have what?"

"I know your secret thoughts, Michael, your dreams. But it is I who will get the sword, who will deliver Jerusalem from these creatures. Nothing will stand in *my* way. No woman, certainly."

"You plan to kill me then?"

"No. You stole my birthright by being born first, but I will not slay you for that. God will give me the sword."

Michael began to laugh. The very things he told himself sounded quite insane when his brother said them. Jacob backed away, offended, and Michael's laughter turned to quiet tears. God had let his son be torn to bits and eaten in the first moments of his life.

And Rebecca. His heart swelled with pain as he remembered her sweetness when she had been a young bride. She had adored him, and he had taken it as his due, not as the fine gift it was. For the first time Michael saw his ambition for what it was. Pride. What an empty thing. He had killed her sweetness with neglect, and left her to perish at the hands of ghouls. He felt sick, sick of himself, and sick that he had not protected the woman who had never done him any ill.

Michael gazed up at the starless sky and prayed for humility. He wept again, for his wife and child, for his beloved Jerusalem, for all that was lost. In his heart he begged to be allowed to return, to free the city and make a decent grave for Rebecca. He prayed to find the girl with the sword of light, wherever she was, and he gave his oath that he would not take it by any force. Then he slept dreamlessly, the fire of his aura making a pillar in the darkness, so his followers whispered he really *was* the Archangel Michael, and felt more secure. Only Jacob derived no comfort from the sight.

XIV

Helene awoke to a pounding headache, a ravenous appetite, and a feeling of imminent nausea. The headache was increased by the constant jarring she was undergoing, and she realized she had been slung across a saddle like a sack of grain, her wrists and ankles bound by thin rope, and her mouth stuffed with a filthy rag. No wonder she wanted to vomit. She turned her head carefully to one side and saw Achilles' familiar neck and head. The movement made the pain in her skull increase, and she let it fall back into its previous position while she tugged at her restraints.

A large hand grasped her hair, yanked her up a little so she squeaked with anguish. She caught a glimpse of eyes like Galatian olives, black and lustrous, but any other features were hidden beneath voluminous draperies. "Lie still, witch." He glared at her, and Helene glared back as best she could. He let her hair go without warning, and her chin smashed on the leather of the saddle. Stars danced in her eyes, and she tasted blood in her mouth.

After a few minutes of dizziness combined with hatred, Helene closed her eyes and concentrated on dealing with her headache and nausea. She visualized a still pool, smooth, clear water, deep, cool water. Twice the picture slipped away and her bodily discomforts rushed back, unbearable. She would have clenched her teeth but for the gag. But she struggled back to the thought of the pool, and was rewarded by the cessation of the worst of her pains. All the hours she had spent in Hiram's library, reading moldering treatises on geomancy, sorcery, or the powers of crystals, and all she could manage was to fix an upset stomach. But it occurred to her that she had never been able to do that before, and that much of what had happened in the past day or so would be better for some quiet reflection. She chuckled into the gag at this, knowing reflection, quiet or otherwise, was not a skill she had ever cultivated previously. Perhaps it was her position, all that blood falling into her skull. If she had been able, she would have laughed aloud.

I wonder what else I can do? It was an oddly disturbing thought, because she remembered the apple and how she had murdered her father. Helene shut off the memory and concentrated on examining herself as if she was a quiver of unfamiliar arrows. Each arrow, her archery master had taught her, was slightly different from every other, and a good bowman knew his arrows like a hen her chicks. Some flew a bit to the side, others straight. Some flew a few lengths further than their fellows. She knew by feel the characteristics of every arrow she used in practice, as if they were living extensions of her body. Genesius had often said she was the best student he had had in many a year.

Helene found her thoughts drifting towards the little statue of the lady with the arrows, and wondered if she had known her weapons well. It seemed likely. It was comforting. She remembered the spider-mage, and the strange weapon that had come out of the curious thing she had taken from her father's body. Her disgust at shape-shifters and at males in general left a sour taste in her mouth much nastier than the wretched rag that silenced her. She pictured herself cutting the heart out of the black-eyed man who had pulled her hair, dragging the still throbbing organ out of his chest, and enjoyed the vision for a moment. Then it repelled her. She remembered that taste of the first bite of the apple and knew that life was too precious to destroy over pulled hair. She would have to wait for the man to give her a good reason—which she did not doubt that he would supply.

Who were her captors and where were they taking her? By the swathings of his head and body, the black-eyed man was one of the desert people, but there were literally hundreds of tribes scattered across the arid regions be-

tween Byzantium and the sands of Araby. Few, if any, of
them would have spoken to her in Greek, as he had. She
listened to the occasional remarks of the horsemen around
her, a guttural gabble she barely recognized as a dialect of
Aramaic. She understood just enough to know they were
uneasy about a number of things, not the least of which
was her. Helene caught one comment that they never
should have left Antioch, and a response that the Black
Folk had probably not left a stone standing, which was
both revealing and puzzling. What Black Folk? Some
invasion from Sheba or Egypt? No word of it had reached
Byzantium, and that seemed strange.

There was a shout, and her horse was led into a narrow
defile that then widened out. She was pulled off the horse
and dumped unceremoniously on her already bruised bottom.
She glared at the tall, robed figure above her, and he
backhanded her sharply. Tears sprang unbidden into Helene's
eyes, and she clenched her small, torn hands. The hand
swung back for another blow, and another hand stopped it.

"Cease. Jalael wants her."

"What care I for Jalael's base lusts? We should have
killed her where we found her."

"Base lusts," came a silky voice. "Is that what you
think of me, *habiba?*"

Dazed as she was, Helene recognized the insult. She
blinked to clear her eyes and tried to see the new speaker.
Half a dozen almost identically garbed men in voluminous
white robes with veiled faces stood in a semicircle around
her now, and her black-eyed tormentor had a hairy hand
on the hilt of a long knife that stuck up above his sash.

"You want her for your own ends," he snarled.

"Do I?" replied the smooth voice. Helene searched the
veils for a clue to the speaker. "And what might those
be?" She still could not identify him.

"You want her to do foul witcheries for you!"

There was a faint laughing noise. She found it came
from a man somewhat less tall than the rest but otherwise
no different in his garb from those around him. If he was
the leader, he had no mark of it on his person. "And you
would like to plunge into her womanhood."

"Never!" Black-eyes sounded both shocked and horrified. "Couch a female with fire-hair. Only *you* would risk
mounting a demon. I say cut her throat and be done."

Helene did her best to look pathetic and helpless. The
desert people were superstitious, and they feared redheads
and lefthanders, amongst others. The shorter man shook
his head.

"You have the brains of an ass, Yusef. Bring her to my
tent. Are you afraid of one small, skinny girl? She doesn't
even have tits."

"She will ensnare you."

"No. She will serve me. It was intended. The All-
Powerful intended me to find her and use her. She is no
threat. A few sessions with the rope and the rod and she
will do exactly as she is bid."

The voice was so seductive that Helene almost believed
his words herself. The man seemed to be a natural charismatic, someone who needed no spells to enhance his
charm. Even the promise of punishment sounded right and
proper. He would beat her and she would permit it. She
shook her head to clear it, and realized he planned more
than a few beatings, that the rod he referred to was a
euphemism for that foolish dangle between a man's legs.

Helene was not shocked, but she was frightened. Her
training with Byzantium's men-at-arms had exposed her to
the rough sexual chatter of the barracks, the boasting and
bragging and outright lying that seemed to be very important to them. She had never thought about rape before
because no one in the city would have been stupid enough
to touch a mage's child. Rumor had it that the desert men
had a marked preference for the buttocks entrance, and
that knowledge left her breathless with terror. Sweat beaded
her brow and rolled down her dirty face as a tribesman
picked her up and carried her towards a huge tent. She
trembled in spite of herself and he laughed.

She was plopped down on a thick carpet and quickly
surrounded by robed men sitting down in a circle. They
drew their veils aside and grinned. They looked like an
audience at the Hippodrome expecting excellent entertain-
ment. Helene pulled herself into a sitting position and was

promptly knocked down by a large hand. She lay on the carpet and hugged her arms against her chest. A single tear betrayed her terror, and she brushed it away.

They seemed to have lost interest in her as the faint murmur of water boiling on a small brazier mingled with soft conversation. She smelled sweat and horse and dirt, and over it the warm scent of desert *kayva*, the beverage they brewed on any social occasion. Helene had smelled it before in the bazaars and caravansaries of the city. It seemed an ordinary thing, a commonplace activity far removed from rape or death, and she began to feel less panicked. The men seated around her became less monsters than filthy nomads.

I killed two mages today—yesterday, probably—so why should I be afraid of a bunch of desert jackals, she thought. Helene knew she was, and that braggadocio would not get her free, but she went on assuring herself that she was not afraid as the men slurped *kayva* and discussed horses and camels and the fall of Byzantium in a great earthquake and fire, followed by an invasion of fierce northern nomads who spoke a strange tongue. She closed her eyes and listened intently. These men were afraid of the northerners, but more afraid of another group they called the Black Folk who had recently swept up from the depths of Araby and overrun or ensieged the trading cities of the Levant— Damascus, Aleppo, Antioch, perhaps even Tyre and Alexandria. One spoke with some passion of the end of the world, and Helene silently agreed that it sounded rather grim. She was most puzzled why word of the Black Folk had not reached Byzantium, or if it had, why she had not heard it. She drifted into an exhausted sleep and woke to find the tent empty.

A hand touched the nape of her neck and she stiffened. After a moment the gag was drawn away and the hand caressed her sweat-caked hair. A finger stroked her brow and ran down her cheek, and Helene shuddered. She was afraid, but also excited. She felt her loins quicken at the touch the way they had when she had pressed her father's cross between her limbs. She grasped the knowledge and forced herself to focus on it instead of the thrills which now chased across her flat belly.

Hiram had asked her where she got her power, and now she knew. It was something to do with her maidenness. The thing she had torn from her father's corpse became a sword when she touched it to her mound of Aphrodite. That did not explain the other things, the way she had struck out at her father, the transformation of the apple, and certainly not the comforting voice she had heard in the deserted room. Her body writhed with lust as the hands continued to stroke her face, and Helene felt a cold determination that no man would ever take her newfound power from her.

A face swam before her eyes. It was a fair face, beardless and well-featured. Great dark eyes, soft and seductive, looked at her. Gentle lips brushed her forehead, and she felt as if her loins were afire. She felt like a small bird in the grasp of an enormous serpent.

Mother! She shouted the thought, and saw the calm, serene features of the little statue. *Help me, please*. Her writhing hips collapsed against the carpet, and the wild yearning vanished, leaving behind an urgent memory, an unsatisfied desire which ached like a rotting tooth. She would never submit to that, never, never. No man would ever touch her again. The thought left her with a sense of desolation, and the hope that her life would be brief, because the yawning emptiness of such a future was as revolting as the alternative of submitting to the seductive hands and eyes of the man beside her.

He looked thoughtful and puzzled. "You are going to be more difficult to tame than I believed," he said in careful Greek. He gave a little sigh and picked up a thick length of rope. "I do not really enjoy beating women. The screams are so shrill." The voice was full of menace.

Helene felt herself chill. She twisted to roll away, and he caught her by the hair and held her easily. The rope rose and fell. The blow fell on one thigh, and she had never known anything could hurt that much. She heard herself scream and was outraged. The rope came down again, and she felt a wetness beneath her trousers and knew that she was bleeding. She wished the rope were a snake that would slay her tormentor.

The pain came in waves after each blow, but there was an instant between when the agony subsided. Struggling and panting, she tried to focus on that moment. Finally Helene stopped trying not to scream, let her body go limp under the fall of the rope, and thought only of the object. It was harder, more difficult than anything she had ever done, but years of battering in the practice yard gave her the method. She concentrated on the rope, on transforming it, on killing the man.

Jalael gave a soft grunt and rolled her over on her back. "I do not want to hurt you," he said.

Helene breathed as slowly as she could manage. The rope lay limply beside him. She lifted her bound wrists in mute supplication and pleaded with her eyes. A trickle of power quickened her loins and she directed it into the rope. She caught his hand, the hand which had held the rope, and drew it towards her lips as if to kiss it. He loosened his grip on her hair and smiled, running a thumb across her browline. Smugness and self-satisfaction played across his handsome features.

Helene felt the rope stir beside her aching thighs. She gave the man a shy smile and lowered her eyes with as much maidenly modesty as she could manage. "No more, please, no more," she whispered. From the corner of her eye she could see the coils of the hemp smooth out into the satiny skin of a serpent. It moved, and she poured energy at it frantically.

The thing thickened, became rounder than an arm, then more like a leg, and suddenly a smooth triangular head lifted above that of the man. It was as big as a plate. The tongue flickered out and the opalescent eyes glittered.

Something must have shown in her face, for Jalael turned and stared up at the snake coiled above him. He snatched for his knife, but Helene grabbed the hilt before him, and the snake looped around his chest, trapping the arms against the man's sides, and began to squeeze. Jalael made a cry and Helene cut his throat. The snake continued to wrap itself around him, and included Helene in its embrace. She could feel its coils pressing her against the limp, bloody carcass of her most recent victim, and she hacked feebly at it as she tried to think how to reverse her spell. Her ears rang and her head swam dizzily as the snake continued inexorably in its constrictions.

Helene realized the creature was using her own power to go on, and made a great effort to still the energy that was boiling out of her. The stink of blood and sweat filled her senses, nauseating her, and she could barely breathe. The serpent raised its great head and looked into her eyes. Then a mist came into her mind, and she slid forward with the man's body beneath her.

XV

Gooffrey was deep within a dream, a wonderful, pleasurable dream. He had never had one quite like it, and it was decidedly just the sort of dream his monkish teachers would have disapproved of, which increased his enjoyment for no reason he could think of. He had never had a dream which seemed so real. A bevy of Milanese beauties were caressing his body, kissing him and stroking his loins, running smooth fingers in his hair, and rubbing his aching muscles. He could feel their warm breath on his skin. One of them mounted his manhood and began to ride him. He groaned in his sleep.

Then sharp teeth sank into his skin, and he started awake. A hideous face bobbed above him and tangled hair fell on his face. It was a woman, a very real flesh and blood woman, and she thrust her hips against him and clawed his chest. Her eyes were strange, the pupils almost invisible, and her lips were green. The breath that came from her gasping mouth was fetid. It smelled of stale wine and something else, a pungent green smell.

Another face intruded, and hot lips pressed against his mouth, nearly suffocating him. A wet tongue stabbed into his own, wriggling against the roof of his mouth, and he nearly gagged at the taste of heavy wine and the other, unidentifiable flavor of something green and rank.

He tried to push her away and found that hands held down his wrists, incredibly strong hands. The female impaled on his manhood continued her movements, and while his mind recoiled in distaste, his body seemed to revel in it. He wanted to surrender to the sensations.

His rider gave a curious grunt, a long, wild cry, and

rolled away, and strong hands grasped his root and rubbed it like a fire drill for a few seconds. Then a wet mouth closed around it—he could feel the teeth slide across the tender flesh—and he had a fresh rush of pleasure. Fingers rubbed his testicles, and a tongue licked them. There had to be two women down there, nibbling on his manhood. It felt wonderful and was terrifying at the same time. He kept thinking about the teeth.

Another woman mounted him, and he felt the muscles of her femaleness clamp around him in a fashion that was almost painful. The woman kissing him drew away, and he saw the face of his new partner. She grinned at him, but her eyes were empty. She clamped clawlike hands over his shoulders and rammed her hips down, giving a cackle. Her generous breasts bounced up and down, and he watched them, fascinated in spite of himself, until another female thrust her body across his face and pushed a stiff nipple into his mouth. His lips closed around it like a hungry babe, though he could hardly breathe. When he did manage a gasp, he regretted it, for she stank of heavy sweat and wine. A hand coiled in his hair and pulled, and another clawed across his chest.

Geoffrey felt the skin tear and knew warm blood was welling from the cuts. The breast in his mouth pulled away, and he saw the contorted face of his partner—blank eyes and yellow teeth within wine-stained lips. A fire filled his loins, and there was a moment of indescribable delight that blotted out all thought. A volcano burst within him, and he knew nothing for what seemed like an eternity.

A hand raked his cheek, slashing the skin above the beard, and she screamed something unintelligible at him. He realized he was screaming back. Something stung his thighs and he saw a whip of greenery descend behind the woman. She lowered her head and sank her teeth into his shoulder.

He was revolted, both by his attackers and by his own body. The sight of the empty faces ringed around him was obscene. Geoffrey wanted to get away. The thought filled him to the exclusion of all else. He wished he were somewhere else, and—more—that he were someone other than himself. He felt like a worm, and wished he were one.

The accursed women were doing something to the worm between his legs, something awful and wonderful. He felt the sting of the green whip, the probing of fingers, the wet touch of mouths, and wanted to cry. He hated them and hated himself for being powerless to defend himself. If only he could think of something.

For a moment he saw a picture in his mind, a picture of his mother with a huge snake coiled around her body. It was one of the illuminations in his aunt's book. But it seemed alive, animated. The serpent was moving. He could see the skin ripple and flex.

Geoffrey focussed on the movement and felt his body still. It was a sickening sensation, like dying, and then a surge of something seemed to pour into him. He felt his body as it changed. His arms and legs seemed to fall away, his skull lengthened, his torn flesh smoothed. Long, sinuous muscles flexed, and he was barely aware of the wild women screaming and howling. Sound was faint, and the world was rock and sand and a bare foot kicking at his eye.

He pulled away, coiled great muscles, rolled onto his long belly and lifted a huge head to the eye level of his assailant. She was round-eyed with terror. He felt the slap of the green whip somewhere along his length and turned a slow gaze towards it. He felt a tongue slide out between huge fangs and tasted sound and smell. He moved towards the pink figures and they screamed and fled.

Geoffrey felt the warm sunlight against his skin as he stretched his length out. He slithered on his belly. It was right. He was a snake. He had always been a snake. Not a hero, not a savior, just a snake. The sun was too warm. The light was too great. He would remain like this until he died. No one would ever know the shame he felt.

He oozed around rocks, along the trickling stream, seeking a cool, dark place out of the light. He remembered things—a horse, a book, a woman singing in the garden—but they seemed unimportant. He was just a beast. It was that simple. No one would ever record his exploits in a fine chancery hand or illumine his adventures on sheets of parchment. That seemed a good thing.

Geoffrey came to a hillside and crawled along its contours until he found a hole. He thrust his wedge-shaped head into it and flickered his tongue out. He tasted damp and rock and lichen, but nothing else, no threat. It was cool and dark. He slithered in and felt the earth around him.

It was a good sensation. The stone had a little song he had never heard—or rather, tasted—before. He liked it. Dimly it came to him that his mother knew this song, that he had heard it in her bones while he floated in her belly, and that, before her, his father's mother had heard this music. It was a minor thing, this knowledge, but he approved of it.

The tunnel opened before him, and he could see the vague form of a rock. His eyes were poor, and more so in the darkness, but it was enough. Geoffrey crawled onward. He would go to the heart of the earth, he decided, where the music of the stone must be the greatest. Perhaps he would find the serpentine great-grandmother so vividly pictured on a page of the book. No, she probably would not want to meet so wretched a descendant. It would be better if he just went on, listening to the stone song, until he died. He banished all hope and memory and plunged into the darkness.

The rock beneath him turned to gravel, then to sand, and Geoffrey slithered to the bank of a river. The water was dark and he could sense the cold lurking in it. He was not sure if serpents swam, and could not imagine how to do the task, so he paused and turned his wedge head from side to side. He could see little, and the air told him nothing. Finally he crawled off to the left. Beside him, the water flowed, but made no sound.

When he came upon the boat drawn up on the shore it surprised him. A loud, raucous noise came at intervals, disturbing the silence, and he coiled up to discover the source. His vague thoughts of despair and melancholy vanished with his curiosity.

A man lay in the bottom of the boat, snoring. Geoffrey peered at him, and, as if aware that he was under observation, the fellow gave a final snort and opened his eyes. He gasped.

"Well, I never . . . of all the . . . I don't suppose you have an obol there about your person—er, serpent?"

Geoffrey swayed back and forth. The man was old, bent and work-roughened, but he did not seem afraid. For some reason, this pleased him. He flowed into the boat and rearranged his lengthy body in a tidy coil at one end of the craft. He could feel the movement of the current against the end of the boat, but the surface of the water seemed like dark glass.

"No, no obols. Well, at least you won't tire me with aimless chatter. My passengers are dead bores." He gave a ghastly chuckle.

Geoffrey realized that this was a jest, and gave what he hoped was a reassuring hiss in return. Apparently it wasn't, because the man jumped and eyed him uneasily. Geoffrey began to appreciate the difficulty of being a beast, but could not imagine how to return to his former self. It was as if he had lost Geoffrey d'Avebury beside a sunny stream on an unnamed island.

The man recovered his aplomb. "No offense meant, to be sure. Everyone's got a job in this world, and I oughtn't complain of mine—though the hours are dreadful and the pay is miserable and I never have a holiday. Not that I've had a lot of business lately. People are still dyin', but they ain't comin' here very often. Had a passenger a couple days ago, a pretty thing. She didn't say a word, but kept looking back as if she expected someone to join her. Golden hair and azure eyes. Almost as fair as the Lady herself, though I should not say it. The Lady's a bit jealous of her beauty." He had unshipped the oars and pushed the boat away from the water's edge. "*She* had not a coin to pay her fare, but she sang quite nicely, so I took her." He snorted. "Songs and snakes. My service will turn into a charitable organization if I don't watch it."

He spat into the dark waters, and it sank without marring the glassy surface. "But at least she did not moan and groan about deeds undone and grandchildren yet unborn like some. I tell you, serpent, you really get to know life in my job, and a pretty poor thing it is too. As if immortality was some bed o' roses. I been rowing this damn boat back an' forth across the Styx since I don't know when, an' I'll go on doin' it that long again. Never had a choice nor the opportunity to better myself, so all their pissin' on about the things they never got to finish really gets my goat—or it would, if I had a goat.'' He cackled again. ''No one ever laughs at my jokes, so I have to do it myself. Had a passenger once, some playwright fellow, famous for his comedies. Eubalus, was it, or Menander? After a time they all blend in my mind and the waters sweep them away.''

He savored his philosophical point for a moment, plying the oars, while Geoffrey swayed lightly and peered at a faint glow that appeared to lighten the horizon. ''Well, I thought, finally, I shall have an appreciative audience for my jests. Hah! I barely got my best ones dusted off, when he starts in about the indifference of the audience, the parsimony of his patrons, the stupidity of his actors, and the infidelity of his lovers. I could write an epic about the indifference of my audience, could I but read or write. And I'd make all those twitterin' ghosts listen to it too, just to show 'em. But I never had the learnin'.''

Geoffrey would have laughed if he could, and wept too, and if he could have spoken, he would have told the ancient ferryman that learning did not help. Instead he hissed again.

''Still, I s'pose you got your own worries. Not dead, are you?''

Geoffrey thought about that for a moment and moved his flat head back and forth. The glow on the further shore increased.

''Thought not. Ferried a few live ones in my time. Full of questions. They did not listen to my jokes either. Here we are. Them's the Elysian Fields, if you care for that sort of thing. Pretty enough, I s'pose. Too quiet for my taste.'' He beached the boat and slipped the oars back into place. ''The worst part of bringin' someone over is I gotta go back. Good luck, in case I don' see you again. You're a real handsome serpent.'' He chuckled to himself.

Geoffrey crawled slowly over the end of the boat and slithered across the smooth grass. Flowers blossomed here and there. He peered nearsightedly at them, and recognized them as poppies. There was a faint squeaking noise which he could not identify, and he nosed forward.

There were stands of trees, groves of cypress and myrtle and yew, and small pools with willows about them. Despite the vegetation, he could sense none of the green taste he had gotten from the grasses of the world of sun, and the whole place seemed quiet and still.

He heard a faint melody, far away, and moved towards it without knowing why at first. Then he recognized it and his heart seemed to clamp between his mobile ribs. Aenor's song.

Geoffrey found her sitting on a rock. He rose and swayed, watching her sing. She appeared as she had when he was a child, all rose red and gold, and not as she had looked on her sickbed. Aenor seemed bemused, almost unaware of her surroundings. He remembered the tale of her long captivity in the caverns of the White Folk and wondered if she thought she had returned to them.

Geoffrey coiled at her unshod feet and lay his huge head across her lap. Aenor paused in her song and looked down. She put a warm hand on his brow. He felt safe, as he always had as a child, and he wished he could tell her how much he loved her.

"Dylan?" she asked, and the spell was broken. He felt his muscles flex in rage. Even in death his father stood between them. The skin of his body seemed to dry with the heat of his anger. He gave a convulsive twist and pulled his head away from her, squirming across the grass. He struggled with the conflicting emotions and felt them tear his skin apart. Great sloughs of scale slid onto the lifeless grass.

After a minute he looked back at her. She was watching him, clearly troubled, and he realized she was waiting for his father to join her in death. He felt ashamed of his anger and his jealousy, and a sadness filled him. He had failed to prevent her death. Although he had known he could not keep her alive despite his earnest desire, he had not experienced it in his bones and flesh. It seemed to course out of his heart, and his cold blood burned.

Geoffrey writhed and fought. The torment seemed endless and unendurable, and he would have screamed if he could. His flesh seemed to char, the skin curling off in great patterned patches.

Aenor knelt beside him and put a gentle hand across his brow. He felt tears leaking out of his eyes, and heard his sobs before he realized he had returned to his own miserable body. He was a mass of scratches and welts. Aenor hugged him against her breast and kissed the top of his head as she had when he was little.

"There, there, my love. It is all right, dearest Geoffrey." And although she was dead, and nothing would be all right again, he was comforted.

Still rather dazed by his experiences, Geoffrey sat on the ground, naked, and leaned his back against his mother's knees. Aenor had gone back to singing her song, and he sensed that she was waiting for his father. With his back to her, Geoffrey found he could almost pretend that she was still alive. He felt battered and tired and more profoundly angry than he had ever been in what he realized was a very angry life. He tried to sort the rage into tidy, rational bundles in his mind, and it kept spilling out in disorderly, chaotic feelings.

She came across the grass quite calmly, as if she were not the author of his misery, and she was as beautiful as he remembered her in the garden. The fine linen gown she wore was blue turning into black above her sandalled feet, and a white cord bound it against her breasts. Geoffrey lowered his head and stared at the ground.

"Do not sulk. It ill becomes you."

He hunched his scratched shoulders. "Go away. I don't want you."

"Come. We will talk."

Geoffrey found himself standing and was enraged. He looked back at his mother, but she seemed unaware that he had left her side. That hurt. She was waiting for Dylan. Nothing else was really important to her.

"Don't you realize she must hate being in the earth?"

he demanded, to relieve some of the pressure of his emotions.

"Certainly. I have been a prisoner here myself, you know. She will not tarry long. And she suffers not. Truly. Time has stopped for her once again. No power in the world can keep her from your father's side, but it will be some little while in days or months before he joins her in the Blessed Isles. The passion of your line is such that death has little sway, that once bonded you are forever joined. It is a remarkable thing."

"My *line*," he said bitterly. "I wondered, when I read the book, if we were just breeding stock, mere cattle to you. That's it, isn't it? We are only some toys for you old gods to play with. I must be a great disappointment."

"No. But I fear I have disappointed you and failed you as a guide and a foster mother. In many ways, you are the culmination of your kin, and you have capacities that were not anticipated. Your pig-headed logic, for instance. Who would have suspected that you could turn out so intelligent and so stubborn? Intelligence is not a useful aspect in a man, especially a warrior."

"Me? A warrior?" Geoffrey began to laugh in spite of himself, and went on laughing until tears rolled down his cheeks. "If that is what I was bred for, you must be really disappointed," he said, when he could finally control himself. "It serves you right for meddling. You lied to me and let me think . . ."

"Yes." It was a whisper, and Geoffrey looked into her face and saw pain in the great eyes. "But I did not make your mother come to her time to bring you to the shouldering of your burden. I do not create death, I merely administer it."

"Shoulder my burden?"

"Each of us has a task. Yours is before you, to take the Sword of Light and wield it against the Shadow, as your father and grandmother did before you. And you had immured yourself within the tower of your intellect so completely that I could barely reach you. Your dear father has a great deal to answer for. He should have told you, taught you, led you. He wished to protect you from the horror he endured. I hope you will be wiser with your own offspring.''

"Unless I got a child on one of those . . . creatures, there will never be another d'Avebury." Geoffrey remembered the delightful babes he had envisioned and felt a terrible pang. Still, he was determined. He would never touch another female—or male, for that matter. He would not be a pawn in the game of the gods. If he ever saw the light of day again, he would seek the closest monastery, and though he had no belief in the Savior, he would spend the remainder of his life praying and trying to forget screaming wild women and being a serpent and riding a hat across a choppy sea, playing his flute. Mostly he would attempt to forget how, for a moment, he had loved the young god. I would follow you to Hell, he had said in his passion, and here it was. It was all ashes. The world was an even worse place than the monks had told him.

"It is *not* a game." Her words stung like the lash of a whip. "It is the safety of the world, and, for this generation, it lies in your hands."

"These?" he wondered contemptuously. "They aren't fit for anything but turning the leaves of other people's books."

"Saille warned me how . . . impossible your family is when you are feeling sorry for yourselves, but I just laughed. Do stop being such a fool and listen."

"No. I was a fool to have listened in the first place. I am not the stuff of warriors and heroes. Look at me. I was overpowered by a bunch of *women*."

"And you acquitted yourself nobly."

Geoffrey gaped at her. "Nobly?"

"Your encounter with the Maenads taught you what neither I nor excellent Hermes could accomplish—to transform yourself at will. You must know how to do that to complete your adventure. And you did it without harming them, which would have angered Dionysius a good deal."

"The Devil take Dionysius—and the rest of you. I am not having any more adventures. The whole world can go to Shadow, for all I care."

"Even your sister Margaret?"

"That isn't fair!"

"No, it is not. Geoffrey, the world is not fair. Look at me. I must forever divide myself between my mother's flowery realm above and my father's shadowy domain below. I have no choice."

Geoffrey was distracted from the substance of their argument for a moment. "Your father? I thought Hades was your husband."

She gave a little shrug. "It matters not. He is the master here, and I the mistress."

"I don't understand. But if you think I can save the world, you are crazy. I don't know what to do."

"Are you certain?" She held out an object. "Do you know what this is?"

Geoffrey looked at it. "It appears to be a section of the snake skin that I sloughed."

"Yes." It changed in her hand, became thick and hard until it was a recognizable sword sheath. The pattern of it was something he had known all his life, though he had never seen it before. It had been a part of him once, and still was, and it connected him to a grandmother he had never met, and beyond that to the Serpent of Earth who was his ancestor. Geoffrey felt a sense of incredible revelation. He knew who and what he was, and he found he did not like it at all. "It takes some getting used to," the goddess added softly as she held out the sheath.

He found his hand was closed around the surface despite an intention to refuse it. It tingled under his fingers. He knew, somehow, the sword that fitted it, and the small strong hand that wielded it. Such a formidable hand. And the weapon itself was incredible. He ached to possess it, and was terrified at the same time. The beard bristled on his chin. Then he lifted his eyes and found her regarding him with a grave expression.

"Persephone," he said, naming her for the first time, and reluctantly accepting her as a part of his life, "you are a bitch."

"Oh, pooh. That is what all men say when they know a woman is right. Now, I must tell you of the Shadow. Your grandmother drove it out of Albion, and your father from

Franconia, but it has arisen again in the east, in Araby, and it has swept up the Levant like a torrent. Its forces have captured many cities and changed many people. Jerusalem is fallen and you must help restore it.''

More out of pique than reason, Geoffrey said, "I thought I was going to Byzantium."

"Byzantium is gone, though not fallen to Shadow. But the reign of the mages is broken, and the city is a smoking rubble overrun with tribesmen who have no notion what they have destroyed. They came from the heartland of Asia, driven by the press of others behind them."

"Why is the sword important?"

"These things of power were made out of the heart of the world, to keep it and protect it, in the time before time." Persephone furled her brow. "They are strong, by the spells of the smith who forged them, but they are profane. When your grandmother gave the Fire Sword into the keeping of Arthur of Albion, it became sanctified, and so too with the Sword of Earth when it was surrendered to King Louis. It is fortunate that neither Dylan nor Eleanor were overmuch attached to the objects. It will be more difficult for you to bestow the Sword of Iris, for so great is your affinity for it that you have carried its sheath within you all your life. You will know when to give it up, and to whom to give it, but I do not know if you will succeed."

"And if I try to keep it?"

"It will destroy you, child." She brushed his tumbled hair off his brow. "You must go now. Call me in your need—if you can. It will be hard. You are so proud. And you are so good."

"But not sacred enough to possess the weapon that fits this thing."

She gave a giggle. "You would not enjoy being a sacred king, Geoffrey. It's very limiting. And, besides, goodness is not the same as sanctity. That is a monkish confusion. Evil can be sanctified as easily as good. You will understand, I hope, someday. Now, go. You will find Marina and your belongings ahead. Wear my favor as you have before, and I shall be content." She was gone, and he was alone at the mouth of a cave, with the sound of the sea in the distance.

XVI

Helene returned to herself feeling exhausted and drained. The smell of Jalael's blood on her clothing and her fear-charged sweat was revolting, and the wonderful bath she had taken seemed a lifetime away. She used the knife to cup open the ropes that bound her hands and feet, and swallowed several times. She drank some water and splashed some on her face. It was warm and brackish, but it tasted and felt delightful. There was some lamb on a platter, cold and a little greasy, but she wolfed it down and felt less unsteady.

She stood up and sat down again almost immediately. Every movement was agony. Helene undid her trousers. The rope had cut her skin and the fabric had adhered to the blood that had flowed, so they tore as she lowered the garment. She gave a little moan. There were bruises and ugly wounds along her thighs. She wished she could bring Jalael back to life so she could kill him again. She wanted to lie down and just hurt for several days. There was no time for that. At any moment, one of the nomads might decide to check on Jalael.

How was she going to get out of the camp? Grow wings and fly? It was very quiet, and she assumed that most of the tribesmen were asleep, but Helene was certain there would be some sort of guard. They hadn't come when Jalael cried out, but they probably thought he was . . . she stopped the drift of her thoughts. Men were vile. No one would ever touch her body again. The resolution made her ache with loneliness. Helene shivered and hugged herself.

She stretched out on the gaudy carpet, exhausted. Helene needed strength, and she had none. Her mind drifted aimlessly for several minutes, as if she had almost fainted or fallen into a light sleep. It seemed to Helene that she could feel the hard earth beneath the carpet, and almost hear it. It was so strong, and could endure so much. If only she could reach into the heart of the world.

The trance deepened. She lost all sense of her pain-wracked body and of time. Her bones seemed to sink through her flesh, and fall into the earth itself. She could feel a steady throb along her spine, a slower rhythm than her heart, and it seemed to buoy her. It grew and grew, until she sat up, sharply aware of everything around her. Helene was revitalized, but when she looked at her injured limbs she knew it was only a temporary recovery. She could still feel her exhaustion, and knew it would return. But for the moment she had enough strength to continue.

Achilles! She could almost sense the horse, almost see him, and he would come to her whistle as he had since he was a colt. Helene closed her eyes for a moment and tried to "see" him. Rather to her surprise, it worked just the way it was described in several of her father's books, despite the fact that she had done none of the various rituals that supposedly permitted one far-vision. She didn't pause to ponder this, but studied the camp as well as she could. It was a little hazy, but she could make out the tents, the horses, the starless sky, and a pale sliver of moon darting behind huge clouds. The silver light seemed to touch her, and the fatigue dropped away. She knew it was illusion, but she didn't have time to mull it over.

Achilles was still saddled, and she suspected that the nomads had been unable to do more than stay out of range of his hooves. Her helm and the curious cross she had removed from her father's neck hung from the pommel. Helene chewed a swollen lip and winced at the pain, furled her brow, and decided she needed a diversion. Something to frighten the horses, she decided. She stared sightlessly at the blood-sodden rope beside the corpse of her most recent victim and cast her mind about.

A wolf. The thought seemed to crystallize, and she remembered the animal that companioned the small figure she had brought up from the catacombs. Unless the nomads had removed it, it was still coiled in the diaphanous gown she had snatched as she fled Hiram's tower. It struck her as funny that she had grabbed something so useless, and she let a tiny giggle escape. It felt good. She had been a little afraid she would never be able to laugh again.

Helene focused her mind on the statue, visualizing it as clearly as she could. Sweat beaded her forehead and she became giddy from holding her breath. Nothing happened. Her shoulders ached with tension. She paused, rubbed the back of her neck with one hand and wiped her brow with the other, and made herself breathe slowly in and out.

She could feel the earth beneath the rich carpet, and she let herself reach down into the sensation. In a blinding insight Helene realized that her father and the other mages had cut themselves off from the power of earth with their tall towers, and that this, in part, had led to their downfall. Air and fire were the forces the mages commanded, and although she could recall some mentions of earth and water in a few of Hiram's volumes, these elements were dismissed as unworthy of attention.

Earth had renewed her a while before, and now Helene returned to the slow steady rhythm that had vibrated in her very bones and tried to draw it into her. She could sense the enormous energy, but she could not grasp it. A large tear slipped down her grimy cheek and the salt of it stung her lips.

Go to earth. The command chimed in her mind, and for a moment Helene had no idea what it meant. Then she realized she had been trying to dominate the power she sought, as her father had commanded air or fire, and that it demanded submission. She remembered how she had felt she was sinking into the earth; as if it was closing over her like a grave. Her skin roughened in fear, and the breath caught in her throat. No wonder the mages avoided earth. How could you breathe? She felt hot and suffocated.

Helene struggled with her terror and made herself think of the earth as a kindly mother, as womb instead of tomb. It was difficult, because she seemed to shrink into near nothingness as she bowed to the will of the soil. Sweat ran down her legs despite the chill of the desert night and it made the cuts hurt more. Then it was as if the point where her spine rested on the ground was alive and vibrant. She went to the earth, and earth filled her.

Concentrating on the wolf, Helene let herself fill up with the power of the earth. A slow pulse beat in her blood, and she wondered if it was the heart of the world she heard, or her own. Beyond the walls of the tent, she could "see" the clouds scud away and the moon silver the landscape. Its light touched the horses, the robed figures of several tribesmen, the saddle on Achilles, and the cross that hung from its pommel. The luminescence seemed to thicken and curdle and a shadowy shape formed against it.

For a moment there were huge eyes shimmering in the darkness, and then a head coalesced around them, huge slavering chops and fearsome teeth, and an enormous body, thickly furred and gleaming in the moonlight. Helene was surprised at how large the beast appeared. It gave a growl that sounded as loud as thunder. Then it leapt forward like an arrow and snarled at the tribesmen's horses.

Helene pursed her lips to whistle for Achilles and discovered they were too swollen to perform the task, but the big stallion reacted as if she had made the sound, swinging his head around and charging for the tent wall just as the wolf reached the horses and set them panicking. Nomads jumped up and ran for the horses as Achilles nearly smothered her by knocking the tent down around her. The ridgepole missed her by a second as she slashed the thick cloth with the still bloody knife and missed jabbing her horse with the point by a hairsbreadth.

With an enormous effort, she vaulted into the saddle and kicked Achilles. He bunched his great hindquarters and jumped free of the tangle of fabric and thundered away. Tribesmen who emerged from their tents were ridden down, and one who leapt for Helene lost his hand in the process. Afterwards, she remembered the expression of startlement as Jalael's knife cut through flesh and bone and a fountain of blood spattered over them both. Then he was gone, the camp was gone, and they galloped up the wadi, away from the shouts and whinnies behind them.

At the mouth of the ravine, Helene reined Achilles in

and wondered which way to go. She had no idea where she was, and she was afraid of either getting lost on the trackless terrain or encountering another group of nomads. Then she felt a sort of tug within her, and turned Achilles off to the left. The clouds obscured the moon again, but she could sense it behind them, and the earth beneath her, and she felt a profound gratitude swell inside her. She reached a hand back and patted the bundle behind her.

"Thank you, Lady," she whispered.

At first Helene set Achilles at a canter, terrified of pursuit, but the light was poor and she slowed to a trot. Breaking her steed's leg or her own neck over an unseen obstacle seemed a greater danger than the nomads for the moment. With any luck, they were still trying to catch their horses or arguing over who would be their new leader.

The air was cold and clean. It had been a long time since she had smelled air that did not reek of smoke or magely incenses. Except for Achilles, she might have been alone in the world. A night bird hooted. She had never been beyond the walls of Byzantium at night and unescorted. It was a peculiar sensation, pleasant and a little disturbing.

All the strength she had seemed to fade away, and the pain of her body was almost intolerable. The hard leather of the saddle rubbed the dried blood on her trousers into her cuts and bruises, and each step of Achilles' hooves seemed to jar her bones. Her belly revolted and spewed up the greasy lamb onto the parched earth. She fell forward against the horse's neck and hung on grimly.

Helene let her thoughts drift over recent events in a sort of exhausted muse. She was too tired to concentrate, and her thoughts seemed to skip around distractedly. One moment she would remember the taste of the apple, the next Hiram withering before her eyes. The smell of the spider-mage and the vile scent of her own fear would mingle, then fade into the loathsome flavor of the gag in her mouth and the feel of the rope across her thighs. She rubbed a finger against the cuts beneath her filthy trousers.

How had she done those things? Where had the power

come from? The little statue? She put a grimy hand on the bundle still tied behind her saddle and felt no tingle of the energies which had consumed her earlier. Women could not be mages. Helen had known that for as long as she could remember. Perhaps the Council had been wrong. Or lied. Still, there had been nothing in her father's library to indicate that females could raise the powers of the elements. And she had done no rites or rituals to prepare the way, only summoned the energy the same way she drew a bow from her quiver. She had had no teacher except herself and Hiram's library, and everyone knew that an apprentice mage must study for years to learn even the simplest spell.

Helene curled her fingers around the curious artifact she had removed from her father's neck. She could feel the complex traceries against her palm, a mild whisper of movement against the scraped skin, but nothing like the surge of energy she had received when she touched it to her womanhood. She held it up to catch the muted moonlight and saw a pale glimmer of color against the night. It curved out of the handle and looked too insubstantial to cut a hair, let alone a solid, stinking mage in beast form. She shuddered. How could anyone transform themselves into an animal? It was disgusting.

Achilles gave a little snort, and she let the object fall from her hand against its cord and patted his neck. "Not you, old fellow. You are entirely noble, and better than any man I have ever encountered. Well, Jerome and Hippolytus were not so bad. I wonder . . ." She drifted off into another thought about the fate of her former companions-at-arms. If they were fortunate, they were dead; if they were not, they were the captives of the army which had camped outside the walls of the city. Helene hoped for the first, and found, to her surprise, that she was genuinely grieved as she could not be about her father's end. She hoped every mage in Byzantium had shrivelled and perished, and that the earth would never again bear the tread of such men. She wished there were somewhere on earth where she might go and never again hear the voice of a man, lay down the burden of her newly found powers, and dwindle into a profound silence. She looked at the thing dangling from the pommel with distaste. Whatever it was, she wanted no part of it. And, if she must bear the company of men, then let them be farmers and herdsmen, simple folk who knew nothing of raising great powers and turning themselves into beasts.

Helene was so busily involved with abjuring magicks and her kind that she did not notice for several minutes that Achilles had left the uneven ground of the plain and now trod an ancient roadway. A tumble of pillars lay on one side, and an intact structure appeared on the other. It was a villa, by the look of it. Helene came alert, listening for voices and sniffing the air for the smells of animals and woodsmoke. Some small beast scurried between the pillars, but the place seemed deserted otherwise.

The avenue broadened, and there were more buildings, granaries and villas, an empty stable, and an old marketplace. There were some faint indications that the recent earthquake had made itself felt here—a couple of cubit-wide cracks in the road and some disturbed stonework that appeared fresh—but the place seemed to have been deserted for a long time. The dawn breeze ruffled her matted locks and she smelled the sea—and something else besides.

Helene looked west, the rising sun behind her now giving her a sense of direction, and saw a dark haze on the horizon. It looked like a storm cloud, except it was almost flat with a sort of dome in its center. She could not immediately decide what might have caused this, and her eyes stung. Her mind felt like cold mush and her body hurt everywhere. She was too weary to go any further. Achilles seemed to share her exhaustion, hanging his great head a little.

She urged him forward at an aimless walk. There were most buildings, villas for the most part, and they looked to be in decent repair. She picked one at random, dismounted, and led the horse up the wide stairs and into the central courtyard. The small plots of vegetation were overgrown with weeds and it was obvious no one had lived there in quite a while. She looked in some of the rooms off the court and found the floors thick with dust. She could see mosaics beneath the dirt, and a family of mice stared at her from the corner of one.

Helene unsaddled Achilles and looked for the cistern. The water in it was surprisingly clear, and she pulled a copper bucketful up and washed her face and hands. She tasted a mouthful and spat it out, but it seemed fine. Perhaps the water system of the city still functioned. She would have to risk it. She refilled the bucket and watered the horse. Achilles sniffed it, then slurped eagerly. She rubbed him down a little with the saddle blanket and gave him some feed from the sack.

Helene stripped off her garments and poured several buckets over her body. Her skin goosefleshed in the morning chill and she shivered, but it felt wonderful to have some of the filth off. She rubbed herself dry with a corner of her cloak, washed out her tunic and trousers and spread them to dry, then forced herself to eat some very dry bread. She was too tired to be really hungry, and she was afraid of pursuit. Her eyelids drooped. She folded her cloak, put her head on the saddle, and stretched out. Achilles would warn her of any danger, she thought as she slipped into an uneasy doze.

XVII

Damascus was flooded with refugees, and the din was incredible. Michael ben Avi loathed it. The Damascenes screamed at one another, at their horses and camels, at his ragged followers, and even at their hammers and anvils as they continued to ply their skills as the finest steel makers in the world. They seemed unable to converse at less than a shout except when they huddled in conspiratorial bunches and whispered as he passed. He wondered how they could hear one another above the racket.

More, he wondered why the city leaders refused to listen to his warnings of imminent danger. Jerusalem, they told him, had been inadequately defended. Even the Jews of Damascus dismissed him and returned to their commerce. It had not helped that Jacob had spoken to them before him because he had felt his first task must be the plight of his followers. He had found physicians for the injured, food for the hungry, and even a few families for the orphaned. It was not enough, and if the dreadful Darklings who had taken his city attacked Damascus, it would all be for nothing.

Michael was exhausted, but he was almost afraid to sleep. He was afraid of what Jacob might say or do while he rested, and he was afraid of his dreams. Whenever he closed his aching eyes he saw the small girl with the sword, but worse, he saw the stern-faced woman who stood between them, one small breast exposed, and holding a bow in her strong capable hands. In his dreams her eyes seemed to pierce into him, as if she could see the corruption of his heart. Michael needed no scholar to tell him she was one of the many she-demons of old, the female goddesses his forebears had tried to destroy for centuries. He had traveled to Egypt in his youth and seen the temple of Isis in Alexandria, and he knew her for a jade and a betrayer. She had set the brothers Osiris and Set against one another for her favors. Harlot. Why were women such whores? He must sleep soon, or go mad with weariness. He must banish the evil goddess from his mind.

The day was grey, and to his tired eyes the twilight was increasing. This was a clear sign that the forces of Darkness were approaching, and perhaps it would help him convince the Damascenes of their peril. Why was he bothering? These people were not worth saving.

Michael entered a small temple created by the Jewish community for their worship and washed his hands and face. He suppressed a shudder of distaste, for it was gaudy within, a sort of cheap imitation of the grandeur of the great temple of Solomon. The pillars were painted in bright colors, and the tiled floor was a pattern like running waters that dazzled his eyes. He sank to his knees with a groan. Every joint in his body ached, and his skin felt like fire.

He bowed his head and closed his eyes, but the dancing blue and white patterns on the floor remained etched in his mind. Michael waited for the solemn presence of Adonai to touch him even while he doubted that the Almighty would enter such an over-decorated place. That was the problem, he realized. Doubt. It ate at him, eroding his belief and confidence. For the first time in his life, he doubted God, and it made him angry and terrified. He *knew* God. He had spoken with him since he was a boy, and had been answered. Or had he? Perhaps all he had heard was the voice of his own enormous ambition and pride. Had he been humble before the Lord, or just giving lip service for his own ends? Perhaps he was being punished for false humility.

Michael opened his eyes and looked up towards the altar. There was a sound which he could barely hear above the continuous clamor in the street, a kind of hum. It was a murmur of bees, and he could smell the deep sweetness of honey. A sign. God was giving him a sign! His heart raced with joy.

A white dove flew into the temple and alighted upon the altar. Michael smiled as he was sure the patriarch Noah had smiled on Ararat when the dove returned with the olive branch. The muscles of his face hurt, and he would have laughed aloud if he had dared. One did not laugh in the house of the Lord, even such a shabby one as this. The bee sound increased, and the scent of honey almost drowned his senses.

The dove seemed to flicker, a woman stepped off the altar and came towards him. Michael shrank back in horror. She plagued his dreams, and now she invaded the sacred precinct. Her bare breast and long, shapely leg aroused no lust, but a blinding rage.

He stumbled to his feet. "Get out of here!" He lifted a clenched fist as she continued to approach him, growing taller with each elegant step.

Michael's knees betrayed him and he slipped back to the tiled floor as she towered over him. She reached a shining hand out, and he covered his face with his sweating hands and cowered. He felt his hands fall away, and a little strangled scream escaped his throat. A luminous finger touched his eye and seemed to enter his brain.

You cannot deny me.

"No, no!" A flood of tears and sweat drenched his face.

Yes. You are mine. I claim you, and you will serve me.

"I serve only Adonai. I shall have no other gods before him. Begone, evil phantom." Michael's deep voice cracked and quavered.

She smiled. He could taste honey in his mouth, as if he had been kissed, and he wanted to choke on the sweetness of it. He wished he could crawl away and hide from the terrible sweetness, for he was filled with a joy he had never tasted, and it revolted him. Michael wanted to rest his head on the magnificent breast as he had never done with his own mother. He tried to wrench his head aside, disgusted by his desire, by the bliss coursing along his veins, but he was unable to move. He could only stare helplessly at her stern face which seemed to him more beautiful than any other. He memorized the features, the grey-blue eyes beneath dove-wing brows, the long, proud nose, and the smiling lips as bright as roses. He loved her, even while he feared and hated her.

Then she vanished, and Michael could still taste the honey in his mouth and hear the bee song in his mind. He rubbed his eyes to destroy the image of her, and dragged himself to his feet. He spat the honey taste onto the rippling tiles of the floor and turned away.

In the outer courtyard he stood awhile, breathing slowly. He lifted a hand and touched his eye. It felt tender, as if it had been bruised. Then he sternly banished all memory of her, set his shoulders straight, and determined that no one would ever guess that God had betrayed him. He would be the Deliverer in spite of that.

Michael glanced at the sky and knew it was darker. Suddenly he was uneasy. He would make one more attempt to convince the Damascenes of their peril, and then he would gather as many as would follow him and lead them away. He must find that red-haired girl and her sword. Only then could he overcome the forces of Darkness. It was the will of God.

XVIII

It was night again when she awoke. For a moment she did not know where she was, but she saw Achilles' comforting shape across the courtyard. He was munching on some weeds in one of the flower patches. The moon had risen above the roof of the villa, a finer crescent than the night before, but the sky was not so murky as it had been. A breeze blew from the west, smelling of salt and the other smell she could not quite put a name to. She had pulled the cloak around her in her sleep, and it was cold.

Helene put her clothing back on, ate a little more of her meager food, and wondered what to do next. She had no idea where she was, except that she was somewhere near the coast. By the size of the moon she guessed it had been three nights since she quitted Byzantium. It felt like a lifetime. She watered the horse again, then resaddled him and led him out of the villa.

She did not mount up, feeling stiff and achy, but walked beside him until they came to a truly monstrous agora. Even by her Byzantine measure it was enormous. Helene crossed it, finding the emptiness of it vaguely disturbing, and followed one of the wide streets which led out of it to the north. She could see the dark bulk of a mountain against the night sky and hear the vague hiss of the sea as the road veered westward.

A great forest of pillars rose before her and Helene paused. She had no difficulty recognizing an antique temple—there were a few in Byzantium and she had seen drawings of others in her father's library—but she had never imagined anything so immense. They must have used up several quarries just to get the marble. What deity had merited such expense and labor?

She was about to pass it by when a sudden sense of urgency surged over her. Helene felt compelled to enter. Reluctantly she began to mount the steps. She felt odd—excited and frightened at the same time. She stood between the first rank of pillars for several minutes, tingling with eagerness and filled with trepidation. Something within the place beckoned her, demanded her presence, and she had a sinking certainty she wasn't going to be pleased with what she found.

Helene turned to retreat and found she could not move. She heard a titter of laughter and realized the sound was only inside her head. Her feet itched as if her boots were filled with ants, and her belly twitched as if it housed a swarm of locusts. There was a murmur, like bees, in her ears. The itching became intolerable, and she yanked her boots off to see if there was something in them.

The discomfort vanished, except for her stomach and the maddening bee sound. She let her boots fall and padded forward stocking-footed between the graceful pillars. A pale light shone on the floor somewhere ahead of her, and finally she saw that part of the central roof had broken and fallen inside.

The center of the temple was shadowed by a great figure. She crept towards it, feeling smaller and smaller with each step, barely daring to look up. The bee sound grew more intense, and a heavenly scent of balsam filled her senses. She stubbed a toe on a piece of marble and bit back an oath.

Carved feet rested on a pediment at the level of her eyes. Above them rose a columnar form, a single leg adorned with small figures of some cat-like creature. The torso bellied out in many globes, so it looked as if the garment was stuffed with oranges. A serene face wearing a squarish crown stared out at the temple. Just above the crown the sickle moon was visible through the hole in the roof.

Welcome, child. The murmur of the bees changed to a voice and remained still the hum of insects. *Why are you afraid?*

Helene was not afraid. She was dumbstruck with a

terror she could neither explain nor control. It rolled over her until her knees shook. Sweat drenched her despite the chill of the night. Despite the friendliness of the greeting, she was overwhelmed by a sense of something so powerful that it made everything she had known before into nothing. She felt as if she might wink out and disappear altogether. Her knees gave way and she huddled before the pediment and stifled small mewling noises against her scraped palms.

Child, child. The words in her skull were clearly intended to be soothing, but Helene became even more agitated. Her heart pounded against her ribs and her breath came in short painful gasps. *Why are you afraid? I would not harm you.*

Helene struggled to calm herself, and to answer the question. She had *not* been afraid of the presence in the little statue, perhaps because of its familiarity. The voice beating in her mind was even the same voice, but it was so immense that it was as if the cosmos were shouting at her. It was such an enlargement, such a magnification, like the difference between a garden spider and the spider-mage. And there was another element. She could not quite put a name to it. She wanted a mother she could cling to, who would comfort her. There was nothing comforting or safe about the presence she huddled before. Helene felt like an insect, like an anonymous bee.

I never did have the common touch. There was a sort of sigh in the words, an infinite sadness and an overwhelming loneliness that could not be cured. *My sisters all had their little favorites, Athene her Odysseus and Perseus, Aphrodite her Adonis and Aeson. I never could manage that.* Immense regret came with the words. *But I do love you, as best I can.*

Helene felt that, and knew it was true, but it was a vast, impersonal emotion, a love for the world and every creature in it. She wanted more, to be loved for herself, singly and specially, the thing she had always sought from her father and which he had denied her to the last. She was certain now that she would never have that precious affection. She was just a little redheaded orphan and no one would ever love her. She had been a fool to expect it.

What do you want from me? Helene let that thought form and crystallize, and realized that she had been brought here for some purpose. In her experience, other people's purposes were always unpleasant. She was filled with great wariness and suspicion.

Yes. I have a task for you. Another sigh. *And you are not going to be pleased with it.* A sound like laughter, bitter mocking laughter with no humor in it. *But it is needful.*

That is what my father said when he proposed to use me for a sacrifice. She was shaking with terror, but with anger as well. *Everyone wants to use me!*

Yes. What you say is true. But that is the nature of nature. How my brother Apollo would laugh—if he knew how to laugh—at my poor philosophy. All of life is about use. It does not even end with death, when great Gea takes us back unto her bosom, and the worms feast on the flesh. Thousands have used me over the centuries, cried out to me to ease the pain of their child-bearing, begged for my favor in the hunt. On festal days they would raise me up on groaning ropes to the opening there behind you, and the people would shout my name and praise me—and ask for more. Oh, they were grateful for my blessing, in their pitiful way. But I was feared, not loved. And you, with your poor, battered heart, and the great task yet before you. You will not believe me when I tell you that your efforts will have reward.

The bee song of the voice was maddening, and if she could have managed the feat, Helene would have crawled out of the temple and never looked back. *Do I have any choice?*

None. You were made for the venture yet to come. You have some liberty in how you will accomplish the deeds, but none at all in the ends themselves. Though it will not be so unpleasant as you will think. Someday you will rejoice in it.

Helene was filled with an itchy impatience. "What do you want?" The sound of her own voice echoing in the temple was a surprise. She felt less helpless not to be dumbstruck.

Take the weapon you took from your father and give it to the man with the flute.

That sounded simple enough, and much too straightforward for so much effort and equivocation. Helene paused, waiting for the other sandal to fall, but there was only silence. "Is that all?" Her voice sounded shrill and hideous, and she found she was drenched in icy sweat.

A bee sigh murmured in her mind. *I never approved of all this bedding and wedding, and it has always been to me a most untidy way of arranging the matter.* The voice sounded rather peeved, as if it was being forced to say things it would prefer to avoid, and Helene was a little less fearful. *Oh, very well. Even the gods must serve. Though it seems a frightful price to pay. Dear child, when the sword is given, you must give yourself as well.*

"What? Why? That is cruel. I do not even want that thing —and I most certainly have no desire to have some . . . some man I have never met before . . , no, I will not. Find another servant. No man will ever, ever touch me. They are all beasts, even the best of them. If he wants that accursed sword, let him take it and be done, but leave me out of the bargain. I will not sacrifice my body. It is mine. It is all I have." Helene crouched and hugged herself.

Oh, my child! You cannot be spared this. It is your destiny.

Helene felt the pain and empathy in the words, but she hardened her heart against them. "He will have to force me," she screamed.

No.

"I will kill myself first."

No. It was an inexorable command. Helene felt her mind crushed under it. She saw a face, a weary, bearded face, great blue eyes rimmed with shadow and red with crying, a strong, straight nose and curly brown hair beneath a stained hat with flowers on it. He did not look as if he knew one end of a sword from the other.

What is he?

A man. A mage, though he knows it not. A shapeshifter, though very new to it. A musician such as would be welcome in the halls of Olympus itself.

Helene listened to this roll of attributes and wished the earth would open up and swallow her. No wonder the mages denied the gods. They had a vicious, cruel sense of humor. How dare they demand she lie with this stranger! She'd plunge a dagger into his heart before she submitted to such a wretched fate.

That small flame of rebellion was snuffed out in a moment. Helene was trapped within the will of the goddess who gazed serenely down at her. She was dragged to her feet, and something hard pressed into her hand. Then she was standing beside her discarded boots, clutching a pillar, sobbing uncontrollably, with no memory of leaving the temple.

Achilles stood patiently on the steps. She reached for her boots and discovered she was holding a small stone. She started to toss it away and found her arm would not move. Helene peered back into the temple and saw the statue staring at her, compelling her to do as she was told. Her mind struggled, but she could do nothing. Finally she dropped the stone in her belt pouch, took her boots, and walked back to the horse. Re-shod, she mounted and sat unmoving in the pale moonlight, her heart filled with bitterness and rage. She would never be free and never be loved. She brushed her tears aside and urged the horse down the stairs. It no longer mattered where she went. Whatever she did would be meaningless.

XIX

Geoffrey sat on a dark boulder and stared out at the sea. He had been doing this for quite some time, despite more and more urgent demands from his belly and bladder, and an occasional nudge in the back from Marina. He was exhausted, confused, and—he finally realized—more than a little angry. He knew he had been tricked and used, that he was part of some Great Plan, that he had a rare opportunity to save the world, and he did not care. Aenor was dead, and his father dying of grief, and the world could go hang itself for all it mattered to him. He could not generate any enthusiasm for the future, no matter how hard he tried. He wondered if this was how the plans of the gods went awry, and wished Hermes were there to discuss it.

He had emerged from the depths of the earth on an island, perhaps the same one he had been shipwrecked on a day before, and found his horse and belongings waiting for him. He had put on his clothes, eaten a little, and sat down for a moment. A deadly lethargy had come over him. Night had come, chill and damp, with a slender crescent of the dying moon in the star-specked sky, and he had lacked even the energy to fetch his cloak. The blood of heroes must run very thin in his veins, and he found it difficult to imagine how his grandmother and his father had accomplished their great deeds.

All he could feel was a vast emptiness that his mother had left the world and his father would soon join her. How could Eleanor have gone on, after the death of her spouse? He knew the answer immediately. She had had his father in her womb. Women were very fortunate in that. And his grandfather had returned from the grave—because it was part of the Great Plan for his father to have sisters, just as he did, just as his children would. He was just a stud, waiting to do service to a filly he had not seen yet—because, when he got right down to it, he was simply part of a long-range breeding program and not important as a person at all.

Geoffrey felt the hard knot of rage twist in his guts. He hated the sensation of being a nobody. He felt he had never amounted to a heap of beans before, and never would now. It was all very well for his tutelary Lady of the Poppies to say "go here, do this, do that," with the vague promise of a pair of delightful brats squealing on the floor as eventual reward. It would not fill up the void in the world left by Aenor's passing. It was as if she had never existed, except for the snatches of her glorious song that remained in his mind.

He sighed deeply and finally surrendered to the demands of his body enough to relieve himself. Though his stomach growled, he had no appetite. But after several minutes he took out his flute and began to play, letting the memory of his mother's song drift through his mind, until she was almost palpable. Geoffrey did not notice the tears slipping down his cheeks, nor the small bits of vegetation that began to sprout around his boots and from the rock he was sitting on. He did not hear the approach of hooves and ignored Marina's warning nicker. The music was all that mattered.

Something prickled on the back of his neck, a little tendril of fear, or perhaps a bug crawling across his skin. Geoffrey disregarded it for several seconds, intent on capturing an especially haunting air, but the itching became intolerable, and he paused. He heard an equine snort that was not Marina's and turned.

A small figure stood behind him, glaring out of glazed green eyes, a scrawny midget of a very dirty female. Geoffrey, a little shortsighted and still involved with the music, did not instantly register the dagger she held over her tousled red hair or the fact that she seemed frozen in the moment. He dispassionately watched her struggle against some unseen power and thought her probably the single least agreeable looking girl he had ever seen. Why, she barely stood as high as his heart.

Then she broke free, and her knife arched down towards his chest, and, without thinking, he brought the flute up in a tidy garde and parry that would have pleased his oft-despairing arms instructor. A bright flash nearly blinded both of them as the flute and the blade met, and she dropped the hilt and swore in oddly accented Greek while rubbing her palms against her boyish breast. She suggested a number of unlikely and downright impossible anatomical degradations which would have shamed the Milanese guards he had heard using rough language, and he was impressed.

And amused. The feeling pierced his despondency as the knife would have done to his heart. "You swear like a trooper, girl."

"Is that all you can think of to say, you . . . you mooncalf. Well, don't just stand there. Get it over with." She was flushed with anger, so her high cheeks colored and her green eyes sparkled. It made her almost pretty. Not beautiful. She would never be beautiful, he decided, and found a peculiar pleasure in the thought.

"Get what over with?" Geoffrey tucked the flute into his belt and prepared to be entertained. This was an error. She boxed him soundly on one ear and was going for a second blow when he caught her wrist. She was remarkably strong for such a small person, and her face was not even remotely pretty. About as lovable as a stoat, which, with her bared teeth and narrow eyes, she resembled very closely. She went rigid at his touch and stood breathing shallowly.

"Aren't you going to violate me?" she screamed.

Geoffrey considered this with as much gravity as he could muster, despite a huge bubble of laughter which threatened to fountain out of his chest. Odd. A few minutes before he had thought he would never laugh again. But having three younger sisters, he knew that to laugh at their rages was the gravest insult imaginable, and he guessed this strange child to be a very serious thirteen or fourteen. If this was the future mother of his children, the gods must all be much madder than he had ever imagined himself to have been. He found that where the fear of insanity had long lurked in his mind, there was now a profound serenity, and he was surprised.

"I cannot say the idea had even crossed my mind. I am not in the habit of violating little children, but perhaps I do not know the customs of this country."

"I am *not* a child," she blazed at him. "I am sixteen. And it is the only way you will get me, so there," she added sullenly. "I do not care what *She* says," followed in a whisper.

"I am glad *that* is settled."

"You brainless dolt. Are you as stupid as you are big? *She* made me come here. It was like a big hand inside my head. I had no choice, because it was all decided for me, probably centuries ago, as if I was a nothing. I only wanted to be something, and they would not let me. And they are all dead—and I killed them—and I'm still just a nothing and a nobody. Just a game piece to be shoved about to please . . . *She* wouldn't let me go!"

Geoffrey had no doubt that the "She" of this garbled tale was another manifestation of the meddling goddess, and was intellectually curious as to which one, while simultaneously almost moved to tears by the anguish of the tiny woman before him. He wanted to spank her for her incoherence and hug her and smooth her hair and tell her it was all right, all the while knowing it was not. Hairsplitting theological argument was poor preparation for dealing with an exhausted, confused, and righteously angry young woman, and he wished he knew better what to do. I suppose I will just treat her like I would Margaret. The thought of his favorite sister steadied him.

The girl was trembling. Her face was screwed up, trying not to cry.

"How long has it been since you ate or slept?"

"I do not know. I left the great temple and got on Achilles, and we rode and rode. Finally we came to this causeway, and it led to this island. It is sort of a blur."

"The gods are a bunch of busybodies. Sit down. I have some bread—I think." He looked around vaguely.

The girl gave a sharp giggle. "*She* said you were a mage."

"Did she? What is that supposed to mean?" He pulled open his leather bag and looked inside.

"Umm. Forgetful and otherworldly, I think."

"Yes. Once I was going to be a scholar. Then . . . then things went awry. I really should not be here. I mean, I am not very good for adventures. Hmm. These quinces are a little withered, aren't they?" He held out two wrinkled brown fruits.

Geoffrey felt his fingers tingle. His palms itched. His scalp felt like fire ants were swarming across it, for just a moment. Then an odd blue light danced along his arms, down into his hands, and over the fruit. They glowed, plumped, swelled, and the skins turned golden. The bittersweet scent of quince overwhelmed the smell of salt air and damp earth. His mouth watered. He was more hungry than he could ever remember. He offered one quince to the girl and lifted the other to his lips.

She snatched it without brushing his fingers, and sank small, even teeth into the succulent flesh. A drop of amber juice ran down her grimy chin. Geoffrey bit into his own quince, fascinated and repelled by her eating all at the same time, and then lost interest in anything but the flavor in his mouth. He had cuts on his lips and the tart juice stung them, but the discomfort was meaningless compared to the delicious taste. He ate it down to the core and pips, and found himself satiated and content. He felt, indeed, almost happy, and that shamed him and—more—terrified him. He liked the feeling and wanted it to continue forever. Then he noticed that his sense of well-being extended to his loins, and that the thought of pressing between the thighs of the girl was quite pleasurable. Silently he cursed quinces, magicks, and Cyprean Aphrodite for a jade and a whore, and heard a vast gust of mental laughter that did nothing to relieve his lust.

The girl sat across from him, and Geoffrey saw her fingers were curled into her palms and her lower lip was caught between her straight, small teeth. At least he was not alone in desire, but he felt a certain contrariness, a need to be in command of his fate and not thrust onto the couch of Venus just to suit the schemes of others.

He cleared his throat. "I hope you feel better now. I am Geoffrey d'Avebury, by the way. Will you tell me your tale?" He wanted to get her speaking before he said the wrong thing. Suddenly it seemed very important that he treat her well and with some respect, that he curb impulses he could easily blame on the deities, as those wild women who had attacked him probably did.

The girl stared at the ground and poked at it with a stick for a time. She pushed the remains of her fruit into the hole she had made, covered it up, then toyed with a pebble.

"I am called Helene. My father, Hiram, was a mage of Great Byzantium, and of my mother I knew nothing, for she perished in the hour of my birth. I slew her, and him too, in the end. I did not wish to. I wished only that he should love me, but he hated me because I was a useless woman and not the son he had desired. I strove to please him, for at first I did not understand that a female is nothing. I learned all I could of his art, though in truth I thought the whole business of magic very dull and boring.

"Then the Death came to Byzantium, and none of the arts of the Council of Mages could allay it. The wards which had protected the city for centuries began to fail. The crops withered in the fields, the populace dropped like flies, and there were riots and burnings which the city guards could not contain. Several mages were lost as they attempted to control the problem. The Council was diminished.

"One day—an ordinary day of fires and destruction—my father struck me, and mage fire leapt from my fingers and struck him. I did not understand what had happened at first, but Hiram was angry, then very pleased. All know that women have no power except to bear children, but there were records—I had read them myself—describing certain antique rituals whereby this power, by the careful sacrifice of the female, might be used to restore the balance in the elements and bring the wards back into being. This my father proposed to do."

For a moment Geoffrey was so enthralled with the

rhythm and delightful symmetry of her style that he did not grasp the meaning of her words. Then he was outraged. He could not imagine any parent doing something so loathsome, and his heart went out to her. He shifted his weight angrily, all thought of desire fled.

"Here, at last, was something I could do that would please him, make me useful, and I could not do it." The formal, impersonal words were spoken in a voice full of anger and sorrow. "I fled to a place I had found as a child, a tiny temple from the time before the gods were banished from Byzantium, and there communed with some power. I nearly wish I had not. *She* came to me in sleep, the Lady of the Wild Things, and I was strengthened and comforted. I was a child, and She a mother.

"Determined to preserve my valueless life, I returned to the tower. I encountered my father." She paused and rolled the stone in her fingers. "He was so pleased!" Her hand fisted around the stone and the knuckles showed white. "Hiram tried to snare me, to make me do his bidding, and I . . . I still do not know what I did, but it stopped him."

Helene gave a little laugh. "So, I took a bath."

"You what?"

"This amazes you. In memory, I too am astonished. But it felt needful. I wished to wash the stink of his spells off me, and I was very dirty from the temple." She glanced down at her filthy clothes and grimy hands. Helene made a futile wipe at her face and left tracks across her brow.

"He came again, as I arose from the water, and I defied his edict. I was very hungry, and I took an apple from the plate, and it turned fresh in my hand, as you did with the quince. That may be commonplace for you, but I had never done such a thing, and I could not understand it. But I ate of it, one bite, and felt renewed. I was enthralled by my own power.

"Hiram summoned his magicks to entangle me, and I took another bite of the apple and spat it into his face." She closed her eyes and all the color drained from her skin. "He shrivelled. In a moment he aged a thousand years and all the spells that kept him ageless broke. I cried out and begged forgiveness, and held his bones. There was a thing about his neck, hidden by his clothing, and I took it, and carried it away as his tower began to crash into rubble, for the spells which sustained him held it as well.

"I took some few garments from the stable, and Achilles, and rode as the earth began to shake. There was fire everywhere, and buildings collapsing, and mobs of frightened people running everywhere, but near dawn I reached the land wall. An army was camped beyond that wall, and I departed towards the sea wall. Have you water? I am parched."

"Parched? I am exhausted, just listening to you." Geoffrey smiled as he spoke, unaware of how handsome he looked when so doing, and got her some water from the little spring he had found nearby. He rummaged in his food bag and found some bread and cheese. He spread out a linen napkin, its edges stitched by his sister Margaret's exquisite hand, and put the hard, dry loaf and the bricklike cheese on it, between them. Then he held his hand out, rather doubtfully, and waited to see if anything would happen.

Helene watched his movements. He had, she decided, wonderful hands, long and well-formed, and he was not old or ugly, at least. He had a special quality, and she struggled to put a name to it. Innocent. That was it. What an odd thing to think about a man. She saw his brow furl slightly beneath the heavy brown hair and the rather vague blue eyes narrow as she watched the mage fire blossom on his hand and race across the bread and cheese before vanishing. The bread now plumped and steamed, as if fresh from the oven, and the cheese was free of mold and smelled delightful.

Geoffrey looked at his large hand, turning it back and forth as if seeking the source of the energies he had just expended. "Do you think this is how Jesus fed the multitude on loaves and fishes?" he asked. "I have never been able to do this before." Then he blinked, gestured at the food, and smiled once more. "Please, eat, and go on with your tale. I admire the manner of your telling, as good as a book. I always liked tales of adventure, but I think I do not like the actual thing as well. I am not very good at outdoor things," he added apologetically.

Geoffrey glanced at the horses, then studied them with a knowing eye. "I believe your big fellow there is getting rather familiar with Marina, so perhaps I better unsaddle them both."

Before she could stop him, Geoffrey was on his feet and had reached for Achilles' bridle. Helene tried to swallow the chunk of cheese and bread in her mouth—before he got a painful bite on the hand or arm—and nearly choked.

Achilles bared his great teeth and jerked his head. Geoffrey said something too quietly for her to hear, and the silver-tipped black ears swivelled forward. The horse regarded the man with an expression of equine astonishment, and gave a snort. He moved his hooves restlessly. Geoffrey laid a long hand along the tremendous neck and spoke again, and Achilles gave a shudder of skin and a brief neigh, then stood quietly while the man removed the saddle and bridle neatly and efficiently. He pulled a cloth from his own belongings and rubbed down the big, black horse while Helene swallowed her astonishment and more food.

The dainty grey, Marina, stuck her nose in and demanded attention, and Geoffrey laughed and said something to her in a tongue Helene did not know. The two horses drew away together and began to crop on some bushes.

"That is a fine animal," he said, folding up the cloth and resuming his seat. "My father . . . would like him." His face shadowed, the smile faded, and he looked towards the horizon for a long time. "Pray, will you go on with your wondrous adventure?"

Helene nodded and finished her mouthful. Achilles barely suffered the grooms he knew quite well to touch him, and never a stranger, but she decided not to say anything. She was beginning to like this young man, and it made her irritated.

"Yes. Where was I? Ah. I remember." She felt herself shudder. "I was making towards the sea gate. A great spider crawled out of a street and coiled silk around me. It was a mage the Council thought had perished. There is nothing more loathsome than a shape-changer, and the Council had long ago decreed that no mage should ever practice that revolting act.

"I could hear him speak in my mind as he dragged me out of the saddle and across the pavement. I caught the thing I had taken from my father's corpse as I came down and clutched it in my hands." Helene's breath came in short gasps and a line of beads formed across her brow. "He knew I had some power, and he wanted it. He called me his bride and hissed in my mind his conquest of me.

"The thing in my hand—here, this." She held up a cross-shaped object that was thrust into her belt, and Geoffrey leaned forward and peered at it. He felt it tug at him, call to him like some ancient Siren, and he knew that he could never touch it without peril. When he made no move to take it, she put it back in her belt. "It made a stream of light of every color, and I saw it was a sword. No, in truth I saw nothing then, but swung the blade and hewed off one of the filthy legs, and then put out his eye. I heard voices, and knew nothing for a long time.

"When I awoke, I was bound and gagged and hung across Achilles and was far from the city. My captors were some desert men who called me a witch. Most of them wished to slay me, but their leader planned to use me. Power. I hate the very word. I never wished to possess these things.

"He beat me with a rope, and I was helpless." Rage made her voice tremble and Geoffrey could tell she was fighting tears. "I somehow made the rope into a great snake. It coiled around him, and I used his own dagger to slit his filthy throat. I wish I could have killed him a hundred times for what he planned to do to me." She dug small fingers into the earth before her. Her shoulders sagged and she looked so forlorn that Geoffrey longed to hold her and tell her she was safe.

Helene took a ragged breath. "I swore I would never be helpless before any man again, and escaped on Achilles. We rode all one night, and at dawning came to a great city, quite empty. We rested through the day—I slept like the dead—and went forth again after dark." She bit her lower lip and winced at the pain.

"There was a temple, and I entered it against my own desire. *She* crushed me like a grape, and held me enthralled until I came here. I hated her as I have never hated anything in my life—and loved her still." Helene rubbed her temples as if her head hurt. "Can you turn water into wine?" she asked with a wan smile.

Geoffrey gave her a shy grin. He understood how she hated feeling helpless, his own recent experiences still raw and fresh in his mind.

"I do not know. I have never tried. I am not accustomed yet to transformations, and, indeed, if I read the tale aright, I should not be able to. The women in my line have the power in that, and the men another." He looked at his hands and shook his head.

Helene watched him think and considered what a gentle creature he seemed. Still wary, she found she wanted to trust him. She felt betrayed by everything, and that made her helpless. She needed to trust something, someone, or else her fear and sense of aloneness would drive her into madness. But he was probably only pretending to be nice, until he could lull her defenses and ravish her. Why had she asked for wine? What stupidity. If only he did not look so guileless. And if he would just stop smiling at her so kindly.

"Aha!" The exclamation broke into her thoughts as he plucked his flute from his belt and refilled the cup with water. Then he sat for several seconds, his head cocked slightly, as if listening to some unheard melody. He put the flute to his lips and a liquid, merry gush of notes wafted down the column. Helene felt her skin tingle all over, and experienced such a sense of refreshment that all the fatigue seemed to pass out of her body. No blue fire flared, but the water in the cup began to darken into amber. A smell of honey rose in the air, bringing with it a memory of the bee voice of the goddess. It hurt like a spearthrust for an endless moment, so she felt her heart was pierced, and then it was gone, and some part of her was whole again. She found her cheeks were wet and brushed them with her dirty fingers.

Geoffrey stopped playing and looked down at the cup, frowning. He made a face. "Honey wine. I did *try* for something of the grape, but I seem to have missed the mark. In Italia 'tis a bedding cup, this wine, served after weddings, but I vow it will not be that here, except by your leave."

Startled, she gaped at him. "What provokes such an oath?"

"Your father wished to kill you, a spider threatened you with violation, some nomads probably the same, and I am not so unworldly that I do not know how wine enflames lust." He turned a splendid scarlet.

His painful embarrassment disarmed her in a way no ordinary male posturing, as she knew it from her time with the city guards, could have. She liked him, though he was unlike any man she had ever known, liked his eagerness to please, his easy confidence with horses, and his mastery of the flute. Helene was not ready to submit to the will of the goddess, but she was starting to think it might be almost pleasant. "You are a very good man, Geoffrey d'Avebury."

"No, not really. I am a thief and a coward, and a dreamer, and probably a liar too."

"That sounds like the beginning of a tale. So speak." She sipped some wine and found it less sweet than she expected.

"As you wish. 'Twill not be so elegantly spun as yours, but I will do my best." He paused a moment. "My tale began, I suppose, long before I was born, but I will skip that part, except to say that the thing you have in your belt is not the first of its kind that my family has been involved with, nor, I suspect, is it the last. My grandmother bore the Sword of Fire, and my mother that of Earth; yours is of Air, and logically, somewhere there exists one of Water."

"Are you always pompous when you tell stories?"

"Forgive me. I warned you I was no hand at it."

"Oh, blast my tongue! It was when you said 'logically.'"

It reminded me of my father. I do not approve of logic,'' she ended darkly, brooding over her wine cup.

"No, of course not. I was in Milan, studying at the university, and I had a dream that sent me rushing home as fast as a horse could carry me. I must add, parenthetically, that I have often heard voices and had strange dreams, and that I fancied myself a lunatic for most of my life, which is why I approve of logic, because it gives me a feeling of order in the cosmos. In any case, when I got home, I found that my mother was dying, and that grief would soon take my father as well.''

Geoffrey paused, trying to gather his feelings and thoughts. "I heard a voice telling me to go to Byzantium, and I had read that the mages there had wonderful elixirs. I wanted nothing so much as to save my mother's life, for I loved her most dearly. Also, my father's sister, Rowena, was there. She had come from Albion with a book, a history of the family. I read it and discovered my father was a famous hero, and my grandmother too. It was all most peculiar, for my father had never spoken a word of it, unless it was to my sister Beth, who is the real man in the family. I am just not cut out for heroics.

"It was all very confusing, with voices in my head, a history I had never before heard, my mother dying, my father ill with grief, my sisters weeping, and my aunt being an adherent of the old ways. I got rather drunk and went out into the garden, and this woman came out of the moon and *She* told me to go to Byzantium.

"I've always felt rather useless at home, because I'm not very good at things. My father raises horses, and I was never much use in the stables, and I did not learn to use a sword very well. I felt I had a chance to do something worthwhile, you see.

"So, I gathered some things, stole my aunt's history, took Marina and some money, and rode to Venice to take passage to Byzantium. But all the ships were idle, for there was plague in Byzantium and the Doge of Venice was afraid. I ended up in an inn, twiddling my thumbs.

"A man came to the inn, calling himself Mercutio di Maya, and we became friends.'' Geoffrey gave a sharp little laugh. "He was Hermes. God of thieves and liars. He helped me to escape from Venice in a small ship, but he left me. The ship was wrecked, and I did my first magic song, and saved myself and Marina, and ended up on some island."

Geoffrey sighed. "I fell asleep, and when I woke, I was surrounded by wild women. They . . . violated me, until I could not bear it, and I turned into a snake and crawled away into a hole, hoping to die of shame. I ended up in the Underworld, and found my mother, a ghost, I guess, and met again my moon lady. Persephone. I think I do not like the gods overmuch.

"She told me Byzantium had fallen and that I must complete my real task, to find you and that sword you bear, and do as my father had done before me. I felt betrayed that there had never truly been a chance to rescue my mother and save my father, that I had been bred to do a job for which I was so ill-equipped. And then I came here."

"You are right. You have no talent for storytelling. But it would not have helped you if you had got to Byzantium, for the mages would never have parted with the elixir for the life of a woman."

"I feel very tricked."

"What are you going to do, Geoffrey?"

"My job, my task, no matter how much I feel I cannot."

"Why?"

"Because it is my destiny." And, he added silently, *because I love those unborn babies I saw and want them to exist.*

"That is *not* logical."

They both began to laugh. They chuckled and chortled and laughed until they gasped for air, until tears rolled down their cheeks. When, finally, they got control of their breaths, they looked at each other across the napkin between them.

"Will you come with me, Lady Helene?"

She went absolutely still, waiting for the bee drone of compulsion that had ridden her to arrive, but there was only the whisper of the sea, the rustle of the breeze amongst the sedges, and the munch of horses cropping. He was the most peculiar fellow, gentle and modest, but incredibly powerful as she judged mages. She guessed a great deal from what he had not told her, and liked him for not magnifying either his defects or his accomplishments. And she liked the way his blue eyes rested on her, as if she was precious. No one had ever made her feel wanted that way. She wondered what sort of snake he had been, and found she was intrigued rather than revolted. Perhaps the gods knew what they were doing after all.

"Yes, I will. Where are we going?"

"I think we go to find the war, south in the Levant."

"Yes. Those nomads spoke of some terrible thing that had driven them from their homes. Do you know what it is?"

"Only secondhand. It is called the Shadow or the Darkness. And it seems very terrible. Something to run from, not towards. I wish it was someone else's task. But— tomorrow. Tonight I plan to sleep."

"Then I will go catch some dinner, while you build a fire." She stood up a little unsteadily from the wine, and took her bow and arrows from her saddle, and moved off into the low bushes.

Geoffrey watched her and thought he was a fortunate man, and that the gods, meddling busybodies though they were, had served him better than he deserved. Then he knit his brow over making a fire and forgot about anything but domesticity.

XX

They ate and drank and slept on either side of the small fire in easy comradeship. Rosy-fingered dawn tore it to ribbons when Geoffrey discovered Helene chattered like a magpie almost before the sun was decently above the horizon, and she realized he was one of those contemptible beings who spent half the day merely waking up. They glared at one another over the remains of the fire, both a little headachy from too much honey wine the night before, then saddled their steeds and prepared to depart. Geoffrey decided she was an ill-favored dwarf, and could not imagine how he ever thought her pretty. Helene felt a pang, a little twist of pain, at her awareness of his disapproval, and told herself he was a beef-witted bumpkin, the no-account son of a country horse breeder, and unworthy of her consideration. Then she spent a brooding half hour reflecting on his complete unworthiness as they rode towards the causeway.

They might have passed the whole morning in aggrieved silence if Geoffrey had not suddenly chuckled. Helene glanced at him slouched comfortably in the saddle with his water-stained leather hat wreathed in poppies, and took offense.

"Are you laughing at me?" she demanded.

Geoffrey was instantly serious. "No. I would never do that. I am not much given to laughing at people. But I was just wondering what our children will think when we tell them that you tried to murder me on our first meeting."

"Children! What children? I am not having any, certainly not *yours*."

"That's a shame, for the first two are quite engaging

brats, twins I think, and I was rather looking forward to dandling them on my knee. Do you dislike children, then?'' His mind fastened on the intellectual problem of preference and he was unaware of provoking the girl into a mild fury until it overtook him.

"You . . . you selfish lout. You pig. You conceited camel. How dare you think that—no, you do not think. Men. They cannot think. They just assume that what they desire is their right. I was a fool to believe you were different.'' She jabbed Achilles with her heels and set him trotting ahead along the causeway. The big horse jerked at the reins, snorted, and tossed his head at her. Helene gave a stern yank on the bit. "Behave, you stupid beast, unless you want to be a gelding.''

Geoffrey trotted up beside her. "Please. I am sorry if I said the wrong words.''

Helene glanced at him, which was a mistake. He looked at her so fondly, with such tenderness, that she felt helplessness welling in her chest. It was quite impossible to stay angry when looking into gentle blue eyes. And she wanted to remain angry and distant, to keep herself a separate being. Her virginity, which was a thing she had rarely thought of until the past few days, seemed a fine and precious thing, a font of power over her life. It had brought the sword of life against the spider-mage, and she felt determined not to lose it to the first pair of eyes that smiled at her. The sword itself was nothing, a tool, an artifact, but the power it demonstrated within her was everything. She looked away to the east.

The sky above was a little hazy towards the north, and a dull, uniform grey along the southern horizon, a line of near-darkness as straight as a rod. It was like a wall rising from the earth to heaven, and she had a profound sense of wrongness.

"Look. I have never seen anything like that. Do you know what it is?''

Geoffrey had been trying to find some way to repair the damage he had done, for he had felt Helene's sharp withdrawal like a lash across the face. He felt clumsy and awkward and incredibly stupid. Oh, dear Hermes, what do I do now, he thought.

You really cannot expect me to guide you in seducing my only rival, you know. I thought to steal you from the goddess, and forgot that mortal women are much more dangerous.

He was heartened enormously by the cool echo in his mind, gladdened to feel that his beloved young god had not entirely deserted him. *Rival? How poorly you value the love I bear you, even in betrayal, to speak of rivals. As if my heart was so petty an organ that it had not room for two.*

I am rebuked. There was a sense of great amusement, and affection, and the feel of a light kiss upon the brow, then nothing. Geoffrey tilted the hat back and looked where she pointed.

"Yes, I think I do. The Darkness my aunt's history speaks of casts such a shadow over the world, and it is that which we must battle. Can you recall anything those nomads said about what they fled?"

Helene gave a little shudder, and he knew that remembering was painful for her, that escaping had not lessened her sense of terror and helplessness. Then he watched her square her little shoulders and grip the reins a little tighter, and saw a faint glow suffuse her flesh and curdle the air around her. It was, he felt, a kind of bravery he could never match, and his wretched cowardice rose in his throat like bitter bile. There would be no children. He did not deserve such a woman. She shimmered like some ancient battle goddess, Pallas Athene or wild Artemis. Helene required a hero, not a nearsighted, half-baked scholar who had no business there. He did not, could not, love the awesome figure beside him, but cared only for the woman-child he had glimpsed the day before.

Geoffrey, you have a heart as brave as any roaring lion, if you would only know it.

You, ma donna, are a liar and a meddling hussy, he told the voice in his mind, but felt a little heartened nonetheless.

"They said that a strange war had come out of Araby with the spring. The warriors were like dead men, and when they could be slain, the bodies corrupted in a moment. One said too that it was like a sickness that took one man but passed another without cause.''

"Yes, that is like enough to the description in the book. If you can manage Latin, you may read it when we camp tonight.''

"I read seven tongues," she replied stiffly.

"Do you? I have only mastered three myself: Greek, Latin and Italic, though I can muddle through Frankish if I must. This is Albionese Latin, however, and not always grammatical."

"My father's library held many volumes, and I read them all. Some were in Latin, but others were in Arabic and Aramaic, and even Egyptic, which is most difficult."

"If we ever have the opportunity, will you instruct me?" he asked, his humbleness disguising a hunger for knowledge. He was quietly impressed with Helene's achievements, although he had little experience with literate females. Of course, women had no need of such things, since they were not intended as thinkers or scholars. His mother could read, but rarely did so, and his sister Beth could muddle through a stud book, but little more. Margaret was the most inclined to read of his sisters, but she rarely seemed to have anything to say about it. Egyptic. Imagine that. He could not, and was about to enquire further, when he reminded himself sternly that this was neither the time nor the place. He thought of his shabby room in Milan with infinite longing, and wished he could fly back to it, to peace and quiet study, away from gathering Shadows and filthy adventures. With a small start he realized he could, that his body knew how to form wings as well as it had made scales and snaky slitherings. Air held no terror for him. It was his natural element, as earth was his father's.

Geoffrey looked down and saw his left hand was half an eagle's claw, and felt a pressure in his shoulder blades as if wings were about to sprout. I would be a griffin, he thought. Then he made his body still, let his left hand assume its ordinary shape, and studied the looming darkness. I will not fly away from this, no matter how tempting it is, he decided. He rubbéd Marina's warm, familiar neck and let his mind settle into safe, ordinary thoughts of food and rest.

Helene watched him out of the corner of her eye, and almost followed his thoughts. She saw the eagle's claw shimmer into being and was both revolted and fascinated. The second feeling surprised her. Shape-shifters were disgusting. It was the most debased sort of magic. She knew that as well as her own name. The thought of being touched by hands that could be paws or claws, by a body which had admittedly been serpentine a few days before, should have been nauseating. Instead it was peculiarly enticing, and she shuddered. She was more disgusted by her own inconsistency than anything else, one moment determined to preserve her virginity at any cost, the next imagining how it might be to couple with an eagle.

They rode the causeway in silence, each embroiled in his own thoughts, and came to the mainland almost without noticing it. The terrain was dry and rocky and the growing greyness depressed the spirit. After a time they found the cracking remains of an ancient highway and rode towards the south and the menacing shadow.

Several leagues along the road they came to a little village and set the local dogs to savage barking. One, bolder than the rest, rushed out and snarled at Marina, who, unused to such rudeness, took affront and reared, startling Geoffrey from his reverie. Clumsily, he got Marina back down on all four hooves, then looked at the dog, a shaggy brute with a lolling tongue and strong teeth.

Be silent! he ordered, and the beast gave a shrill yelp and backed away as if it had been struck. Then it recovered, and began to growl again. Geoffrey felt a sort of burning in his chest. It spread out into his arms, down his torso into his legs, and finally up into his face. His whole body tingled, and he growled back at the dog. The shaggy thing began to whimper, and then fawned. Geoffrey turned away. He never had cared overmuch for dogs.

An anxious-looking man came out of one of the sun-baked houses, and gave a nervous little head bob that passed for a bow.

"Greetings," he muttered. He shifted from foot to foot. A boy of nine or ten, doe-eyed beneath a mop of black hair, darted forward, and the man seized him by the shoulders and hissed imprecations under his breath. The boy wriggled, curious, eager, and unafraid. Geoffrey wished he had ever had such easy confidence.

"Greetings to you," he answered. "Are you the headman?"

The man seemed puzzled by this query. "I am Elias. You are strangers. What do you want?" He sounded more worried than hostile as he held the squirming youngster.

"Some food, for which we will pay, and some news if you know any," Helene answered. The man looked doubtful.

A shrill voice came from within the house, characterizing Elias as a fool and a coward and ordering him to invite the strangers in *immediately*. An immense female heaved through the doorway, flaccid breasts resting on a wobbling belly, bright, piggy eyes staring from the roundest, fattest face Geoffrey had ever seen. Her garment strained at the seams to cover her grossness, and her plump hands were swollen around crude rings, but for all of that she still carried a remnant of what must have been great beauty in some earlier time. The black hair was streaked with white and none too clean, and the great eyes were rimmed with shadows, but she sparkled as she quivered like a Lombardy custard.

"Excuse my worm of a husband, good strangers. Please, enter our home. Elias is afraid of everything, even his own shade. Not like my Davos here. Such a good boy." She ruffled the child's hair affectionately. Her voice was high and hideous, like an ungreased axle, but she moved with grace. "He would battle a giant if there were any." She sounded mildly regretful at the lack of giants. "Come in. Come in. Stop standing there like a stump, Elias. Fetch some water so our guests may wash."

"But, Yasmina, we do not know . . . ."

"Faugh. Do not begin telling me the things I do not know or we will be standing here until the world ends. I may only be an ignorant old woman, but I do know guests when I see them. And if my lentils get burnt because you made me stand out here in the sun and argue, I will make you eat the ruined portion. Go fetch the water. Come, come. You are welcome to my house, such as it is. Elias only married me to get my poor house.'' She patted the wall with the same cheerful affection she had shown the boy. ''And he lets it fall to bits on our heads. Was ever a woman so tormented? Still, it is better than living in a tent. Is it not, Elias?''

He sighed. ''Yes, my dove. It is better than living in a tent.'' He sounded less than convinced, and Geoffrey understood why he had looked puzzled when asked if he were the headman. He exchanged a swift glance with Helene and found her green eyes alight with suppressed merriment.

They dismounted and entered a large single room. The walls were white, and narrow windows let in a little light. A carpet covered the floor, a complex blaze of color and pattern, and sturdy cushions rested against one wall. The woman began dragging them forward, but the boy pushed her aside, and she kissed the top of his head and went to crouch over a smoky brazier and stir the pot on it.

''Who are you? Where do you come from? Where are you going? Can I go with you?''

''Davos!''

''Oh, Mother!''

''It is not polite to ask questions,'' shrilled Yasmina. ''Our guests will tell us about themselves in good time. After they have washed and eaten and rested.''

Elias staggered in with a bucket, and set it beside a basin. The shadows of several other villagers darkened the doorway until Yasmina scolded them away. Helene put some water in the basin and removed the worst of the grime from her face and hands, and Geoffrey followed her lead. He was a little uneasy, for the roof was no more than a handspan above his head, and he wondered if the villagers would steal the saddles off the horses. He dried his face on a little towel, then looked up to find Helene had vanished.

The panic that gripped him was incredible. He glanced

in the corners and started for the door while his guts twisted. She returned and smiled at him, and he wanted to shake her for scaring him, and hug her against him, all at the same time. From the way her eyes widened she understood his feelings.

"I was only putting the horses behind the house," she said quietly.

"Yes. I know. I know you can take care of yourself, probably better than I can take care of you. Just tell me where you are going next time, please."

"Poor Geoffrey. Yes, I will." She put a small hand out and patted his arm. "You really deserve some nice girl who'll let you . . . I have been too much with men-at-arms. I do not know how to be a woman, and I do not even know if I wish to learn."

"But I like the way you are. I do not wish you to be different." The words surprised him as much as they did her.

Yasmina ordered them to be seated and served small bowls of steaming lentils mixed with quince and spicy lamb and curious flat pieces of bread which served in place of spoons. She dolloped a white, quivery substance on top of each serving, which Geoffrey tasted cautiously. It had a peculiar tang and he was not certain he liked it, but he followed Helene's lead and scooped up a mouthful on a piece of bread, mixing everything, and decided it was delicious. It seemed like an age since he had eaten a proper hot meal, though he realized after some calculation that he had only left Venice a few days before. Perhaps. He was not certain how time spent in the Underworld was counted.

Geoffrey turned his head slowly, mentally following the sun's course to the west, and stared at the whitewashed wall as if he could see beyond it, across the sea, all the way to his home. It was as if some great lodestone drew his mind towards the place of his birth. Unbidden, he saw his parents' bedroom, and Dylan, shrivelled and wasted, lying upon the pillows. Rowena, her hair unbound, stood beside the bed and wept without sound. His father seemed to rouse for a moment, opened his eyes and smiled. He spoke one word, "Aenor," closed his eyes, and the light faded from him.

His throat closed and his eyes stung. Geoffrey swallowed. He was certain he had just seen the moment of his father's passing, and was both piqued and moved that Dylan's last thought had been of his wife. He had a sharp pang of empathy for his aunt. In a savage bout of self-satire he thought of himself having a lovely time, getting shipwrecked and nearly stabbed by a hop-o'-my-thumb girl, while his poor aunt had to sit and watch her beloved brother perish. These ideas kept the realization of death at bay for a moment or two, but the pain rushed back.

Geoffrey found, to his surprise, that where he had accepted Aenor's shade with quiet grief, he wanted to howl like a wolf for his father. It was a knot in his chest, as if a hand closed over his heart and stilled it for a moment. He wished it would stop forever, so he could join his parents in whatever place their spirits now abided, but knew there was no room for him between them. There had never been. It seemed the saddest, most terrible thing in the world, a love so powerful that it excluded all else. He forced himself to think of his three sisters and his aunt, and wished he could be there to comfort them, instead of where he was, on a ridiculous adventure he had no proper business in. He felt his aching heart swell with a bittersweet emotion of affection and sorrow until it nearly choked him. He wondered if he could send the feeling across the leagues to home, and if the air could bear so heavy a burden.

Hermes! Take my love to my sisters and my aunt! He felt no response, except a lightening in his chest, and was promptly shocked at his peremptory ordering about of the young god. Too late. He wondered if he had given offense, then shrugged. Automatically he brought another mouthful to his lips, and knew that the tang of quinces would always remind him of death now.

Helene was studying him from beneath a quirked eyebrow, green eyes wise with worry or something like it. She gave him a tentative smile, and Geoffrey remembered the way her teeth had broken the firm skin of another quince the day before, and how the golden juice had dribbled from the corners of her mouth. She seemed infinitely precious to him in that moment, and it filled him with a kind of terror that he might lose her in some fashion. Bittersweet. It was so unfair. He had not come for a maiden, and he had no desire for fame and glory. All he ever wished for was to be loved by his parents and to pursue a quiet career in scholarship. That was all smashed beyond recall now. He was different, a stranger to himself. He could do things he had never dreamt of and did not particularly want. He had his father's capacity to transform, and his mother's earth song rang in the very bones of his body. They were gone, but they remained a part of him, and he would pass them on to any children he fathered.

Geoffrey almost laughed aloud. *What a peculiar fellow I am. I have the power to change the world, and my greatest ambition is to be a father.* He felt comforted. He could not imagine why. *The worst part about adventures is that they make you change—but that is the best part too,* he thought.

I could not agree with you more. What deity echoed this agreement he was unsure, but it hardly seemed to matter. He knew what he wanted, and would move heaven and earth to achieve his simple desire. The problem was going to be moving Helene.

"Did you find out anything in there?" Geoffrey asked as they rode out of the little village.

Helene looked at him. Mounted, they were at eye level, her larger steed compensating for her fewer inches. "What happened to you in there?"

"Happened? I washed my face and had a delicious meal while you gossiped. You did gossip, didn't you? I have no gift for it myself, not being female, but you might not either, being reared around mages."

"I was nursed on gossip. What happened?"

Geoffrey shrugged and shifted in the saddle. This must be how Prometheus felt when the vulture ate his liver every day. She was so fierce. Helene's intensity seemed to vibrate in every cell of her body, in her fine green eyes, and in the fiery nimbus of her aura. It made him uneasy. It was as if she was angry, but it was more than that. She was passionate, he decided, and he was uncomfortable with that.

He was always careful, so careful, to keep his own powerful feelings hidden and well-controlled, lest they overwhelm him and send him reeling into the abyss of himself. Emotions were untrustworthy things that led one into impulses like running off to Byzantium to save his mother's life. Emotions let you *believe,* and it seemed as if every time he tried to believe, he blundered. He had believed his Poppy Lady, and she had lied, and he had let himself love the young god and been betrayed.

The fault, he felt, lay in the feeling, in passionate hope. He had hoped to save his parents, and they were gone. He was terrified to hope for the glorious children he had glimpsed, afraid they too were another betraying ruse of the deities. He had failed to save his parents, and he did not deserve charming babes spitting up on his tunic and wetting his lap. His sisters had done those things innumerable times, and for some reason he had always found it completely endearing rather than repulsive.

Geoffrey had been three when Beth was born, and big already, four when Margaret had arrived, and nearly six when Orphiana made her quiet appearance. His father had been agitated at each lying-in—afraid he would lose his beloved Aenor in childbed, his son now guessed—and his mother had seemed dreamily distant, handing the girls over to a wet nurse and returning to her garden as quickly as was decent. He had sat by the cradle happily, changing linen napkins with clumsy little boy fingers, holding the delightful, squirming pink bodies every chance he got. The aching loneliness he did not have a word for vanished when he hugged them. The strangers they became as they grew up, Beth toddling after Dylan into the stables, Margaret bending over her broidery frame, or Orphiana, the baby who never cried, becoming a girl who rarely talked, whose eyes were focused on some other place or time, wrenched him back into dreadful isolation. Back into voices no one else heard and people no one else saw; back into madness. He knew now he was quite sane, but it was cold comfort. He still felt mad and frightened, and they were powerful, passionate emotions that refused to bow to clear, logical thought.

It made him angry in a way he never had been before. After several seconds Geoffrey realized he was angry at his parents for dying, and, more, angry at them for loving one another more than their children. Maybe he was not sane. Surely only a madman could be enraged at dead parents. It was not logical. The whole world was crazy, and this infuriated him. And he wanted to hug a baby and not feel so utterly lonely any more.

Geoffrey returned his attention to Helene and realized he would like to hold her, not out of lust, but out of loneliness. How unmanly! He was disgusted with himself. He had let Hermes know how alone he had felt, and look what had happened. He had vanished. He made a passionate, irrational resolve never to let anyone know that he was afraid of being alone, and watched it go up in invisible flames under Helene's demanding gaze. Curse the girl. Why did she have to look at him like that?

"I think my father just died," he said in the remotest voice he could manage, hoping she would not guess that it was anything important. "I never knew him very well, and now I never will."

Helene reached out a small hand, a callused, roughened hand, and curled her fingers around his right hand. "I am sorry. At least you did not kill him." Her touch was so warm and strong.

"I might as well have. My mother was the world to him—and I could not save her."

A man emerged from the rocks on one side of the worn road and scuttled towards them like some monstrous crab. A thin sound came from between his cracked lips, and his eyes seemed to glow with a nauseating yellow light. He gave a little cackling cry and bounded towards Helene, clutching at her foot. It was a fatal mistake on the man's part, for Achilles struck him in the chest with an iron-shod hoof before Helene even had time to draw her blade. He reared a little and came down on the man's skull, squealing furiously. A smell like an open sewer filled the air, and a thin yellow rivulet of stuff leaked out of the broken cranium.

Helene jerked on the reins and gagged. She pulled her horse away from the corpse, which was decaying before her startled eyes. Geoffrey joined her, his eyes tearing from the incredible odor.

When she could speak, Helene said, "What got into Achilles? I have never seen him attack without command unless he was unmounted."

Geoffrey leaned forward and laid his hand along the still quivering flesh of Achilles' neck and murmured the soothing sounds that he had known since he could toddle, nonsense words he used even when he had been terrified of his father's graceful animals. Achilles swivelled his ears around, rolled his brown eyes, and bared his enormous teeth, a comical expression on such a fearsome beast. Then he blew through his mobile lips and snorted.

"I think he has an instinctive revulsion for creatures of the Darkness."

Helene had been watching Geoffrey calm her horse, wondering how anyone so profoundly gentle could be expected to survive into old age, caught between growing admiration and a fear that something might happen to him. Now she tore her fascinated gaze away from the movement of his hands to look at the rotting corpse.

"Is that what it is? They could slay their enemies with the stink alone. Anyone with sense would be riding as fast as they could in the other direction."

Geoffrey shrugged. "It does not matter which way I go. I am afraid all the time anyhow, and I always have been. But you, my dear Hippolyta, should not be daunted by a little smell."

Helene knew she was being teased, but only because she had heard the guards in the barracks indulging in it. No one had ever poked fun at her or joked at her, and she was not certain she liked it. And she realized that she was sure she did not like Geoffrey admitting he was afraid or calling himself a coward. Men were supposed to hold high opinions of themselves, not the opposite. He seemed so humble. Pride and arrogance she was accustomed to, but his gentleness disarmed her, and she did not wish to be disarmed.

"Hippolyta? Why call me that?"

"She was Queen of the Amazons and the second wife of Theseus, and you are the nearest thing to an Amazon I ever hope to see. I only regret I am hardly a heroic figure like Theseus. Well, he was not really a very nice hero, and he never would have found his way out of the Labyrinth without the aid of Ariadne, whom he abandoned soon after. But I am sure that Hippolyta was very like you, even to the red hair."

"Perhaps. I do not know those tales very well, for they were forbidden in Byzantium. Some of the storytellers used them in the marketplace, but rarely, and very quietly."

"Forbidden? Why?"

"Because they spoke of the gods of ancient times, and the gods were banished by the mages long ago."

"Banished? How does one banish a god?"

"I do not know, but I can understand why they did it, now." She gave a little shudder. "Are we going to find more people like that man?"

"I am afraid so."

"I do not know if I can stomach it."

Geoffrey's laugh startled her, and she realized that her serious remark sounded like a joke. It was a good sound, a clean, human noise, and it lighted his sober face in a pleasant way. Had Hiram ever laughed? She could not remember. She did not think so. They turned their horses towards the deepening greyness in the south.

XXI

It was nearing dusk, though it was difficult to tell beneath the overcast sky. The land was rough and there were no sharp, distinguishing features either of them could pick out. They were both uneasy since their encounter with the man, eyeing the vague horizon anxiously and riding fairly close together.

The air was chill and Geoffrey was thinking of finding a place to camp and wondering whether they could risk a fire. The aureate scintillations of Helene's energies flickered against the darkening sky like a beacon, and any foe could see it if he looked. Those creatures of the Darkness, on the other hand, had no body radiance and could creep up unseen.

"Let us stop, and I will hunt a coney while you start the fire," Helene said.

Geoffrey started to protest against the idea of her scrambling around alone in the twilight without him, and quelled himself. She was much more capable of protecting herself than he was. They had goat cheese and flat bread, a parting gift from Yasmina, and that would do for supper. He was about to offer this alternative when a sound split the air that raised the hairs all over his body.

It was a howl, an enormous nerve-rasping scream that chilled the blood. A moment later a thing sprang out before them, some enormous beast, though all that was visible were two great luminous eyes. Several small figures materialized around it, gobbling meaninglessly. They rushed forward, and Marina reared and screamed in terror.

Geoffrey slipped from the saddle and rolled onto the stony ground. He was dazed for a few seconds, and when his head stopped swimming the gabbling brutes were all around him, striking him with their pallid hands and rough cudgels. Their touch chilled his flesh, and he felt himself retreat before it. With an enormous effort he staggered to his feet and clumsily pulled his sword from its sheath. His greater height gave him some advantage, and he thrust into one of the attackers as a blow struck his other shoulder.

The metal of his weapon entered the flesh of the enemy with little resistance, as if he had stabbed a loaf of spongy *panetone*, and he pulled it out and turned to another as a cudgel barely missed his head. He flinched and nearly tripped. A stick struck his kneecap, sending stars of pain along his leg.

His leg collapsed and suddenly he was on the ground on all fours, while sticks and kicks battered his back and sides. He saw his own death reaching for him, and he was helpless to prevent it. Geoffrey felt pain and growing cold and defeat.

A noise came from his throat, a sound he could not name, a belly bellow that tore the cords of his voice, and a doorway opened in his mind. Years of unspoken rage fountained up from his guts, and a heat raced along his blood that was almost more terrifying than the foul brutes who battered away at him.

His flesh seemed to contract, then explode, and the world changed. Geoffrey felt his hands become claws, his skin become hide, his jaw become a great, deadly beak. He was barely aware of his clothing ripping away, or of the huge wings that rose from his bleeding shoulders. All he could feel was anger.

Great hind legs propelled him off the stony ground, and a clawed fore-member tore the head off the closest attacker. He felt strong. He would rend the world. The wings behind him flapped furiously, creating a draft that knocked one brute down. Geoffrey set a hindpaw on the chest and gutted the fellow without thought. He would kill and kill, until the world was empty of all life, down to the last worm, until his rage was sated.

A great dark horse shape reared in the twilight, and Geoffrey almost flew to tear its throat out. Where was the rider? The question twisted around in his brain while he casually clawed the face and chest of a thing he barely realized was female. Helene! Where was she?

A scream came from his beaked face, a brazen challenge, and he flapped his wings and felt his feet leave the earth. Aloft a few man-lengths, he saw the swarm of little figures like black ants, and the horse smashing his way across them.

A paler steed lashed out at something and screamed in panic. Under her belly a fire seemed to be guttering out.

The beast she screamed at was like some misformed wolf and it nosed towards the paling fire. Marina stood her ground above Helene, and Geoffrey dropped like a stone. He settled onto the back of the beast with a flap of wings. It turned its head and spatters of yellow drool flew through the air.

Cold touched him. Geoffrey could feel his powerful hind legs turn to stone. The breath of the beast curled out in a filthy yellow mist, a perversion of everything that was light, and his claws felt leaden. His heart slowed. In a moment it would stop.

The world stilled, and for an eternity he clung to the foul fur of the thing, growing colder and colder. His rage was gone. His terror was gone. He was empty, as vacant as the void. The yellow eyes of the beast looked into him, freezing him.

With infinite slowness he lowered his beaked head and sank the cruel hook of his mouth into the obscene orb that drank his soul. The point sank into the eye, penetrating the oily surface, and a bitter fluid spouted out. He jerked away from the substance, and felt less frozen. He reached over the head, catching slimy nostrils with his talons, and ripped back. A satisfaction gripped him as the flesh parted and the beast howled with pain, a loathsome pleasure that heated his loins.

The beast collapsed and began to rot, and Geoffrey sprang off, lustful for more slaying, only to realize that there was nothing left to kill but two horses and a girl. The burning in him demanded quenching, and he eyed the living in a red haze of desire. He'd have them all.

The girl stirred and sat up groggily. She rubbed her forehead and looked around. She was so tiny. He could hold her body with one claw and peck her eyes out one by one while he mounted her. She stared blankly at him, sheltering under Marina's belly, and then her eyes widened.

"Geoffrey? Is that you?"

The name drew him back into a calmer time, when he had borne a name and lived a simple existence. Disgust rose in his throat, a loathing for himself and the beast he could become so easily. Being a snake had been strange, but nothing so shameful as he was now.

He felt the wings wither on his back, the well-muscled hindlegs lengthen into ordinary limbs, the taloned forepaws fade into hands, until only the throb of his groin remained to remind him of his vileness. Crouched on his hands and knees, naked and bleeding, he spewed his desire onto the dry earth. Then he crouched off into the low bushes and tried without success to empty his belly. Nothing came up but foul, bitter bile.

He spat the filthy taste out and wiped a running nose with the back of one hand. Geoffrey noticed the tears along his cheeks and brushed them away. Finally he struggled to his feet and staggered back onto the road.

Helene still remained where he had left her. Marina had moved a few feet away and was touching noses with Achilles, exchanging equine comfort. The stink of decay was incredible.

Geoffrey knelt beside her. "What is it? Are you injured?"

Helene looked up at him uneasily and made a little mewling noise. "I am cold," she moaned. Her body's light was pale, faded and weak.

He pulled his cloak off Marina's saddle and wrapped Helene's small form in its folds. He felt exhausted, but he lifted her up and staggered down the old road until he was away from the nauseating smell. Then he found a little hollow in the rocks and set her down as gently as he could. She clutched at his hand.

"A very poor Hippolyta," she muttered. For a second Geoffrey could not imagine what she was talking about.

"You are a magnificent griffin," she whispered. Then her large eyes closed and she was still.

Geoffrey had a moment of terror and panic much worse than anything he had experienced before as he looked at her, until he saw the faint pulse in her throat and knew she slept. Still, he was worried. She did not look right. He tried to think what to do and finally realized he was shivering with the chill of the desert night, and still naked.

Unsaddling the horses, he got his spare tunic and hose out and put them on. He piled both horse blankets together and put Helene on them, and added her cloak to his own over her. He tucked her bag of belongings under her head for a pillow, and she gave a little murmur in her slumber. He built a small fire, gave the horses a handful of grain, and sank down, too weary to eat or move further.

The cold ate at him until finally he crawled over to his sleeping companion, moved her to one side, and lay down, drawing her back against his chest and resting his legs behind hers. Helene's flesh felt cold to his touch, and he folded his arms around her and held her tight, willing her to take some warmth from him. He pulled the combined cloaks more closely around them. Me, a griffin, he thought, and then sleep claimed him.

Mist like ice swirled across a sunless world. Eternal twilight stretched from horizon to horizon over a barren plain. No wind moved the mist and no life stirred the empty sands. There was only an ache, a memory and a longing for a single leaf or the murmur of a bee. But there was only silence.

Then, a single noise, so distant and faint it seemed unreal, a single tear falling onto the sere, dead earth, a crystal shatter in the stillness. It spoke of all the waters of the world in one moment, the last remaining note of the song of waters. If only the melody would return. Longing reached, stretched, groped, and clutched for the lilting, rushing gurgle, the sparkle of fountains beneath the forgotten sun.

The man muttered in his sleep, and the woman turned and placed her head against his chest. She heard the steady drum of his heart and the throb of blood as it rushed along the rivers of his body. It entered the dream and became part of the song so yearned for.

My dear, brave children. The voice was sonorous and sorrowful, and they both dreamt that a great mother held them close, until the patter of droplets on their faces woke them.

"Wha . . . ?" he groaned. Helene's hair tickled his nose, and she was a warm, cuddlesome weight against his body. The top of her head looked like a good place to plant a small kiss. In his waking stupor he faintly heard the sound of water running over stones. Geoffrey felt completely parched, as if every drop of fluid had been baked out of his body during sleep. He remembered the dream, mulling it over slowly.

"Are you always a brilliant conversationalist in the morning?" Helene demanded, wriggling out of his grasp and letting chill air fill the warm place that had existed between them. She sat up and looked around. "I *think* it's morning. It is hard to tell. Ah, you found a spring. No, I do not believe it is actually morning. The fire is still glowing, so it cannot have burned through the night. Why did you not pull off my boots before you put me to bed? My feet are all swollen. And my mail too." She crawled out from under the cloaks and put some fresh sticks on the fire while Geoffrey contemplated strangling her. She was clearly some malevolent dwarf sent to plague his existence. His head was full of straw—dry straw—and if she didn't cease her chatter he was going to stuff a rock in her mouth. His whole body ached and his eyes stung with a desire for sleep. Now she was talking to Achilles. Good. He could doze off again.

Geoffrey rearranged the coverings and put his head on the makeshift pillow. It had a hard, funny lump in the middle of it which always seemed to be under his ear no matter how he moved. His thirst became unbearable, and he gave a huge sigh, pushed his warm nest away, and staggered up, stubbing a hose-clad toe on an attacking rock. It was wonderful how the inanimate world always became actively hostile when he was half-awake. He swore and knuckled his bleary eyes.

A brisk breeze dashed sparkling droplets across his brow, and his sluggish mind informed him there had been no source of water nearby when he had chosen this hollow. Geoffrey felt a dark disapproval of mysteries in the middle of the night. He did not much care for them in full daylight, come to think of it. He stumbled towards the gurgling sound.

A smell enveloped him, a clean, refreshing scent finer than all the perfumes in the world. He followed it, and came to a bubbling spring. He knelt down and peered at the sparkling water for a moment before reaching out a hand. The water seemed filled with light, as if the moon shone on its surface. He cupped a palmful, and silver leaked through his fingers.

Geoffrey tasted the water and felt he had never tasted it before. It filled his senses completely as drops rolled down his throat and beard. It smelled like life, like every field of spring-mown hay and also the earthy scent of harvested corn; it tasted of light, if light could have a flavor; it felt warm as a kiss and cold as new-fallen snow as it flowed into him. The sight of it quickened his pulses and stilled them in the same moment.

When he had drunk his fill—a mouthful or two—Geoffrey sat beside the spring and listened to it. The music in the water whispered along his nerves, and he fell into a waking dream. He heard the rush of waves against the shore, the roll of rivers past peaceful banks, the roar of cataracts. It all wove together into a paean that awed him and inspired his musician's heart. He forgot everything but the water, until something healed within him, and his still weary body demanded attention.

Helene was brooding by the fire, her brow knitted. She looked up as he stumbled into the light, her glass green eyes conveying nothing. Geoffrey wanted to talk to her, but he was too full of tiredness and water music for speech. Instead he pulled the book from his belongings and offered it to her wordlessly. He took her cloak from the bedding, handed it to her, and stretched out, pushing aside the bag and pillowing his head on one arm. Content, he drifted into sleep smiling.

Twitching her cloak around her shoulders, Helene glared at Geoffrey's resting shape beyond the fire. Her mouth ached for water, but she resisted the siren song out of sullen stubbornness. One glance at the spring when she went to the horses had told her it was no natural occurrence. It shone too brightly, smelled too sweetly, beckoned too persuasively. She remembered the dream, and the voice which had spoken to her, and she knew the water arose from the goddess. That meant it had a purpose, and Helene was dumbly determined to thwart any schemes or plots the goddess had involving herself. No one was going to push her about ever again!

Helene shivered, not from cold, but from the fresh memory of the foray on the road. She was furious and ashamed. She had hesitated for a moment in the attack, choosing between her own sword and the peculiar weapon she had torn from her father's corpse. The wolf-thing had thrust its vile snout towards her and breathed. That was all. Just breathed.

She had fallen from Achilles' saddle like a stone, toppled to the hard earth without sensation, felt her horse charge into the fray and the more timorous mare come to shelter her body while the thing slavered towards her. She had felt nothing, not even fear, just a mute helplessness that infuriated her. The wolf had seemed unable to come closer to Marina than a pace or two, and now Helene wondered what curious virtue the sweet, silver mare had which Achilles did not. Then the griffin had fallen upon the wolf from the leaden sky, and she had *known* it was Geoffrey. She had watched the struggle in silent terror when the griffin began to turn to stone before her eyes, and felt a fierce rejoicing when the huge beak rent the wolf's muzzle. And he called himself a coward. Men were incomprehensible. He had saved her, and she resented it because she had not been able to do it herself.

Helene opened the book he had given her to take her thoughts away from herself. She tilted the page towards the light and began to pick her way through the unfamiliar hand and tongue, counting six rhetorical errors in as many pages before the tale itself caught her up. As she became accustomed to the style, she read more quickly, her eye racing down the text and barely pausing over the exquisite illuminations. Her eyes ached and stung from the smoke of the fire, and her feet fell asleep from sitting cross-legged, but she went on, fascinated and repelled by the events she discovered there.

When she came to the final page, the wedding of Dylan and Aenor so recently deceased, she felt a great sadness that she would never know them. Helene closed the book and pulled her knees up under her chin, folding her arms around her shins and wriggling her toes. Pins and needles pricked her feet and lower legs for a moment, but she barely noticed, staring into the fire.

The sound of the water drew her, and the dreadful thirst she had resisted seized her. She glanced down at the book and wondered why she had been picked to be in the third part of this adventure. How had the grandmother, Eleanor, become a mage, and why had the Council insisted that females could not learn the ways of power?

Helene knew with a kind of deadly certainty that she could do anything Hiram could have, now, and felt only a vast indifference. She did not care for power. She just wanted to never feel helpless again. A kind of heat seized her, a fever in her bones, until the merry tinkle of the nearby spring was unendurable.

She rose and picked her way carefully towards the scintillating pool, then stood glaring at the shining waters, until the heat within her soaked her chest and sweat ran into her eyes. Her clothing was vile. She felt dirty right down to her soul. She was dizzy with heat.

"You win, curse you," she said, and pulled off her clothes with near eagerness. If she had had any others, she would have burnt these.

Helene plunged into the spring and felt the water froth up between her legs, caress her flat belly, and flow over her tiny breasts. The waters barely cooled the fever in her blood, and she slipped her head beneath them. She had an impulse to inhale, to draw the water into her lungs which burned in her chest, to drown the heat and herself. Dead, she would never feel helpless again. What did life hold for her but further humiliations, defeats, and terrors?

She hung, suspended, balanced between a painful past and an uncertain future, for an endless moment. Then she opened her mouth and drew the waters into her body. They were sweet and bitter at once, and they filled her up until she felt like a brimming cup. Joy such as she had never imagined raced along her blood, and an anguish too, as if they were the same thing. The joy was terrifying and the pain a comfort.

Gasping, Helene thrust her head above the surface and watched the drops like molten silver fall from her cheeks. After a moment she realized she wept, silently, and that her tears were bitter with salt and fiery with passion. It was a beast she had prisoned up in her heart, a violent, loyal, prideful beast which raged at denial and humiliation. It had hated Hiram for denying her the smallest scrap of affection, for lying to her and deceiving her, for injuring her need to trust, but it hated the goddess of the little statue too, for promising love and then forcing her to turn to Geoffrey.

Him, perhaps, the beast hated most of all, for the very gentleness which wore away at her mistrust, which threatened to destroy the fortress she wanted to hide herself in. Why couldn't he have been some noisy braggart, some stupid, murderous man she could have slain without regret? He was nice, and she despised niceness. And he was brave and thought himself a coward. He was a shapeshifter, and if the tale in the book was even half true, his children would also be.

Helene shuddered at the thought of carrying something in her womb that could turn into a griffin or a huge snake at will, a lifetime of servants' stories and taught anathemas gripping her mind. She refused to be dazed or seduced into mute submission by the plans or wills of the gods. Then she realized that if she was thinking of bearing a shapeshifting babe in her belly, she had already lost. She might just as well crawl under the covers with him and let him plunder her body.

Except, of course, he would not. She had seen the

aroused lust of the griffin, and had been both terrified and
fascinated. She had seen him struggle with it, deny it,
overcome it. She had almost longed to have him mount her
in that shape, so she could hate him completely. She
wanted him to be the beast she hated in herself.

With a sigh, Helene pulled herself out of the pool and
sat naked on a smooth rock. If only everything were not so
contrary and complicated. She wanted clarity and yearned
to feel clean, simple emotions. She had come to the goddess prepared to offer love and utter trust, and found
instead she had a mare's nest of anger and resentment. Did
you betray me, or did I betray myself?

A little of both, child.

"Why?"

*We have such imperfect understanding. And, as you
have guessed, the Cosmos is a muddled thing, not nearly so
tidy a place as philosophers and mages will pretend.*

"Why is it not?"

*Ah, my cuckoo-child, even wise Athene cannot answer
that. Perhaps because Creation never stops, and that is a
very messy business.*

"Creation never stops?" Odd, she had always thought it
rather had, once the world was made and time began.

Every moment is unique.

Helene felt her mind shiver as this thought penetrated it,
like a spear piercing the face of the water. The pool was
still, smooth as a glass, and the image of the moon rode on
its surface. It drew her eyes and plucked her heart, erasing
the past and the future into a simple present, a *now* that
went on forever. It was a trap. She knew it down to her
bones. And it was complete liberation. Helene knew that
as well.

She reached out a small hand to the pile of garments
beside her and pulled out the cross she had removed from
Hiram's body. Helene plunged it into the still water and
watched the image of the moon shatter as the bounds of
her mind smashed into shards with it. For an instant she
beheld the chaos underlying all, a second of violent madness, and then she was holding a sword in her hand.

Helene rose and held it up. The blade was slightly

curved and the metal was tinted with many colors. She
touched the blade with a tentative finger and found it quite
real and substantial. She could not quite grasp what had
occurred, but something eased within her chest, and she
felt refreshed and invigorated. She wanted to go wake up
her companion and tell him . . . what? She was not sure.
She could not tell what had happened to her.

"I am different," she said aloud, and began to shiver
violently. Helene picked up her clothes, revolted at their
smell, and dashed back to the small fire. Picking up her
trousers with disgust she wrinkled her nose as she started
to don them. She dropped them hastily.

All the tedious volumes Helene had studied in an effort
to gain her father's affection rustled in her mind. She
remembered the apple that had freshened in her hand, as
she shivered in the night's chill. Drawing the cloak around
her, Helene examined each incident of magic over the past
few days, furling her brow to comprehend some pattern
that seemed just out of reach. The mages prepared for their
magicks with solemn rites, and never had she done such
rituals, though she knew the forms. It was as if all she had
to do was desire a thing, and it was done.

Surely it was not so simple. She felt her bare feet resting
on the cool earth, and remembered the sound of the heart
of the world as she had lain upon the floor of Jalael's tent.
The power was there, both in her and around her. She
could draw upon it at will. What use were rites and rituals?
She could alter the world as she chose.

Chewing the inside of her cheek, Helene realized that it
was the choice that was the problem. So far, she had been
fortunate, and the goddess had watched over her and guided
her hand. But the power she had found in the pool, in the
waters, and in herself, needed to be used with care. Instinct was not enough. She had too much power, and it
made her afraid of herself.

Helene had a moment of insight that Geoffrey was
afraid of himself as well. She looked over at the sleeping
man, at the rainbow light that enveloped him, and saw as
well the lineaments of a power that would destroy him if
he did not control it. I must learn to use this, not as the

mages did, selfishly or to prolong life just to exist, but carefully and wisely, she thought. But where shall wisdom be found? And I must teach Geoffrey.

She felt very small and very helpless, and she hated that. Helene hated having to choose and realized she always had, whether it was which garment to wear of a morning or which blow to use in mock combat. It made her uncertain. She could move mountains, but she would have to decide where to put them. That was too great a thing for her. Instead, she picked up her filthy clothes and smoothed them out across her knees, her dainty nose curling at the foul smell of fear-drenched sweat. She focused her attention on the odor, and banished it like some small demon.

To her delight and astonishment, the color of the fabric got a little lighter, and the foul smell vanished along with the creases. She gave a little crow of pleasure and pulled them on, then repeated the small magic with her quilted tunic. It smelled as clean as new. For some reason she could not quite grasp, she felt less helpless than she had in days.

Every moment is unique.

"Do you always have to have the last word, Lady?"

Only the wind answered her.

XXII

Morning was a greyish smear against a leaden sky. Geoffrey lay looking east for several minutes before his bladder forced him out of the horsey smelling warmth of the bedding. He knuckled his eyes and stumbled away from the campsite, bashing unshod toes and cursing the loss of his boots. He had a faint recollection of getting up in the middle of the night and drinking some water, but it seemed very vague and dreamlike, and he was not sure it had been real.

When he turned and came back towards camp, he saw a blaze like the rising sun, which, after several blinks, sorted itself out into the small fire and Helene's body light which shone like a beacon in the miserable twilight. It was, he decided, absolutely magnificent, and would probably attract every creature of Shadow for leagues around, so they would spend the day in peril of their very lives. He banged another toe and decided he hated adventures. He wanted a hot bath, a real bed, and a quiet breakfast.

None of these materializing out of the air, he sat down across the small fire from Helene and prepared himself for her matutinal chatter. For once, however, she was silent. Indeed, she appeared to be asleep, sitting upright. She looked different somehow.

It took his sluggish morning mind a minute to focus on her cleanliness. Her hair was no longer matted with sweat and dirt, but shone like burnished copper, and her face and hands were free of grime. Her garments, too, looked less dingy.

Geoffrey was trying to puzzle this out when his eyes fell upon the sword which rested across her knees. The hilt he recognized, but surely there had been no blade before. It was very beautiful, and his palm itched to hold the hilt, to feel the lines of energy traced upon it. It was like the horrid lust he had felt the day before, endless and tempting. The sword would make him a hero. It would make him like his father. Brave. He wanted to tear it from her grasp. Geoffrey had never desired anything more in his life.

Except those unborn babes. The thought startled him. *Oh, Hermes, beloved friend, thank you for letting me glimpse those children. Even if they are another lie, a fresh deceit, I thank you.* The desire to seize the sword lessened. It remained, but he could control it. In his mind he heard a small, sad tune, a melancholy melody that comforted him. He would not be possessed by any bit of metal.

I have my own wisdom, do I not?

Geoffrey could hear a kind of longing in the answering thought, a need to be worthy that echoed his own. The young god desired such respect as he wished for himself, and had never received it. *You are most wise, and most generous.* He felt a rush of warmth at these words, as if he had given a gift and received a great reward.

He admired the beauty of the blade in an abstract way, but now felt no desire to wield it. He was more curious as to how the metal could be colored like the rainbow, but even that was too great an effort above the rumblings of a mutinous belly.

Helene opened great green eyes and smiled at him. Geoffrey's throat constricted, and his heart—a usually steady organ—tried to hammer its way out of his chest. He never thought anyone would look at him like that. It was the look that Aenor gave to Dylan, an expression of such tenderness and intimacy that his childish self had always felt excluded—indeed, an intruder. If she would promise to smile like that, she could chatter at him every morning until the world ended. He smiled back, then extended his big hands toward the fire to disguise his feelings.

''You snore,'' she said.

Almost relieved to be back on the secure ground of mild

hostility, he replied, "I am sorry. I do. My sisters have often told me so."

"No, I like it. It was such a real sound. Last night the world was very faint and distant at times, and I felt a little lost. Then I'd hear your snores and know just where I was. Look what I did." She lifted the sword up before her face. The slight curve made a crescent shadow across her cheek.

"I am happy to have been of service." He was rather touched. "It dazzles the eye. One moment it looks like metal, the next like light itself. But I wish I had my boots instead. My feet are freezing. I suppose they are torn to pieces back where we met those Darklings."

"I will wager you could whistle yourself up a new pair if you wished."

"Huh? Oh, my flute. I had not thought of that. Later, after I eat something." He stood clumsily and found his pack. As he took out the bread and goat cheese, his hand touched the silky scaled surface of the sheath which he had found amongst the remnants of his serpent's skin. He removed it, glanced at the exquisite traceries of interlace that twisted across its surface and the brilliant blue star stones in the intersections, and brushed it across his tunic to dust off a few crumbs. It curved exactly as the blade Helene now carried.

Geoffrey took the food and sheath back to the fire and resumed his seat. He set the sheath aside and offered Helene some food. The cheese was dry and salty and the bread was coarse, but they both ate like wolves. Helene passed the waterskin, and the taste was sweet after the cheese. He mused vaguely, and she kept silent for a time.

"Geoffrey?"

"What?"

"Thank you for holding me last night."

"I am glad you did not mind. You were so cold. I had a dream that you were lost somewhere. It was a dry, barren place. I could not bear your being lost." He mumbled the last and felt uneasy. "Here. This belongs with that sword." He held out the sheath.

Helene looked at it, but did not reach to take it. "If I

have apprehended your book aright, the two should not be joined until we are.''

"The Devil take the schemes of the gods! You cannot dash all over the Levant with a naked blade against your leg. Be sensible for once.''

"And you are supposed to take my submission before they are joined—and I am to gift you with the sword,'' she said provocatively.

"Submission!'' he roared, stung by the hateful memory of his griffin lust. "I never want to see you subservient to me or any other man—or woman or goddess either. It would be a lie, a snare, and a delusion. I never want to see you helpless, as you were yesterday. Take the sheath and keep the sword as well, for I am a poor hero to carry a thing like that. I will . . . play a merry tune while you cut a wide swath through the Darkness.''

"Will you play a dirge if I perish?'' Her green eyes met his blue ones with the force of a blow.

Geoffrey felt his breath leave his lungs for a moment. He shook his head to clear the dizziness. "No. I'll pipe a song to end the world.'' He felt defenseless under her gaze. It was just not fair. He was not awake enough to behave rationally. She was probably going to bedevil him every moment for the rest of his life. This depressing thought cheered him immensely.

"You really would, I believe. I think you love me—and I find it most unnerving. Or do you just love those children to come?''

Geoffrey groaned. "Woman, you are a plaguey dwarf. I do not know if I love you. Sometimes I'd like to beat you. And other times I want to hug you and kiss your nose.''

"My nose!''

"Well, your mouth as well, but just to shut you up!''

Helene giggled and her short, curly hair glinted with coppery highlights. She was impishly pleased at herself. Then the laughter faded from her face. "Will you always try to keep me safe?''

Geoffrey trembled. His throat constricted for a second, and his mouth felt dry. "If you will permit me the honor, I will always try.''

Large tears spilled from the wide eyes, and Helene extended a small hand above the fire. Geoffrey grasped it firmly and wondered if he was up to the task. It loomed more monumental than all the forces of Shadow yet awaiting them. He had her submission—as much as she would ever give, and more than he would ever desire—in that moment, without the carnal bonding. It was enough. He handed her the sheath, and she accepted it.

They rode along in the oppressive gloom, uneasy and watchful. To his quiet delight, Geoffrey had his boots back, as good as new, thanks to Helene's growing magical talents. They had returned to the place where they had met the wolf-being and found only dried bones that looked years old and the remains of Geoffrey's clothing. Helene had gathered the pieces of his boots, and stared at them fixedly for several minutes until they came together. They felt different somehow, but he couldn't put his finger on how. Still, it made his heart feel almost light in spite of the hideous overcast.

A little after midday there were voices, and before they could find cover, a half dozen men on light-hooved steeds were around them. They wore capacious robes and cloths tied around their brows, and had small veils across their faces. Geoffrey had never seen anything so odd, and he had to quell his scholar's curiosity in favor of vigilance. However peculiar their dress, they might be dangerous. At least they looked like real men, and had none of the lusterlessness of the things they had met the day before.

One spoke and pointed at Geoffrey's flower-laden hat, and if he did not understand a word, he still knew he had been insulted. Geoffrey felt his cheeks burn. The speaker pointed at Helene and said something.

"Who are they and what do they want?" he asked.

"Nomads—robbers, I would guess. The leader . . . has just offered to fight you for me. Actually, he said a great deal more than that."

"Do you know your eyes change color when you are angry?"

"Geoffrey, this is not the time for discussing my eyes! Are you going to fight him?"

"If I must to keep you safe. I am just not very skilled at arms. I'm afraid you did not make a very good bargain back over the fire."

"Will you be unmanned if I fight him?"

"No. I would be relieved."

"Good. When I asked you to try to keep me safe I did not intend that you should ever fight my battles for me. And this is about *my* honor. I do not understand it. I never before have aroused such lust as I have these past few days."

Helene turned and spoke a long guttural speech, and the veiled man registered outrage. His followers muttered, and Geoffrey wished he understood the tongue. The man shouted something, and whatever Helene said seemed to infuriate him to the point of foolhardiness. He whipped out his curved blade and kicked his horse.

This was a grave mistake, because Achilles gave one of his brazen cries, and the man's horse reared and nearly unseated him. Geoffrey was certain he heard someone laugh, though the veils prevented him from seeing who. The leader heard it too, for he turned and glared at his men once he got his horse under control.

Helene looked absolutely calm, sitting easily on her horse, apparently unconcerned. She might have been carved from alabaster. The man spoke again, and her reply made the face above the veil redden with fury beneath the bronzed skin. He jumped off his horse in a swirl of draperies and clearly demanded combat. His men pulled their horses back into a circle and waited.

She gave a careless shrug and slipped to the ground, which made her short stature apparent to all. Helene looked like a child facing a full-grown adult. Geoffrey felt sweat run down his torso and wished he had been a better student of arms. It did not seem right that she should have to fight, even if it was her own virtue which was at stake. Logically, she was better equipped to do battle, but his emotions refused to behave logically.

Geoffrey felt his hairs prickle with the beginnings of

another shape-shift, and resisted it. He leaned forward to see around Marina's head, and his flute poked him in the side as the man raised his sword above his head with both hands. He closed his fingers around it and felt a tingling in them. Perhaps his beloved would like some music while she fought. The thought was both ludicrous and urgent, and he could almost feel the presence of the young god, showing him another path, a different solution than senseless killing. Helene, too, seemed to hesitate, and he saw her hand go from hilt to hilt of the two swords she carried.

The nomad charged, bellowing, and Helene stepped gracefully into his path and ducked, catching him in the midsection with her shoulders as the descending arc of his sword cut the sullen air. He gave a surprised grunt as she used her body in some fashion to tumble him heels over head onto the ground. Her ordinary sword came out of its scabbard in a single, smooth motion as she straightened up, and the flat of the blade smacked the robes around his thighs.

The man somersaulted and came up as Helene smashed the pommel of her sword into his lower face. There was a dull sound and blood darkened the veil as the man staggered back a step. He shook his head as if to clear it as Helene aimed a booted foot and gave a solid kick against the left leg. The voluminous robes deflected some of the force of the kick, but she connected with a hidden knee and he gave a howl of pain. Drops of bright blood flew from his mouth as he lost his footing, slipping to both knees. Helene danced out of reach, then darted in and struck his brow with her hilt. He slumped to earth, half-stunned.

The nomads gave a bloodcurdling cry and urged their horses forward to run the girl down. Geoffrey raised the flute to dry lips and blew a single note that screamed along the nerves. A horrid, twisted melody rose out of his breast and flowed down the column of his instrument as all the horses panicked. Beneath him, Marina whimpered and shook with terror, and he pressed his knees against her heaving sides to try to reassure her, wishing he had an extra set of hands for the reins.

The steeds of the nomads went wild, and their riders clamped brown hands against their ears and bellowed with pain. Only their years astride kept them mounted, and two were unhorsed almost immediately despite this. Another turned and lunged away from the hideous cacophony, nearly breaking a leg in the effort. The rest were too busy trying to shield their ears and control their animals to pay further attention to Helene. She stood over her fallen victim with a slight smile on her pale face, as if she almost enjoyed the music Geoffrey was creating.

The riderless horses plunged away, and the men pursued them, screaming and cursing. Those still ahorse decided that this sort of combat was not to their liking and followed. After a few moments, Geoffrey ceased his playing. Marina turned and nipped at a toe to display her displeasure, and Achilles pawed the dry ground and snorted his.

The man Helene had bested groaned, sat up, tore away his veil, and spat out teeth and blood. He wiped his face against his sleeve and demanded something of her. Her reply made him flinch, but he showed no further desire to fight.

"What did he ask?" Geoffrey queried, determined to disguise the terror he had felt and the conflict still raging within him.

"He asked me why I did not kill him."

"And you answered . . . ?"

"That I would not dirty my blade with a poor creature such as he." She gave Geoffrey a cold, green look that brooked no argument.

"It would have been kinder to have slain him."

"I know. But he tried to touch what was not his. And now he must pay the penalty."

"You are not kind, *ma donna*."

"No," she whispered. "I am not kind; only just."

XXIII

The bazaar in Aleppo was a monstrous assault to the senses after two weeks of the quiet of the wild. Geoffrey was trying to decide if the smell or the noise was the worse affront when he noticed a man gesturing vigorously, apparently trying to convince a circle of doubtful listeners of whatever he was saying. Geoffrey looked, blinked, and looked again. The man was like a pillar of fire, and his incredible light seemed to pierce the sullen greyness which was now an oppressive but everyday occurrence.

A moment later Geoffrey also registered that the man was physically a veritable Adonis, which seemed both appropriate and unfair. Whatever he was urging, his audience remained restlessly indifferent, and he stepped off his stone perch with a hasty gesture of dismissal and strode towards Geoffrey and Helene. Geoffrey looked at his companion and found she was staring at the man with a kind of awestruck admiration that made him want to grind his teeth.

The man, however, ignored Helene, and marched up to Geoffrey and Marina, and began speaking urgently and incomprehensibly. Expressive hands moved dynamically, and a sensuous mouth curled around fluid sounds that were delightful even if he could not understand them. He was tall and well proportioned with strong Levantine features, huge doe-like eyes rimmed with ebony lashes, wavy black hair, a pronounced nose, and a square black beard. He asked a question, by the sound of his voice and the lift of heavy brows, and Geoffrey felt like an idiot. Helene answered in the same tongue, and the man ignored her. The man repeated his question as if she had not spoken.

Since Helene looked ready to explode, Geoffrey quickly asked, "Do you speak Greek?"

The man stiffened for a moment. "I do not like to foul my mouth with the tongue of sodomites."

Geoffrey took a violent dislike to the fellow, despite his obvious attractiveness. "And I do not like to waste my time on rude fools," he snapped.

The man eyes blazed. "Surely you are the one I have awaited, who was promised to come in my dreams. Surely you have brought me the sword against Darkness. I must have it, to free Holy Salem from the hands of the despoilers. I must have it to raise my army!"

"No, I have not. And did I possess what you speak of, I would not bestow it upon a prideful, discourteous man who accosted me in the marketplace."

"Prideful! I am the humblest of the servants of the Almighty. Do not test me, *angelos*."

Geoffrey almost grinned at being called an angel, though he knew the man meant messenger, not heavenly being, but restrained himself. The man resembled all too closely the fanatical monks who occasionally made appearances on the streets of Milan, spouting hatred and sedition until they were dragged off to rot in the Duke's dungeon. They were humorless and righteous and convinced of their missions.

"I do not test you, stranger. I have no sword to give. That of which you speak belongs to my companion, and it is hers to give, not mine." Helene, he realized with a sinking heart, was still free to bestow herself however she chose, and from the way she had looked at the man, he could have her however he wished. It occurred to him again that he had come on this adventure upon the false promise that he could prevent his mother's death, and that, perhaps, the beautiful dream children which had given him hope and courage were another jest of the gods. If only he were handsome and dynamic.

"I do not speak to *bints*." The man spat the incomprehensible last word out like a mouthful of pips.

"What did he call you?"

"A cunt," Helene replied brutally, looking as if she had

been struck. She gave Geoffrey a small, forlorn glance, then a shrug. "If this is the man who will sanctify the sword, I would as soon cast it into the sea. The gods must be moon-mad."

"I am the Chosen One! I will save the temple!"

Geoffrey reined Marina to one side. "You are a raving lunatic. Come, let us find some place to stay."

The handsome features of the man twisted, and he made a leap for Helene. With an almost casual carelessness, she brought the hilt of her short knife down onto his brow, and rode away as he staggered back into the dust. Raucous laughter rose from the nearby booths, and several shouts of approval rang out. Despite his charisma, the man was obviously very unpopular.

Helene negotiated for the rent of chambers in the caravansary, and together they settled the horses in the quarters of the ground floor before climbing the stairs to an airy suite of rooms above. Brilliant tiles covered the floor and lacy grillwork covered the windows facing the bustling street. They put their meager belongings in the inner room, which featured running water in a glazed pool and had several mattresses rolled up in one corner.

"What do we do now?"

Helene's small face was cold and remote. "*I* am going to bathe."

Geoffrey removed himself into the outer chamber and stood before the window, looking sightlessly at the stream of people below in the narrow street. He could hear the splash of water behind him and was aware of the travel-grimed state of his own body. His clothing, despite the magicks Helene had worked on it, was nearly rotting off his body, and he wanted nothing more than to burn it. Everything was going wrong, and it was his fault. He looked at the people below and realized that many of them were as lightless as the wretched creatures they had encountered in the wild. They scurried along in the shadows of the buildings and darted across patches of light like insects. They were the sort of folk his father had slain in the cleansing of Paris, a business which had revolted Dylan then and which repelled Geoffrey now.

Despair rose in his throat. The strange man in the bazaar troubled him deeply, and he wondered if there would be another betrayal. The man bore no resemblance to young King Arthur or Louis of Franconia as they existed within the pages of Rowena's book. Still, he had not been there, and only knew of events second- or thirdhand. Arthur seemed headstrong, and Louis imbued with a profound belief in the Savior that Geoffrey was unable to share, but they both appeared as kindly men. The man in the bazaar had been heroic in appearance, but was lacking in some intangible that he could not put a finger to.

Persephone, what is going on? The thought came unbidden to his mind.

I thought you would never ask. There was an infinite sweetness to the voice he heard within, and he felt a lightening of his spirit. Geoffrey felt the love swell in his heart, in spite of everything, and accepted a complexity that was entirely against the logic of his mind. He experienced a return of the delight in her presence that he had had as a child, and had a sense of trust that startled him. How could he trust her? How could he not?

You are a jade, ma donna. Your mother should have beaten you when you were a babe, so you would have better manners.

I am very spoilt and have been much indulged, though none but you has had the wit to perceive it. I think that is what drew me to your cradle—those clear, blue eyes that would see through all my vanities and love me still.

And what is the love of one mortal to you?

Oh, Geoffrey. It was a sigh. *Everything. To have a place in your heart is everything. Even if I must share your affections with swift Hermes and your mettlesome Helene. Now, be patient and bide a day. Rest and refresh yourself, for the greatest peril is yet ahead. And pay no heed to false prophets.*

She was gone, and Geoffrey silently cursed the cryptic utterances of all deities and relieved his feelings by glaring out the window. He turned at a sound behind him, and Helene drew back sharply at his expression.

Geoffrey drew a ragged breath and stared. Helene had

put on a garment that did nothing to conceal her slender body, and after two weeks of sleeping beside that body, with the sword laid between them like a wall, he was astonished at how desirable she was. She looked good enough to eat.

"I could not bear to wear those other clothes again," she said hesitantly.

"I understand. I would burn these if I had any others."

"My wits are failing. We can have new garments made. I will run downstairs and . . ."

"Not dressed like that, you will not!"

"No." She plucked at the gossamer fabric. "I grabbed this as I escaped the tower. Very impractical."

"But lovely," he answered.

"Is it?"

"You are, Helene. Very lovely. And if I catch you looking at any man the way you did that lunatic in the market, I will cut his heart out and use his stripes to beat you."

"You do not own me!"

"No, I don't. You are quite free to do anything you wish. But I simply will not watch."

She came up and put her head on his chest, slipping an arm around his narrow waist. "I know. And I will not provoke you. It was only that he was so handsome. You are the only person I have ever trusted, and you have been very patient with me."

"Please, do not make me regret I treated you like a lady instead of a whore."

Helene lifted a hand and covered his mouth with the palm. "Go bathe, and I will send for some food. Yes, I will decently conceal myself from lusting eyes—though yours almost started out of your head when you saw me."

"Minx."

Geoffrey removed his filthy garments and eased into the heated pool, delighting in the play of water. He leaned back and thought of nothing. Then he thought of the days and nights in the desert, while Helene had shown him the paths of magic as she knew them from her father's library. If he was indeed a mage, he was a different sort than those

of Byzantium. Some simple things, ripening fruit or freshening bread, he could do quite easily, and in the past few
days he had learned to make a ball of fire appear in his
hands. But, for the most part, his magic was in the air of
his breath, and in the songs he made with the flute.

Geoffrey heard voices from the outer chamber which he
did not bother about, and generally relaxed. When he
opened his eyes, the first thing he saw was a small statue
sitting on the back edge of the pool. It was a woman,
carrying a quiver and bow and accompanied by a small
wolf, an exquisite bit of the sculptor's art. It was also, he
was quite certain, Helene's goddess, and he felt mildly
embarrassed at being naked in front of it. Foolish, of
course, but he mentally apologized for any offense, real or
imagined.

Helene bustled in with her arms full of cloth. "Here.
We have a guest. Wear these." She seemed flustered.
"And hurry. He brought dinner."

Confused, Geoffrey climbed out of the pool, dried himself on a fine linen towel, and sorted out the tangle of
garments she had brought. There was a long robe, not
unlike a monk's habit though much finer, and a sheer,
shorter gown to go beneath it. They fit his many inches
easily, and he bound a long sash around his waist a little
clumsily. Over this he put a glorious coat of blue brocade
over-embroidered in silver, and felt quite grand until he
noticed his bare feet. With a shrug, he padded into the
outer chamber, feeling as cheerful as he had in months.

The mood vanished when he saw that the visitor was
none other than the lunatic who had accosted them in the
bazaar. What the devil was Helene thinking of, letting the
fellow into their rooms? And why was she looking side-
ways at him under her long lashes? Had she always had
long lashes? Geoffrey felt an irrational fear, and a smol-
dering rage beneath it that disturbed him deeply. If only
the man were not so handsome and so confident. Despite
an absence of physical similarity, he was reminded of
Dylan.

Several braziers were burning within the room, and
delectable smells arose in a perfectly distracting and mad-

dening way as Geoffrey mentally tried to sort out his tangled feelings from a social situation he found incomprehensible. The tall man seemed entirely at ease in a room with a scantily clad female, several servants, and an unknown male. No, Helene was not barely covered. She had done something to her sheer gown that made it entirely opaque. It had, regrettably, not diminished her desirability a bit.

The man gave a deep bow above a hand upon his broad sash, and Geoffrey returned the gesture awkwardly. When the man stood upright, he realized that it was not the lunatic from the market, but another so like him they must certainly be twins. This one was, if anything, even handsomer, and it seemed almost indecent that two such splendid specimens should walk the earth at the same time.

"I bid you welcome. I am Michael ben Avi. I pray you will accept my poor gifts of food and clothing." He spoke Greek with less difficulty than the other, and his voice was more pleasing.

"I thank you." Geoffrey could not imagine calling the robe he wore a poor gift, nor understand why the man had brought food. He wished it did not smell so good. "I am Geoffrey d'Avebury."

They stood awkwardly for a second, and then the man gestured him to sit on some bolsters that were arranged around the braziers. It was as if Michael were the host and Geoffrey the guest, and he felt quietly resentful. Helene remained standing outside the circle of cushions, and Geoffrey looked at her, puzzled.

A servant offered Geoffrey a brass tray with a small metal salt cellar and a piece of bread on it. "If you will partake of these, you will truly be my guest, and under my protection," Michael told him, and Helene gave him a nod.

Suddenly Geoffrey was infuriated. He felt ignorant and stupid and pushed around in what he regarded as his own house. Who was Michael ben Avi to come into his home in this high-handed manner and play host? And why was Helene looking at Michael so worshipfully? He wished he had never left home.

"Why should I wish to be under your protection?"

"It is the custom."

"Then I must refuse. I have no wish to be your guest, nor under your protection. I did not ask you to come here with gifts, and I do not want them." Despite his growling stomach and his watering mouth, Geoffrey started to get up and go into the inner chamber to remove his finery.

"Geoffrey, please, just do it," Helene asked.

"You want his protection. *You* eat his bread and salt."

"I cannot!"

"Why?"

"Men and women do not eat together."

"Why not?"

"It is the custom," Michael repeated.

"It is not my custom to place myself under the protection of strangers, nor to let my companion go hungry while I eat."

"She will be allowed to eat when we are finished," Michael replied indifferently.

"You are even more arrogant than your brother, and the Devil take the lot of you."

Still completely at ease, Michael said, "Poor Jacob. He is very troublesome. Still, God wills it so. I am, believe me, the humblest of men, a servant of the Almighty. It is true that Jacob is very proud, but I left my pride along the way when we retreated from Holy Salem. Oh, do sit down and cease being stubborn. I am ravenous."

"You can starve to death for all I care. I've a bellyful of you already and could not stomach more."

Michael leaned forward intensely. "This is much too important a matter for petty disagreements. Now, sit down and eat the bread and salt."

There was such compulsion in his words that Geoffrey found himself beginning to comply. His knees bent a little. Michael relaxed, or began to. Geoffrey felt his beast-self rage as it had not done since their first encounter with the Shadowlings. He wanted to kill everything in the room, but especially the smug, handsome man who sat so assuredly across from him.

His breath caught in his chest for a moment, and his

thoughts boiled. Then he forced the beast back down, because he would not kill senselessly and needlessly, and sought some alternative.

Hermes, be my guide.

Change is always possible.

The echo of the words he had first heard in Venice brought back a spate of treasured memories, of the time before betrayal, before death. It had seemed so simple then. He wished it could be simple again.

Geoffrey passed his hand across the still proffered tray, and the bread and salt vanished. Instead, a very large animal dropping sat fresh and steaming on the tray.

"Geoffrey!" Helene cried.

"I do not eat dung. Do you?"

The servant stared wide-eyed at the steaming pat, then dropped the tray and shrank back. Michael ben Avi looked at it and seemed to pale a little, his aura of complete assurance fading. Helene, much to her own disgust, was giggling. As usual, she did not grasp the importance of the moment. She could tell this from the look of disapproval Michael turned upon her. It reminded her of her father. Geoffrey, on the other hand, in his outrage looked like a constipated eagle. Still, he did not glare at her giggling. Instead, he gave her a look of such intensity it made her knees tremble, and began to laugh himself. Whoops of unseemly merriment roiled up out of his belly, shook his chest, and brought tears to his eyes. It was the first time he had really laughed in a long time, and it hurt.

Scandalized, Michael ben Avi said, "Are you mad?"

"Oh, probably," Geoffrey answered indifferently. He couldn't quite recall what he had been angry about. Oh, yes, this fellow barging in and presuming to order him about. Just like Dylan. So certain of himself and so careless of other people. He studied the other man impartially for a moment, looked at the blazing aura of light that surrounded him, and remembered his father's first encounter with Louis of Franconia. The book had described a similar aura, and he supposed it had something to do with a profound belief in the single god and his own mission. How odd, he thought, that our family serves the Lady in

her many guises, and ends up dealing with these sanctified, single-minded saintly men. What a mystery.

It was about the sword. It had to be changed, made
sacred, Persephone had told him. The sword had to pass
through his hands—but why? Geoffrey felt as if he was
stretched into infinity, to the beginning of all things, and
realized he was a bridge between the archaic and the
present, that he was a connection between the ancient earth
serpent whose skin was the sheath of the sword and who
was his ancestor, and the new era. For Michael the sword
was a power to slash through the veil of Darkness that
threatened to destroy a world he cared for, and for Geoffrey it was merely an artifact. And it was not his to give,
for he had not claimed it through the body as his father and
grandfather had. He had slept with Helene but never lain
with her, and if he read Rowena's book aright, that was
the pattern. Which meant that Helene could bestow both
the sword and herself however she chose. No wonder I
could not eat his bread and salt. Why would she want me
when she could have a fine, heroic fellow like that?

Geoffrey wished he could shut his mind off, that years
of study and the practice of logical thought would cease
grinding out conclusions he could not bear. The smell of
dung and food mingled in the room, and he felt ravenous
and nauseated at the same time. He wanted Helene, and
those dream children. When they talked, he never had to
explain anything twice. Never in his wildest imaginings
had he conceived of any person, male or female, who
would grasp his meaning so quickly and completely. And
now he was going to lose her because of his own scruples,
because the very idea of unwilling carnality repelled him.

"Geoffrey?" She was beside him, curling a small hand
into his larger one, looking like a waif with her wonderful
green eyes.

"What?"

"Keep me safe."

"Always," he whispered, and hugged her shoulders,
and wondered if she could hear the pounding of his heart.

Michael ben Avi cleared his throat. "I have been discourteous in my eagerness."

Realizing this was as much apology as he would ever get from the man, Geoffrey nodded. "Indeed."

"Can we begin anew?"

Despite his fear, Geoffrey nodded again. "We shall try."

Geoffrey and Helene lay side by side, the sheathed sword between their bodies as it had been for many weeks. By the rise and fall of her breath, Geoffrey did not think she slept.

Impulsively, he reached out and took her hand and felt her fingers curl against his palm. "What do you think of him?"

Helene did not answer for what seemed a long time, and he watched the brightness of her aura against the darkness. "He reminds me of my father," she finally said.

Geoffrey laughed, and she sat up and glared down at him.

"What's so funny!"

"He reminds me of my father too."

Helene's fierce scowl vanished in an immediate giggle. "Why?"

"Michael is so certain of himself, just like Dylan always was, and it makes me feel like an idiot." Geoffrey did not add his private opinion that Michael ben Avi was an arrogant bully, and perhaps just as mad as his raving twin brother Jacob.

"Yes. He thinks his god is on his side."

"If he knew as much of the gods as we do, he would not be so complacent. But do you like him?"

"I think so. Umm. I watched him while the two of you were talking, and he kept sneaking looks at me that I did not like, though. As if . . . I was some prize."

"You are a prize, dear Hippolyta."

Helene's fingers were cool as they caressed his cheek, coiling into the silky beard and touching the skin. "I do not wish to be. It makes me feel as if I was in danger. I have no wish to be coveted."

"What do you wish?"

In the silence that followed his question they could hear

the cry of the first merchants in the bazaar. Morning was not far distant. "Geoffrey, I do not know. Once I wanted Hiram to love me, but he is dead. Once I wanted power, I think, and now I have it, and it seems an empty thing. I can do such magicks as I never dreamt of, and they are nothing. If I make water come from a rock, it is because it is needful, not to show myself. I am confused—and I do not like it!"

"Ouch! You need not yank out my beard in your bewilderment, plaguey dwarf."

"Oh, forgive me." She put a brief kiss on his cheek, a sister's kiss to a brother. Then she folded her knees tailorfashion and set her elbows on them, resting her heartshaped face against her palms, clearly prepared for a lengthy bout of introspection. Geoffrey sat up and faced her, a little uneasy at where his thoughtless query might lead.

"Must I want something?" she demanded.

"No, of course not. But people usually do."

"Well, what do you want, Geoffrey?"

"My ambition or my heart's desire?"

"Both," she answered promptly.

"I want to be brave."

"Geoffrey, you are."

"No, I want to feel brave, and to be more trusting."

"Is that your heart's longing?"

"No, those are my ambitions. My most earnest desire is to be a father." There. He had said it.

Helene frowned for a long time. "A good father?"

Geoffrey gave a nervous laugh. "I would like to be the best father in the world."

She looked at him and large tears rolled down her cheeks. "I think that is the strangest and most beautiful thing you have ever said. I wish you could have been my father."

Not the way I feel about you, you do not, Geoffrey thought as he cleared his throat. "And what is your ambition, then?"

Helene brushed her wet cheeks and chewed her lips. "I think I would know who I am, beyond a plaything of the fates. Do you think Michael knows who he is?'' She put her chin back in her hands.

Geoffrey suppressed a sigh and a spurt of jealousy. Michael ben Avi was handsome, charismatic, and ten or more years his elder. How could he ever compete with that? ''I am sure he believes he does,'' he replied carefully.

''Yes. That is probably the flaw.''

''Flaw?''

''I would like to shake him out of his smugness,'' she answered as if he had not spoken

''I think having his food turned to dung is enough shaking for the time being, imp.''

''Oh, Geoffrey. You were wonderful! I nearly died trying not to laugh and then I nearly died laughing. What do you think is his ambition?''

Geoffrey considered this for a moment. ''To hold this in his hands,'' he answered, pushing the hilt with a careful finger. ''And to save his city from the hands of Darkness.''

Helene reached out and grasped the hilt in one hand and the sheath in the other, and slipped a handspan of colored metal from the covering. The light of it reflected along her small breast and firm chin. It made her green eyes glow in the dimness, and she looked like a small demon. ''I would give it to him, but I do not think he is quite worthy of it.'' Geoffrey felt his heart swell with quiet gladness, and was ashamed of so ignoble an emotion. ''I wish he was, though,'' she added a little sadly.

XXIV

A stall in the marketplace had been set aside for the meeting of Michael ben Avi's subordinates, and to this meeting Geoffrey had been invited, though he could not imagine why. After a breakfast of honey-sweetened *laban* and fruit, he and Helene had entered the bazaar in search of the meeting place. She paused at a cloth merchant's stall to haggle over some new garments while Geoffrey waited, still not completely awake. They had managed, during their travels, to learn to accommodate to one another's matutinal habits, so that Helene tried not to chatter ceaselessly and Geoffrey tried to take some interest in what she did say, but he still found his mind was sluggish for the first few hours.

While he waited, Geoffrey stood near several camels and marvelled at the hideousness of their features. They reminded him of an unbeloved monk he had studied with in Milan. It seemed a lifetime ago, and he was shocked to realize that only a month had passed since he had left Italia. Abstractedly, he reached out to stroke a camel's scrawny neck and nearly lost a finger to square, yellow teeth. He glared nearsightedly at the beast, and it returned the look for a moment, then changed its surly expression. One second it was sneering at him, and the next a long, flexible neck was bending before him and heavily lashed eyes were staring up rather adoringly. He reached out and stroked the forehead that bowed before him.

The camel driver gabbled at him incomprehensibly, pointing and gesturing, which to Geoffrey in his early day stupor was an insufferable affront, but he continued to fondle the camel's eye ridges, scratching it behind the ears and causing it to bellow with ecstasy. Several other camels rose awkwardly and came over to see what was happening, until he was surrounded by ugly heads butting his chest and back, honking and stomping, the sour smell of their breaths enveloping him. His beast-self heard them and understood them, though he could not grasp why the camel drover was so upset. He was not, as Dylan had been, a Lord of the Beasts, but he had enough of the same capacity to cause animals to fawn on him.

"Geoffrey, what are you doing?" Helene's voice broke through the hubbub. "The man thinks you are trying to steal his camels, and he cannot understand why you have not waited for nightfall like a decent thief. It goes against all custom."

He felt his face redden with embarrassment, and he mentally ordered the camels to settle down. Instead a long, raspy tongue licked the back of his neck. A head banged into his back, demanding attention. He started to turn and the flute he had thrust into his belt jabbed him. Geoffrey pulled it out and played a long, low note while he reached in his mind for a tune which hung tantalizingly just a breath away. It came, tentatively at first, then easily, and in a minute all the beasts began to settle down in a circle around him, swaying their ugly heads back and forth.

Geoffrey stepped between two beasts and tucked the flute away. Helene's green eyes seemed to dance with merriment, and he could tell she was trying hard not to laugh at him. What a clown I must seem to her, he thought, his dignity disordered. I am a clown of the gods, a fool and a buffoon.

They crossed the market in silence, and Geoffrey was aware of curious stares and glances from merchants and townsfolk. It made him uncomfortable. Then Helene looked up at him with open trust and affection, and nothing else mattered.

The stall was hung with bright carpets and there were sturdy bolsters set on the floor. Half a dozen men in the garb of nomads lolled on them, speaking and gesturing. Geoffrey was certain he and Helene were a topic of conversation and wished he spoke either Hebrew or Arabic. Helene understood what they were saying, and he hoped she would translate.

Michael and his brother Jacob came in with several other men in the more ornate clothing of town dwellers. Side by side, it was difficult to tell the twins apart except by the discontented expression on Jacob's face. He flashed a finger in their direction and snapped a question.

"He wonders what I am doing here," Helene muttered, standing close to Geoffrey. "The others, the ones seated, are worried. There are rumors that Michael has gotten a mage from Byzantium to help him. That's you, but they cannot comprehend my part. If only I were a man!"

"Nonsense! You are more a man than any of these, despite your woman's body, my Hippolyta."

Michael started to speak before she could continue, and the nomads rose and bowed to him, and then to Geoffrey as introductions were made. They struggled to twist their tongues around his name, while he attempted to remember who was Abner and who was Solomon. Finally they seated themselves, and Michael began to speak while Jacob clasped and unclasped his hands restlessly. Helene knelt behind Geoffrey, outside the circle of cushions, and gave a whispered translation.

At first, the men discussed supplies—camels and horses and swords and food—then numbers of men able to fight. Geoffrey, bored, studied the faces of the men, and then their auras, seeking clues to character. One of the nomads, a quiet, serious fellow, had almost no body light and kept his eyes down. Recalling how King Louis had used his father to sort those afflicted with the Shadow from those not, in Paris long before he was born, he wondered if this was such a man.

A melody came to him as he waited, a dreadful, discordant tune it was almost painful to think of. It was, he thought, something Great Pan might have piped to drive men to madness. He glanced out into the bazaar and saw a knot of lightless men gathering beside the well in the center.

The serious nomad, Tabber by name, looked up and gave a little nod to another man standing outside the booth. The second man gave a shout, and the crowd of lightless men surged forward, whipping out curved swords or short knives, screaming some strange battle cry. They reached the stall almost before anyone could get to their feet.

Geoffrey was up before most of the rest because he had a moment's warning, and Helene vaulted over the cushions and rolled to her feet with the many-hued sword of light in her small, capable hands. Michael ben Avi stood and wheeled around to stand beside her as the first wave of attackers reached the cramped entry space.

Tabber pulled his knife and stabbed the man on his right in the throat, then caught the man on his left with the backswing. Then he lunged for the broad back of Jacob ben Avi who was standing on the other side of Helene, so she was buttressed by the twins. Geoffrey, caught by the confines of the place and his own clumsiness with weapons, kicked out a booted foot and caught Tabber on one leg. The many layers of his garments deflected some of the force, but Tabber stumbled and his blow missed Jacob.

Geoffrey could see Helene dart forward out of the corner of his eye, but he was too busy trying to avoid getting killed by friend and foe to do more than keep on his feet. He ducked under a blow from Tabber's knife and butted the man in the stomach, crashing his backside into another nomad who was trying to escape the madness within the stall. As he came up, Geoffrey smashed a knee into Tabber's groin and had the satisfaction of hearing him scream.

Geoffrey felt his beast-self rise, and at the same time he heard the dreadful melody he had composed. His body yearned to change, to become the griffin, to rend and tear, but his mind, recalling the terrible lust he had felt, was revolted. For a second he was frozen by the two opposing demands. Then he sprang over the bolsters to the back corner of the stall, and pulled out his flute. He jerked back as a knife came through the canvas, and sent a piercing note down the column of the instrument.

Helene was a swirl of light beyond the entrance to the

stall, with the brothers swinging their swords into the screaming mob as she cut off heads and hands. Geoffrey almost lost his breath at the sight, but forced his mind to the terrible song that hovered on his lips and fingers. It came, full-blown and without hesitation, and it was even worse than it had been in his mind.

The bazaar went mad. Men and animals screamed. Camels thundered into the crowd, trampling over people, and merchants ran out of their booths, holding their ears. The stall collapsed as two groups of men tried to exit the cacophony in two opposing directions, the cloth roof splitting with a loud ripping sound. The wall crashed outwards, falling onto the brazier of the copper merchant next door, and caught fire.

The lightless ones were trying to run away, but so was everyone else except Helene and the brothers ben Avi, who seemed unaffected by the din. It was a slaughter, and seeing the fire begin to spread, Geoffrey ended his playing and grabbed a beautiful carpet to beat it out with. He stepped over a fallen body and felt ill as he swung the carpet down onto the flames.

All he knew for a time was the rise and fall of his arms as he smothered the crawling flames. It seemed the most important thing in the world to slay the fire, to still the unsated beast who raged for blood inside him, and to stay the melody that still rilled along the bones of his body. It was his mother's song, and he had done something terrible to it. Then Helene touched his arm, and he saw her wan, dirty face, and felt her fingers brush away the hair across his brow.

The bazaar was restored to some sort of order. The bodies of the dead had been removed and the stalls were being cleaned up. Geoffrey found himself something of a hero for putting out the fire, which pleased him while it also made him redden with embarrassment. Michael ben Avi and his brother, on the other hand, were clearly seen as troublemakers, from the sidelong glances and evil looks they received from the people in the marketplace. Helene they ignored, which Geoffrey found peculiar. He could not adjust to her near invisibility—the way people looked past her or spoke to the air above her head, as if she did not quite exist. He wanted to shout at them. She seemed indifferent to it, so he kept his thoughts to himself.

Michael approached him, brow wrinkled in thought. "You must *never* use that pipe again. It is not seemly. We cannot use such things to overcome the evil that confronts us."

Geoffrey was so startled by this pronouncement he was mute for a moment. Helene was not.

"You idiot! Of course he must use it. It turned the tide for us."

Michael did not reply to her, but said to Geoffrey, "Women should be silent. You will not use your pipe again, and that is that."

Geoffrey had had no intention of ever playing the horrid tune again, but he was furious at being ordered around like a boy. "I will do as I choose, when I choose," he answered carefully.

"No! I am the leader, and the Redeemer, and you will do as I command."

At this point Jacob ben Avi joined in. "You are a fool, and an ass, Michael. I am the one. I should have been first-born. Now, lad, I want no pagan pipes in my army. I am certain you can understand that this is a holy war, and we must conduct ourselves rightly so that the Lord will smile upon us and uphold us, as is promised, that I may deliver Jerusalem and restore the kingdom."

"I do not serve you, your brother, or your Lord." He was appalled at the idea that either of these arrogant men should possess the sword or Helene, and he could not believe that the Lady whom he served, however reluctantly, could have made such an enormous error. How could either of these men sanctify so much as a clod of dirt?

"Who do you serve, if not our Lord?" Jacob demanded.

Persephone, you've got me in an awful mess. Hermes, help me please. Inspire me. "I serve the Light." The words came easily, calmly, and with more dignity than he had ever felt before. He felt as if the two deities he had called upon stood behind him, like parents, and with more presence than Dylan and Aenor ever had. It was all he could do not to peek over his shoulder.

This reply seemed to satisfy the brothers, for they nodded and Michael smiled and rubbed his hands together. "I think it would be best if the girl gave the sword into my keeping. We cannot have females running about waving edged weapons or fighting the enemy. It is not meet or right."

"No, no. It should be given to me!" Jacob shouted.

"I would sooner cast it into the sea than let either of you touch it!" Helene said.

"It is mine!"

"No, mine!"

"I almost wish I had left it around my father's neck," Helene said sadly as the brothers continued to scream at each other. Geoffrey put an arm around her shoulder as Michael brought a large fist down on Jacob's brow. Jacob staggered and slipped to his knees, and Michael smashed both fists down onto his brother's skull.

Geoffrey was outraged. He released his hold on Helene and jumped forward, grasping Michael by the throat with both hands. His own strength was no match for the man, but the beast in him swelled and gave him power he had never imagined. Ben Avi clawed at his arms, but could not break the grip. The large, dark eyes widened in horror as he gasped for air like a fish.

There was a moment when he was ready to snap the neck within his hands, when his beast-self howled for blood and death. Geoffrey struggled with it while he choked Michael for another few seconds. Then he flung the man down on the still bloody dirt of the marketplace.

"The Lord ought to be ashamed of both of you! You are no better than a pair of swine rooting in the garbage. You are unworthy to bear my Lady's sword, or kiss the hem of her gown. You will never overcome the Shadow while fighting between yourselves or ordering me about."

As he stepped back, Geoffrey found himself the awed focus of townsfolk and nomads alike, and realized the mage fire played along his hands, arms, and chest. He could not imagine what had gotten into him, and he was not at all sure he liked this new person he seemed to be becoming. I did not want to change, he thought. I was content with scholarship. Why could the gods not have left me alone to live quietly?

Then he looked at Helene, and she was smiling at him, as if he had done something worthy. His heart pounded a little, and he decided it was not so bad after all. Change was always possible, but not necessarily comfortable.

Michael stood up shakily, and Jacob climbed to his feet and brushed the dirt off his robes. They both looked at Geoffrey calculatingly, as if deciding to rush him together. Geoffrey returned their looks with a nonchalance he was far from feeling. It was, he decided, time to do a little showing off. With a casual gesture he brought a ball of fire into one hand, a trick he had been at some pains to learn while he and Helene had crossed the desert, and tossed it into the air over the brothers' heads. They both ducked as it arched over the well and plunged into the water with a loud hiss and a cloud of steam.

The silence that followed seemed to stretch forever. Then Michael said, "If you will not give the sword to me, its rightful, God-appointed wielder, then I command you to wield it yourself. I will not have it said I let any female aid me. Women are a curse, evil and disobedient by nature."

"No." It was not as simple as he wished it could be, but he had chosen his path, and he was not going to be tempted to abandon it. He could have Helene or he could use the sword, and he wanted the woman. This was something that Michael would never understand. "You will have to accept our help on our terms, or forego it altogether."

"Surely you will compromise, lad."

"Not when compromise means doing everything your way."

The crowd began to laugh, and those who did not speak Greek got told the joke by others, so that fresh nests of guffaws formed across it. Michael glared at them, then raised his hand to one eye as if it hurt him. His skin paled and a light sweat sheened it. He looked as if he was remembering something very unpleasant.

"I suppose I must accept your terms," he muttered.

Geoffrey raised his eyebrows, and knew that Michael ben Avi was lying. He would stop at nothing to possess the sword, even to trying to charm them as he had the night before. For a moment he wondered if it might be simpler just to convince Helene to give it away, and then he realized that he would never do it. He had vowed to keep her safe, and that included letting her reach her own decisions. Relieved to be clear with himself, he smiled at her.

XXV

Geoffrey sat upon Marina and sweated. The air was still, deathly still, and hot, but after weeks of following in Michael ben Avi's track, he was past sweating from heat or exhaustion. No, it was just fear, and he let it sit in his belly and on his shoulders, because it no longer mattered if he was afraid. To have been unafraid in the face of what lay before them would have been madness. Instead, he wondered what day it was, tried reckoning, and concluded it was coming towards the end of September, somewhere about the twentieth. His sister Orphiana had a birthday on that day or the next, and he wished her well, and thought of his home as he remembered it from other harvests, all golden, with trestle tables in the courtyard stacked with bread and platters of fruit and cheese, flagons of wine, the sound of heavy booted feet dancing to viol and flute, screams of laughter, and tired children crying. It was very peaceful and seemed more than a world away from the barren plain under a twilight sky where they waited to do battle.

Astride Achilles, Helene studied the foe, and then glanced at Geoffrey. He was thin, and his face had aged. As always before battle, he was pale and tense. Then he relaxed suddenly, as if he thought of something pleasant, and he was transformed. He had such sweetness in him, and such strength. He did not know it, and perhaps he never would. She had come to understand it slowly, over the days and weeks since the marketplace in Aleppo.

At first, when he had protected her from Michael's ambitions, she had felt like a prize in some strange contest, and she had been uneasy and mistrustful, waiting for

Geoffrey to assert his maleness, to roll over the sword which lay between them in the night, and make her his own. She knew that sometimes he had to struggle to overcome that desire. But finally she had realized that he would fight to the end to preserve her liberty, even against himself. He treated her with respect, and her maidenhead remained intact. No longer did she yearn for her father's affection, for she had discovered something better, safer, and more powerful. There were even a few times when she had toyed with the idea of tempting him, seducing him, but she had repressed the urge. She knew her heart, but she still wished to keep her power over herself, of being separate, for a little longer. And it seemed to her that her little goddess smiled on her decision.

Helene looked right, at Michael ben Avi, and wondered how she could ever have thought him desirable. True, he was more comely than Geoffrey, even more handsome than the blonde barracks Adonis called Demetri, back in Byzantium. He was a wonderful leader, and she admired that when she watched him charm, cajole, or bully people into arming themselves against the flood of Shadow that kept rolling up from Araby. He was an honorable man by his lights, but he would have caught her and raped her and seized the Rainbow Sword if he had seen an opportunity. His brother Jacob was even more so, and she'd had nothing but a sense of relief when he had died in battle some weeks before. It had been short-lived, for Michael's demands for possession of the sword had become even more constant. He had taken Jacob's death as a sign of God's favor, and that had effectively destroyed any affection she might have nurtured for him. She was devoted to Geoffrey, but she could not find the words to tell him yet. She looked from Michael's aura of fire to Geoffrey's fountain of rainbows, and knew she had chosen well.

A sound like a great drum rolled up from the squirming mass of blackness across the lifeless earth, and a terror clutched in her breast. Geoffrey snapped out of his pleasant dream and stiffened, and she could see the color drain from his cheeks. He was always so afraid, and yet, never once in all the skirmishes and battles they had fought, from the shattered quays of Tripoli to the battered sun towers of Heliopolis, had he faltered or hesitated or turned to run as had many of Michael's ragtag army. Sometimes the memory of the cold helplessness that had held her once would immobilize her for minutes, so she could not grasp the sword, and then she would see him casting fireballs or simply hacking clumsily with his sword, and she would be free. Afterwards he would be silent for hours, and she would hear the sounds of his weeping in her sleep. She never asked him why he cried. Michael never hesitated either, but he believed his god would shield him. Several sword wounds and an arrow in his shoulder had not convinced him otherwise.

A wave of darkness began to roll towards them, and Geoffrey felt how dry his mouth was. He looked right, to Michael almost glowing with assurance, and Helene completely at ease upon Achilles' strong back, and wished for her martial skills and Michael's confidence. His bowels were turning to water at the hissing, howling jabber of the Shadowlings beneath the drum's enormous throb. It always made him feel sick, that noise, and the carnage that followed. He could not make himself forget that these screaming murderous creatures had once been as human as he was, and that, perhaps, deep within, they remained so. To most of Michael's followers, this was some sort of holy war against unutterable evil, but Geoffrey saw only the tragedy. This was not a glorious war, or even a war at all, but a slaughter of innocents gone mad with disease. It hit him most deeply when he saw the little forms of youngsters, boys and girls of five or ten, lightless and raving, their bodies starved to boniness, their eyes blank, and when his sword bit into their spare flesh, he felt a pain that seared him. In the night he would dream he slept in his mother's arms, and heard her song—or was it Persephone who rocked him? It did not comfort him or ease his pain. He was glad Helene did not seem to share his constant sense of fear, or the pain it caused him to slay. She and Michael seemed to enjoy it; but being courageous was their natural state. He found it admirable and completely mysterious. The hundreds of men around them who fought in Michael's cause were more comprehensible in their commonplace fears and their anguish when they found a friend or relative amongst the fallen Shadow folk. Michael and Helene suited one another so well too, were so akin in their swiftness and ferocity, that he could not imagine any other outcome but that eventually she would give herself and the weapon of power to the charismatic leader. Hermes must have tricked him with the vision of those darling babes. He was not even angry, for it was the nature of the young god to lie. He pictured the mischief-filled face of Mercutio di Maya and felt his heart warm and lighten in spite of his sense of betrayal. *When we give our hearts, we really give them.*

True. And shame the gods with your steadfastness. The voice of Hermes was lost in the throb of the drum and the rush of feet as the Darklings began their assault. Beside him, Helene drew her bow and began firing off arrows as soon as the first rank was in range. When they struck, mage fire raced across the bodies, so the first line of attackers was soon alight with writhing human torches here and there. Those behind just pushed forward, and soon the terrible confusion of two armies joined in battle was all around them. Geoffrey used a few fireballs, until the danger of slaying their own people was too great and he was forced back into conventional weapons. Michael was everywhere, shouting, fighting, and re-grouping his men.

Something fell from the leaden sky as Helene drew her rainbowed sword from its serpentine sheath. Geoffrey saw the dark movement at the corner of his eye as he fought some distance apart. It was like a bird, a huge misshapen avian, and he could feel its cold. Men screamed and fell beneath it.

Helene was silhouetted in colored light for a moment, the sword above her head, and then she gave a cry, and the light of her winked out like a snuffed wick. Geoffrey wheeled Marina around, cupped his hand as he had learned to do on the long road from Aleppo to this place near the Dead Sea, and sent a ball of mage fire flying towards the cold bird thing. It caught, and the whole scene was illu-

mined in eye-aching blue light as he saw Helene topple
from Achilles' back.

He reached her after what felt like hours, slipped off his
horse, and saw a second dark cold bird float forward with
infinite slowness. It was so close he could feel its wings
stir the air, and he drew Helene against his chest, slipping
an arm across her breasts and hauling her up. She was like
ice, a deadly cold that seemed to seep into his bones. Her
hands still clasped the hilt of the sword, and, desperate, he
closed his hands over hers, enfolding her chill form against
him, shouting something.

The dark thing settled to earth upon the bodies of a
dozen men and snaked a long, featherless neck forward.
Helene, so tiny and light, hung against him like a poppet,
and Geoffrey could feel the cold of her enter his loins and
begin to still his breath. For a moment he was frozen.
Then the rage of all his life rose, from groin to belly, from
belly to heart, from heart to throat, until it fountained in
his head, spilling soul fire from every opening in his body.

Geoffrey raised the sword as a surge of shame and
liberation flushed his body and his being. He did not see
the light that gouted from his mouth and eyes and ears,
terrifying both friend and foe, but he felt the heat of that
which issued from his manhood as he clumsily swung the
weapon. It was the unmistakable pleasure of lust. And he
knew that even if he had not penetrated her flesh, what he
was doing was a violation of Helene. He had broken his
vow to keep her safe.

He gasped for breath and slashed off the hideous head of
the bird thing. He fell to his knees.

It burst into cold fire, and his hands went slack. Helene's grasp opened, and the sword slipped from her icy
fingers as, weeping and cursing, Geoffrey dragged her
away. The sheath fell from her belt, and he did not notice
or care. Geoffrey's only thought was to get her as far away
from the battle as possible. Still breathing soul fire and
looking like a demon, he staggered to his feet and threw
her over one shoulder. He glimpsed the black shape of
Achilles, but the horse reared and trotted away.

Something made him turn. Michael ben Avi's unmistakable form stood outlined against the sky, and in his hands he held the many-hued sword. It flashed to the heavens, piercing the clouds and tearing them to pieces like rags.

"God is with us!" Michael's shout echoed across the plain, and the dark drum faltered. Light—ordinary, almost forgotten light—filled the sky, and, heartened, his followers regrouped for fresh slaughter.

Sickened, Geoffrey drew Helene across his chest, cradling her in her arms like the child she resembled. He kissed her brow. She was so still.

Persephone, if she dies, I swear I will tear the Styx from its bed and strangle you with it. His thoughts were a tangle, but this one was clear enough.

Marina appeared before him, prancing and snorting, as a bolt of lightning struck the earth, making it tremble. Geoffrey grabbed her reins and looked for cover, but there was not so much as a bush. The sky shimmered, and a figure began to form above the ragged clouds.

He felt his throat go dry as he recognized it. His senses told him he was beyond any further feeling, but a terror that was both wonderful and awe-full gripped him as he watched a woman form overhead. Her flesh was lambent, glowing like alabaster, and the face was stern and somber. The brief pleated gown flared about long legs and sandaled feet, and the crescent moon shone in her hair. With a smooth gesture she drew an arrow from the quiver which rode on her fair shoulder, and fired another bolt of lightning onto the plain. It was the woman of the little statue which Helene slept beside, and he would have felt joy if his knees had not been shaking.

"Wake, daughter!" The voice rolled across the plain like thunder, and men fell to earth and clapped hands to their ears, the battle forgotten. "Wake!"

Geoffrey would have liked to have fainted, but he didn't know how, so he leaned back against the horse's side.

"Mother," Helene murmured and twisted her head, as if waking from a troubled sleep. Geoffrey clutched her and found he still had the capacity to be surprised that anyone, even his brave Helene, would dare to address this incredible presence so familiarly. "Oh, Mother." She smiled, and opened her eyes, and looked up into the sky-borne face of Artemis. Then she coiled her arms around his neck and said, "Geoffrey, I had such a terrible dream. And, here you are, to keep me safe, just the way you promised. I am glad."

At this point she burst into tears, and he felt like joining her.

Artemis did not give him an opportunity. Despite the battle being over, she continued to send her bright bolts to earth, until Geoffrey could see that they ringed Michael ben Avi out on the plain surrounded by fallen Shadowlings. He held the rainbowed sword, and his handsome face was cast in sharp relief by the flashes of light. He glared up at the goddess and Geoffrey could almost see the hatred which stiffened his form.

"You have taken what is not yours!" The voice of the goddess boomed out, echoing across the plain.

Geoffrey's knees were unequal to this final injury of sound, and he sat down on the ground with a thump and held Helene in his lap. He was very glad not to be the focus of this goddess' attention, then had the chilling thought that she might be saving him for dessert. The stern expression on the face of Artemis reminded him of how Helene had left her fallen foe crippled but alive in the desert.

"Begone, foul devil! God is with me!" Michael screamed his defiance, and his wonderful voice sounded like a rook's caw. "I banish you!"

The arrow sped from her bow and struck his left temple. "No. I am with you, always, and you have paid the price of pride and thievery and ambition. You will serve me all the days of your life, Michael ben Avi. You will be my lion."

He screamed, and when he turned, Geoffrey could see that his dark hair was now white, and that where the left eye had shone, there was emptiness. Then Artemis was gone, and a rainstorm like the end of the world drenched them, cleansing everything.

EPILOGUE

The entrance into the city was anything but triumphal. The army that had followed Michael ben Avi was exhausted, too tired to loot or pillage, even had there been anything left to practice upon. Jerusalem looked as if a huge hand had clawed it repeatedly, and Michael wept from his remaining eye as he was borne in on the back of a creaking cart. He still held the rainbow-hued sword in his hand. His fingers could not be pried off the hilt. He kept hearing the terrible words that she-devil had spoken above the body-littered plain.

Geoffrey and Helene rode on either side of the cart, and when he lifted his remaining left eye to the heavens, he could see their auras arched above him, all fire and light, a rainbow of the soul. It gave him a sense of loss, though he could not think why. He had never desired the little female, just her weapon. Now he had it. He lifted a trembling hand to his face and felt the burn that ran from hairline to beard, across his ruined eye. Now he had it, and he could not get rid of it. He was being punished for doing God's work. His mind refused to believe what had happened. He had fought and suffered, lost his wife and son, his twin at Heliopolis, been humble, and delivered the city from the Shadow. He was the Deliverer. The sword in his hand proved it. And what did his eye prove?

You will be my lion. Michael ben Avi shuddered. "Take me to the Temple. I will be healed there." He found, for the first time in his adult life, that he did not believe his own words.

Geoffrey started at these words. A smile covered his face, transforming his usual solemnity into something Michael found pure and heartachingly beautiful. He looked like an angel.

"Heal! Always heal. That's it!" He slapped the pommel of Marina's saddle.

"What is, Geoffrey?" Helene asked.

"It is what I am supposed to do, why I am here. It is the lesson my father did not learn. I am not here for any sword, for I am a pretty poor sort of warrior, but to restore the earth. My grandmother did it in Albion." He lifted his hand to the poppy-rimmed hat. The leather was bleached, cracked, and stained, the brim broken on one edge, but somehow it had survived all the battles. "My father did not heal from his own wounds because he did not pause to succor Franconia. It made him a brooding man, old before his time."

Michael struggled to sit upright. "That is not for you. I will do all that is needful. I will do God's will."

Geoffrey smiled. "And I will do the goddess'." He turned Marina aside and picked his way across the rubble.

"Stop him, please," Michael begged Helene.

She looked at him, for the first time without the open adoration he had come to expect, but with cold green eyes. It was as if that unspeakable female in the sky had manifested herself in the small body of Helene. "I do not think that anything can stop Geoffrey once he makes up his mind. No, I do not think I will stop him, or even try."

"I cannot let him bring *her* presence into the holy city." He sat up and tried to lift the sword of light, but it lay across his lap unmoving. Sweat beaded his burned brow. "He has to be stopped. I will have my men slay him if you will not stop him."

Helene looked him up and down, tracing the enormous pillar of fire that still burned above his shoulders, clear evidence of his sanctity, and at the sensuous mouth that had voiced the threat, and tried to reconcile them. "I cannot understand how you can be so vile and so sacred at once, but if you try to harm one hair of Geoffrey's head, I will cut your privates off, one at a time, and feed them to you. Is that clear?"

A sound like a breeze over reeds rippled through the air,

and the sky seemed to brighten. It was a honeyed melody that seemed to penetrate the very stones of the city. Michael felt his weariness begin to fade, then watched in horror as plants sprouted from the earth, bloomed, and went to seed between breaths. The tune seemed to enter his bones, and he hated it, and knew he would hear it every day of his life.

Helene turned Achilles aside and followed the sound of Geoffrey's flute. It seemed to her to be the sound of her heart. A bloodred petal blew past her cheek, and she found him piping on the empty pedestal of some long vanished statue. A whirlwind surrounded him, and poppy petals swirled around in it, rising into the churning air a hundred cubits before cascading back to earth. He was beautiful, and she wondered how she could have missed it for so long. Geoffrey would always keep her safe. Contentedly, she sat on a fallen stone and felt the sunshine for the first time in weeks. He had healed her in some fashion, and now it seemed only meet that he should heal the world. Then she saw the injury he bore beneath his beauty, and knew she could return the gift he had given her. A sense of being embraced in a warm, honey-scented hug, kissed on a tear-wet cheek, enveloped her, a mother's caress, and then, as the grass sprouted under her boots, she stood up to reach for the man in the whirlwind.

GENEALOGY OF THE SWORDBEARERS

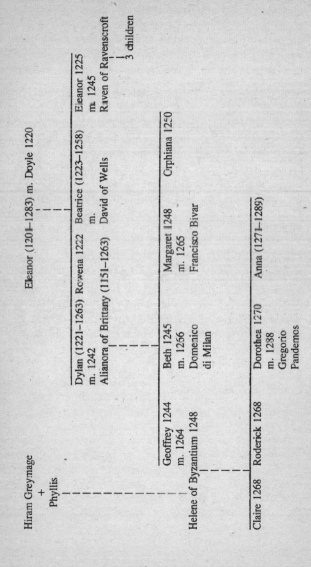

ADRIENNE MARTINE-BARNES is of Arabic–Hispanic heritage, which may explain her lifelong interest in the hijinks of various deities and her mild irreverence for the stuffier forms of sacredness. Her rather off-the-wall interpretations of Celtic and Mediterranean gods—in *The Fire Sword*, *The Crystal Sword*, and *The Rainbow Sword*, all available from Avon Books—will continue into fresh areas: the Orient in *The Sea Sword* and Nordic myth in *The Sword in the Tree*. She wishes to be open-handed in giving offense.

Ms. Martine-Barnes was born in Los Angeles in 1942 and spent an ordinary childhood talking to trees, cats, and other sentient beings. She has written a monograph (*Nekobana, Or Zen and the Art of Cat Arrangement*) which reflects some of these experiences. She is also the author of *The Dragon Rises*, possibly the most peculiar use of Arthurian material yet to see print, as well as two contemporary novels. When she is not writing, she paints, quilts, costumes, makes dolls, and adds to her collection of over 200 hippopotami.